Never before had the Sleeper killed anything more offensively dangerous than a chicken or a duck. A shiver of fierce pleasure ran through him. It was no spiritual thing that he felt, but an actual physical sensation in the pit of his stomach and shooting upward through his nerves until he locked his teeth upon it.

In the ecstasy that rushed through him, he wanted to go straight for the house, beat in the door, and find his tormentor, ax in hand.

What held him back was a most tenuous thread of fear. He must, he decided calmly, go about everything in the most careful and thoughtful manner, for he had made up his mind that he would never leave the place of Trot Enderby until he had in his hand the gun which could not miss.

TWENTY NOTCHES

A JOVE BOOK

This Jove book contains the complete
text of the original hardcover edition.

TWENTY NOTCHES

A Jove Book / published by arrangement with
Dodd, Mead and Company

PRINTING HISTORY
Original hardcover edition published 1931
Ace edition / June 1977
Jove edition / January 1987

ISBN: 0-515-08897-8

Jove Books are published by The Berkley Publishing Group,
200 Madison Avenue, New York, NY 10016.
The words "A JOVE BOOK" and the "J" with sunburst
are trademarks belonging to Jove Publications, Inc.

PRINTED IN THE UNITED STATES OF AMERICA

CHAPTER 1.

THE SLEEPER WALKS

ON A DAY, three tramps sat in an empty freight car. It was a big box car so loose with age that the wheels staggered even on the most level tracks, and the whole superstructure swayed and sagged in going around a bend. It seemed to be shuffled and shaken by the wind, and it maintained a steady uproar, like a waterfall. One sidedoor was open, because it would be a long time before they entered a town or passed a station.

Of the three tramps, one was old, one was middle-aged, and one was young.

The old man was on the road because he was searching, he hardly knew for what; but in truth he was looking for death, because he was very tired of life. Yet he would have been the first to deny such a charge, and he sat up cross-legged in spite of his years, with a straight back, and looked out at the mountain-desert, keeping a little smile on his lips, as one who pretends to be content. The only thing that contented him, however, was the horizon line, perfectly sharp and yet entirely vague, always coming straight down to the earth and yet never meeting it, and bounding the moment with a pale-blue wall which receded, disappeared, and to one who stared fixedly, it became a window to infinity.

This old man was placid in his looks and in his demeanor. He had good features, and once he had been a good man. He was built big and solid, so that one could not suspect in him sufficient agility to swing him onto fast-moving trains, or drop him off again. His back was so straight and his face so open that all he needed in order to make him look respectable in both clothes and skin was some yellow laundry soap and a spare bucket of water.

He was the one who spoke the words which began everything. Two brown hillsides dipped into a shallow gully, and in the middle of the gully stood a distant house with a group of aspens in front of it—like shadowy fingers against the sky—and the tall skeleton of a windmill and high tank at the rear.

"You see that, hey?" said he.

"Yeah," said the middle-aged tramp, chewing his straw. "Yeah, what about it?"

"Well," said the old man, "that's Trot Enderby's house."

"Yeah? What about it?" said the middle-aged man.

They were plugging up a heavy grade. The labor of the engine sent tremors down the train of cars, and the wheels groaned, running slower and slower.

"Well, that's what about it," said the old man. "That's Trot Enderby's house. That's what about it."

He grew mildly excited. Cynics should not show their cynicism to such gentle-spoken old men.

"Yeah?" said the man of no belief. "He's somebody, is he? Maybe he's the first man that ever built a windmill."

He continued to chew on the straw, smiling in half-secret scorn to himself. It was plain from his demeanor that he despised the straw, that he would just as soon have the straw bitten to pieces in a moment—or it would have made little difference to him if the world of our sorrows had been between his teeth. He would have kept on shifting it carelessly from side to side, like the straw, and smiling secretly, and bitterly, and contemptuously askance at any one who suggested, or hinted at, or dreamed of the slightest virtue, beauty, talent, or goodness in any portion of this universe.

His last challenge irritated the old man suddenly.

"Well, you wanta know, eh?" said he. "You wanta know something about him, do you? You never heard of Trot Enderby's twenty dead men, I guess? You wouldn't be interested to know, though. You wouldn't care about a fellow that could kill twenty men. No, no, no, what would that mean to you—and your straw?"

The middle-aged man stopped chewing the straw and for an instant he narrowed all his attention upon the mere face of the speaker, not in too much disgust, but rather in contemptuous mirth. Then, in place of answering, he resumed his chewing of the straw, letting his head nod from time to time in agreement with himself.

"Why, you loon, Trot Enderby's got a gun that can't miss!" cried the old man.

At this the youngest tramp said:

"Well, I wish I had it. I'd like to tap that Denver

3

'bull' on the brain—that McGuire, I mean. I'd like to come up and ask him what he's thinking about, and then before he answered, just as he reached for his gun, I'd let him have it!''

He alone, of the three, had been lying on his side, with his head upon his arm. One could see at a glance that he was the worst of the three. The others were at least capable of crime, but this fellow was capable of nothing. He was one of those sleek, olive-skinned, brown-eyed, black-haired, lazy, idle fellows who are always waiting for the world to turn fast enough to raise a breeze. In cities they are seen on every street corner, smiling at one another. Sometimes they wear silk shirts with yellow, green, and red stripes. That means their mother is providing for them, a widow, pinching and scraping, but always worshiping the handsome darling. One of these fellows is always standing at the door of a pool room. The little boys go by and admire the way he manages his cigarette, blowing out the smoke luxuriously. They admire the flash of the ring on his finger, and they are able, instantly, to see that the pool room is a place where real men should want to be.

This tramp had on the relics of one of those silk shirts. For it was brown, and black, and green, and gray, with grease, dust, and dirt of a thousand kinds. He had been lying on his side and sleeping soundly in spite of the jouncing and rattling of the loose floor boards. Wave after wave of dust and straw powder—the last load had been of baled hay—walked from the farther corner up to him and stepped into his rather greasy black hair, and was drawn into his nose and blown out again by his breathing. Sometimes he smiled and muttered in his sleep, and when

4

his lips parted, some of the straws stuck to them.

The two older tramps had looked on a good deal, but they could not put their eyes on this hopeless, worthless, languid, useless reprobate. The people of this breed are always handsome, but this one was actually beautiful. He was made and finished with the same exact care which a sculptor bestows on an ideal statue—of a god, say. His hands were like the hands of a woman, a beauty, though they were big enough for strength. He was made for strength, too, as all good statues are—that is to say, his neck was big, and chiseled perfectly, round, and smooth, and columnar, and one could guess that he possessed what the book of canons declares must be—neck, upper arm, and calf of leg all of one measure.

Yet size does not make strength, and there was not a little ugly-faced, clean-eyed, red-headed Irishman of half his size who would have hesitated to jump into him as a wild cat jumps into a dog. One would have expected him to simply fall down and lie limp and smiling under such an attack. The whalebone of courage which stiffens a true man seemed utterly lacking in this youth. Or was it not as much a matter of missing courage as it was enormous, incredible, oceanic indifference?

It was for this reason that both the older men were startled when the youngest tramp rolled upon his back and spoke.

Yet he did not so much as sit up. Some dust, dislodged from the rattling ceiling of the car, fell down upon his face, and he merely winked it away from his eyes. His arms lay loosely joggling on the shaken floor board.

"He'd let him have it," said the middle-aged

tramp. "You hear that, do you? The Sleeper would let him have it?"

He smiled at the older man, his eyes remaining wide with scorn, while his smile touched his lips only. Now he had not mere thoughts but a whole human being to despise, and scorn, and mock, and it was better than a meal to him. His gray eyes darkened; his red-painted nose wrinkled.

"You hear the Sleeper talking? He'd go killing, if he had a gun that couldn't miss."

The Sleeper sat up and leaned his shoulder flabbily against the edge of the door. With the jolting, his head wabbled on his strong neck.

"Where's the house?" he asked.

"Yonder," said Doc.

"You better go get that gun," said the middle-aged tramp. "You might need it one of these days unless you wanta be kicked around all your days. You're a sneak thief, so why don't you go and sneak it?"

The Sleeper yawned.

"Why, maybe I will," said he. "I can steal anything. Why not steal that?"

Doc laughed.

"Steal from Trot Enderby? That's a good one! Steal from Trot Enderby! Go steal out the back teeth of a lion, but don't bother around Trot."

"He's a bad one, is he?"

"You ever hear of a man that's killed twenty men and yet he ain't a bad one?"

The middle-aged tramp put in:

"Killed twenty, eh? Twenty what? Twenty rats! Newspapers is where he probably did his killings. A chink and a greaser. That's two. Put a cipher behind a two and you've got twenty. Yeah, I know about the

6

way they work up those things. There ain't any news except bad news. Killed twenty, did he?''

He had grown savage, but he seemed to regret this outburst of emotion, and with an effort he regained his sneering smile, and again nodded in agreement with himself.

"He's got a gun that can't miss, has he?" asked the Sleeper.

"That's what I said, and that's what I mean. I tell you what I saw—I saw Enderby shoot a sparrow on the wing!"

"Luck!" said the middle-aged man.

The boy, however, yawned.

"Well, there may be something to it," he remarked. "It makes rather a long walk, though!"

He measured the distance regretfully, shaking his head a little. He was so greasy, so caked with dust and grime, so marked and scored with it, as with the strokes of a whip, and so inert in his bearing that nothing was more surprising than to hear his easy and clear-clipped speech. Plainly, an education had been thrown away on him.

"Well," he said at last, "it's almost as easy to be walking there as rattling here."

He looked down, then swung himself lightly out from the edge of the doorway and dropped to the ground, running a few easy steps forward to break the shock. The train snorted and groaned its way over the rise, and carried off with it the curious faces of the two older tramps, as they craned their necks and stared back at the boy.

He had turned his face toward the house in the gully.

CHAPTER 2.

THE SLEEPER WORKS

HE FOUND A STICK, to help him up the grade, and this he used, leaning on it almost like an old man. He sauntered as though he knew no other gait.

There was a twisting road, first laid out by meandering cattle, then widened by the wheels of buckboards. It crossed little runlets where the winter rains had washed the surface soil away and exposed the rocks, battered and broken by wheels. It swerved to avoid the smallest hummocks, as cattle will when their stomachs are full. Therefore, this way was exactly to the taste of the Sleeper. He strolled along it with his stick twirling. He paused now and then to look at the rails already well beneath him. They flowed straight across country, like two rivulets of white fire, wavering, and trembling in the heat waves. For the sun was high and fierce.

Its naked face did not seem to trouble the Sleeper. He wore no hat, but this did not bother him. And when he found a great swarming mass of ants building a new nest, he paused for a long time to watch them, noting the busy workers, the big-headed soldiers posted on the outskirts, a squadron of them adventuring upon his shoe. What if they were trodden underfoot, or carried off on his clothes to an irreclaimable distance? It made little difference. The elastic economy of that ideal state would care for such losses quickly. Men, too, might be regarded as a swarm of insects, scurrying here and there, dreaming that they accomplished their own ends but, after all, advancing nothing except the interests of society.

The Sleeper mused upon this thought for some time, and then went on up the slope. As for him, he was not inside the frame of society, but moved upon its verge. He was an observer rather than a participant.

He came to the house of Trot Enderby. It was small, solidly made, and freshly painted. There was an alfalfa patch in front of it, watered from the windmill, now looking pale and naked after a recent cutting. There were a fig tree and a mulberry side by side, and the aspens out in front growing in a depression where, no doubt, their roots could tap underground moisture. Opening on the corral he saw two sheds, neat and solid like the house itself. There was a good strong fence, and inside the fence appeared a pair of half-breed mastiffs which silently followed him as he strolled past.

It was about the hour of lunch. He could smell food, and by the diminishing quantity of smoke that rose from the chimney, he guessed that the fire was dying, the cookery ended. That was the right time to tap at back doors. The dogs, however, discouraged entrance.

He was in no hurry. He never was. He was no

more impatient than a growing tree or slowly flowing water, unconscious of a goal. For, as a rule, there was no goal for the Sleeper except to eat once a day. If need be, he could devour enough on such an occasion to last him for forty-eight hours. His stomach was as elastic and as powerful as the stomach of a wolf.

So now he leaned on the fence and looked down at the dogs, while they looked back at him wistfully. By those animals he knew that Enderby was intelligent, or he could not have picked such a pair; he was cruel, otherwise he would not have selected such watchers; he was suspicious, for the same reason; he was parsimonious, for their ribs stuck out cruelly from their sides.

"Hullo, bum," said a voice from the house.

Behind the screen door, visible as if through clouded water, he saw a man standing. He was short, wide-shouldered, long-armed. Beyond doubt, this was Enderby.

"Hullo," said the Sleeper.

"Whacha want?"

"A woodpile," answered the Sleeper.

Enderby tossed the door open and stepped onto the porch.

"Hungry, are you?" he asked.

He looked more formidable than ever, on a nearer view. His weight was all in the massive shoulders and arms; his waist tapered off waspishly, and his legs were childishly small, and bowed out to fit a saddle the better.

"I'm hungry," agreed the Sleeper.

"Then come on in," said Enderby.

"Call off your dogs."

There was a whistle. The dogs went hastily toward their master, and the tramp entered. He went slowly up the path, looking from side to side. The front gate slammed behind him. He felt that he had entered a trap.

Then Trot Enderby stood above him on the porch, looking into his soul with a cold blue eye. The face of Enderby had a broken, battered look, like one who has felt many fists and much weather. His red hair, sun-faded, stood up high on his head, and his eyebrows arched, giving him a constant look of surprise and anger.

"All right," said the tramp. "Let's see the chow and then the woodpile."

"You'll see the woodpile and then the chow," said Trot Enderby.

He led the way to the back of the house and showed a new and formidable pile of wood, with the shed for its storage to the rear. Inside of this circle appeared the sawbuck, with a reddish pile of sawdust at either end of it. A pair of big-headed axes leaned against the buck.

"There you are," said Trot Enderby. "Step right up and make yourself at home."

By the gleam in his eye, the Sleeper knew that there was a catch. But he hesitated no longer, having committed himself as far as this. Also, he guessed that Enderby would manage to do as he pleased, now that the stranger was in his hands. Yet the Sleeper was very loath. He suspected the bright paint on the house. Even the woodshed was newly doused with green paint, and Enderby himself had a scrubbed look. In the experience of the Sleeper, cleanly people were apt to be hard of heart and of fist.

Yet he entered the circle of the wood.

"Watch him, boys!" snapped Enderby, with a note of triumph.

Instantly, one of the big dogs appeared to the right and the other to the left in the gaps in the hedge of loose wood.

"What's that for?" asked the tramp.

"They'll watch you, that's all," said the other. "They'll keep a good close eye on you, son. If you move out of this here, if you so much as try to get into the woodshed, yonder, they'll go for your leg and your throat. You may brain one of 'em with your ax, but the other'll tear your throat out. I've gotta ride out. Mind you, keep on workin' steady. You don't eat if you set down to think!"

He went off down the little board walk which led from the house to the nearest corral gate. He was whistling as he went.

"Hey, listen!" shouted the Sleeper. "I don't want your handout. I'll get along without your food, Enderby. I'm quitting now, d'you hear?"

The corral gate slammed. Then Enderby turned.

"You saw your way right through any side of that pile. Mind you, don't throw the wood around. Saw your way through. Sixteen-inch lengths is what I want. You'll see some the right size, there by the sawbuck."

He went on toward the barn.

"Listen!" screamed the Sleeper. "The dogs'll tear me up, Enderby! They'll murder me! I don't want your food—I'm through with the job now!"

Suddenly he stopped shouting and sat down on the sawbuck, for he realized that Enderby would never turn back to him. He was trapped!

He made one pace toward the left-hand gap—instantly one of the dogs flung into his path. The eyes of the brute were red with expectancy. The Sleeper shrank back in horror. Those dogs not only would pull him down, but they'd eat him afterward. They were kept with hunger sharp as the edge of a knife.

Then he told himself that being fairly caught, he would have to submit. He picked out a log, dragged it to the sawbuck, lifted onto the buck its three hundred pounds of weight with an amazing ease, and commenced with the saw. Before he took a stroke, he brought from his pocket a pair of old gloves, which he put on, and then commenced working at the crosscut. Silver-bright the long blade went back and forth, biting deeper. The end chunk dropped with a thud.

He went on. He spent an hour working that log into sixteen-inch lengths, and then he looked toward the side of the pile from which he had taken it. The heap did not seem to be in the slightest degree diminished!

Nothing was easier for the Sleeper than to give up. He promptly lay down on the ground. The sun was turning the inside of that little amphitheater into a place of fire, but the Sleeper merely laid a big hollow piece of bark over his head and instantly was slumbering.

The slamming of the corral gate wakened him. He sat up to find that it was evening, the sky black with low-hung clouds, and a chilly wind coming out of the northeast.

"Hullo, bum!" said Trot Enderby. "You didn't work, eh?"

"I worked an hour," said the tramp. "I couldn't get through that wall of wood. Not in a week."

"That's too bad," said Enderby. "You'll be dead

13

of starvation long before that.''

The Sleeper made a pause, to consider. "You mean that you'll keep me here?" said he.

"I'll keep you there, and be danged to you," said Trot Enderby. "Of course I'll keep you there! If every lazy bum in the world was starved, a sight better for the honest men! Get to work, get to work, and stop your whining!"

There was no argument, no appeal from the Sleeper. He recognized the iron hand of Fate, for he had felt the weight of it before this day.

"All right," he said. "Just give me a drink of water. I'm dry to the bone."

"You and water be danged," said Trot Enderby. "You cut your way out of that pile, or I'll hold you there a month—and no water, either! And not a stick of wood moved out of place."

He went stamping on into the house. The two watchdogs wagged their tails and lay down again to keep guard over the prisoner.

As for the Sleeper, a sharp pain burned upward like electric shocks through his brain. He told himself that he would kill Trot Enderby for this.

Then the overwhelming knowledge rolled over him and submerged him in a choking wave—Trot Enderby meant what he said. Trot Enderby had killed twenty men with bullets. What would it mean to him to kill another with—a woodpile?

Even in his moment of trouble, the Sleeper could not help smiling at this. He picked from the pile another log, and laid it on the sawbuck, and began to work.

CHAPTER 3.

THE SLEEPER DECIDES

THE NIGHT DARKENED. There was no star to light him. He shouted for a lantern, but got no response. Then he had to fumble about and measure the wood lengths by touch, and place his saw and guide it straight by touch, also. Once he stumbled and cut his shin on the mighty teeth of the saw.

Then, rain blew up. It did not last long enough to give him a drink. It simply struck him with sudden whip-strokes that bit to his skin, and after the wind whistled in his ear and down his wet back.

He began to be frightened. He thought of pneumonia. And now he worked faster to keep the blood in hot circulation.

It was disagreeable. The gloves saved his hands only in places. Wherever there was a seam in the gloves, blisters began to work up. But at least his muscles were not aching too bitterly. The longer he stood there, swaying the massive length of the cross-cut, the more amazed he became, for he knew that he had stepped long beyond the measure of the strength of ordinary men. He was working for two, and had been working so all the night long. Yet as the rusty dawn began to crawl along the horizon and blacken the eastern hills, he still was there at the sawbuck, rocking with the long, rapid stroke.

It was an extraordinary sensation. He could feel the pull of his muscles, interlinked and interchained from his finger tips to the small of his back, as he tugged on the heavy weight, or dragged it by sheer force through a green place in a log, or where the blade had jammed in a wet and narrow cut. He felt the muscles in his legs, too, from hip to toe, supporting him as he swayed. He began to admire his body as a wonderful mechanism—and still wondered why fatigue did not make him drop.

He had broken through the ridge of the wood wall.

By the time the breakfast was started inside the house, he was picking up the last logs at the bottom of the cut.

When Trot Enderby came out to the back porch, rolling a cigarette and then yawning ostentatiously from the goodness of his breakfast and the soundness of his sleep, the tramp had made a clear passage through, and the wood was heaped up high behind him.

"Hey!" said Trot Enderby. "How was the night for you?"

"A good, cool, working night," said the tramp, smiling. "I enjoyed it a lot. Breakfast ready?"

"Breakfast?" said Trot Enderby. "What've you done?"

He stepped down from the porch, puffing at the cigarette. The smell of coffee, and of the smoke, turned the tramp faint with desire.

"Not a dang thing," cautioned Enderby, "until you've cut through that wall of wood—"

He stopped short, for he had come opposite to the place and saw the steep-sided cut which sank to the very floor, with the mass of short lengths heaped behind the sawyer.

Amazement made Enderby hunch his shoulders.

"How did you—" he began.

Then he checked himself, and his lips curled back in malice, like a dog about to bite.

"What's your name?" he asked.

"They call me the Sleeper," said the tramp, watching, fascinated, the face of the cattleman. He never had seen such hate, not even in a criminal when the hand of the policeman falls on his shoulder, but the hate of the criminal could be understood.

Trot Enderby disappeared into the house and came back with a quart can of water and two pieces of meat. The meat he tossed to the dogs. The water he put on the ground for the tramp.

"There's a drink for you," said he.

The Sleeper picked up the can. He drank off that quart of water at a single draught, and could have drunk again, immediately afterward.

"And the chow?" said he.

"You've worked for water. Now you start in and out through the other side of the pile," said Enderby. "That'll be time to talk about food."

The Sleeper was stunned. "Is it square?" he asked.

"You've got the strength of three men," said Enderby. "Go ahead and use it. Dang you, I know your kind! You're sleeked up with the fat of a lazy life. I'll take that fat off of you faster than a knife. You chicken-stealing, barn-burning dog!''

He left the house. The tramp saw him ride away, only the jogging head and shoulders visible above the top of the corral fence.

He told himself that this was a dream. But he also told himself that there was no chance of escape. The dogs lay on guard, still licking their crimsoned lips. Labor alone could save him, and labor he dreaded more than the surgeon's knife.

He fell to work again, rocking back and forth with mechanical motion. His knees began to sag. The blisters broke. His hands puffed until the gloves burst, here and there. Sometimes it seemed to him that the erect handle of the saw was fire, and the flames were eating up along his arms, reaching to the heart and the brain.

The day brightened, then turned black again, and another northeaster swooped on him. It flogged him with hail, it whipped him with rain, but still he worked at the saw.

He did very little thinking. He had resigned himself, as often before when he clung to the rods, beneath a train in midwinter, and his body turned gradually to ice, while he wondered how long his blue hands could maintain a grip.

In this manner he labored through the day. His lips began to pull back from his teeth in a fixed grin of effort of which he was unconscious. His knees staggered. From the aching small of his back, shooting pains darted up and exploded in his brain.

The sun lowered in the west. The sky cleared. The wind was sharper and colder than ever and blew straight from the north as he reached the ground again through the second cut.

The Sleeper was about to sink to the wet ground, when he heard the slamming of the corral gate, and Trot Enderby came in again, with his slicker like polished steel from the rains through which he had been riding.

He looked at the new cut in the loose wall of wood. He looked at the tramp. And then Enderby laughed like a snarling dog.

He went into the house and came out again with a raw cut of steak and a second quart tin of water.

"There you are!" said he.

"I've got no matches to start a fire and cook this," said the Sleeper hoarsely. He had to swallow twice before he could speak at all.

"Are you better than those dogs?" asked Enderby. "They eat it raw!"

The Sleeper ate it raw, also. He thought he never had tasted meat so tender or so delicious, and the water was a gift from Heaven. He found himself almost grateful to Trot Enderby for such a delicious gift.

Then he leaned back against the woodpile and his chin fell on his breast.

For twenty-four hours he had labored with very slight intermissions. His strength was gone, and he fell into a heavy sleep.

The burning of his raw hands wakened him at midnight. A fine, small rain was falling and he was wet to the skin, but this had not troubled him. It was the hands which hurt him the most.

Wakening, he told himself that this was no more true fact than any fairy tale. As in such a story, he was given a task beyond human accomplishment, but in the tale there was a reward, and here there was merely more punishment.

More clear-brained, now, he pondered his case, but told himself in the end that the words of Doc must be true. No man, no matter how brave, could treat another human being as he was being treated by Enderby, unless the tormentor possessed some rare gift of immunity from danger.

A gun which could not miss!

He was as skeptical as most. He had not come up from the railroad to this house in any actual hope that he could find and steal such a weapon, but the longer he remained in this unroofed torture chamber, the more mysterious appeared the power of Enderby. Besides, there are strange things to be learned in this world. Wireless— What is too marvelous if that can be true? There are, besides, certain fatal superstitions current among the knights of the road. The Sleeper knew them; he could not help but half believe them.

Then, sighing a little, he stared through the darkness toward his hands. In the morning he would be forced to work with those hands again, and how could he endure even the touch of air?

A whimpering sound near him told him that one of the dogs was asleep. The house was black, but the starlight glimmered on the two kitchen windows, so that they watched him like two empty eyes. The Sleeper decided forthwith that he must strike now, or die to-morrow.

He took off the gloves, and his hands burned naked, and so terribly that it was wonderful that they did not give out a light. Then he tore a strip from the tail of his shirt and bandaged his right hand. Next he picked up the nearest of the two axes. Slowly, sternly he forced himself to close his fingers upon the torment. He gripped them so hard that the heavy ax trembled in his grasp.

All the rest of his body felt light. The only weight was in the ax and the hand that held it as he stepped toward the sleeping hound. Keen were its ears, however. It started up as he came with a stride, but the tramp smote down at the rising head and the dog slumped heavily to the earth.

Never before had the Sleeper killed anything more offensively dangerous than a chicken, or a duck from the duck pond. A shiver of fierce pleasure ran through him. It was no spiritual thing that he felt, but an actual physical sensation in the pit of his stomach and shooting upward through all his nerves until he locked his teeth upon it.

He had opened one side of the woodpile to escape, but he had opened a far wider door in his own heart, through which it seemed to the Sleeper that he saw the stars and the mountains for the first time. He had received ten thousand kicks and fist strokes in his day. Now, for the first time, he tasted retaliation.

In the ecstasy that rushed through him, he wanted to go straight for the house, beat in the door, and find his tormentor, ax in hand.

What held him back was a most tenuous thread of fear. He must, he decided calmly, go about everything in the most careful and thoughtful manner, for as he stood there after dealing that stroke, he had made up his mind that he would never leave the place of Trot Enderby until he had in his hand the gun which could not miss.

CHAPTER 4.

THE SLEEPER TAKES HIS PAY

HE STEPPED TOWARD the place where the other brute always had kept watch. Carefully he probed the dark with his eyes, but the animal was not there! If it had seen him strike down its brother, how strange that it had not leaped on the assailant's back? But it was indubitably gone. It had fled off through the misting rain and left the tramp free, with nothing between him and the Sleeper in the house except a locked door.

Yet he did not step out of the circle of the woodpile instantly. He lingered there for a moment, with almost a sense of regret in departing from it, and though he could not tell what had happened to him, yet he guessed that the fire which had burned him here had purged him of a certain dross; at least he was free in a sense which he never had known before. Fear had shackled and manacled him. He was no longer afraid!

He approached the back door of the little house.

His shoes, such as they were, he left on the wet

ground. Up the steps he went, as a cat goes, feeling its way with stealthy feet, soundlessly crossing the flimsy boards until he was kneeling at the door.

Then from his pocket he took a sliver of steel and worked it into the keyhole. It was so simple that the Sleeper smiled a little; the wards of that old-fashioned lock were to his touch like an open, sunlit road, and presently the door gave before him.

He pressed it inward, firmly and steadily, then stepped into the darkness and closed the door with equal slowness behind him.

The starlit night was brightly illumined, compared with this place; it was warm and black as the mouth of a wolf, and the teeth which it held, he knew, could bite to his life in a single stroke.

A light tapping sound began. It walked straight up to him through the obscurity of the room; then he knew that it was the sound of the water dripping from his own clothes, and since his eyes were now accustomed a little more to the dark, he began to go forward.

He could see the table in the center of the room—his extended hands found a chair, circled it, reached a door, and opened this into a narrow hall.

The moment that door was wide, he heard the breathing of Trot Enderby, regular and loud with sleep, and he gripped the ax harder. Some men can see in the dark like beasts of prey; their pupils have the power of expanding to gather in the dimmest rays of light; and the Sleeper possessed this gift, so that he could go forward with a good deal of surety down the hall with his naked, cautious feet.

In the doorway of the bedroom, he crouched to listen and to mark the positions of the furniture in the room. For, looking up at this slight angle, he could spot things more clearly against the dull gray square of the window. In this manner he located a washstand, a chair, and a bed. There was also a bureau, with a streak of starlight on its varnished top.

Where would the gun be?

He hardly had to ask himself, he was so sure that it could lie in only one spot; for Trot Enderby had killed twenty men!

His clothes had stopped dripping. It had taken him half an hour to make the excursion into the region of danger. So he went inch by inch across the floor.

Your consummate housebreaker understands one main essential that the clumsy tyro cannot guess at—he makes his breathing fall into the rhythm of the sleeper whose room he is invading, and this was what the tramp now did. He came so close that he could see the whiteness of the sheet, turned down at the top, and the darkness of the big hands which lay upon it.

The face of Trot Enderby was turned toward him, and for a moment, thinking of twenty dead men, the Sleeper shook with fear.

This spasm did not last long. He found himself saying that fear was an old, dead thing in his nature, to be remembered out of the vague past. Fear and his former self remained behind him inside the magic circle of the woodpile. There his frightened ghost could lie, chin upon breast, and sleep soddenly through the remainder of the night, but the real Sleeper was here kneeling beside the bed of Trot Enderby, and his twenty men!

No mouse could have moved so furtively as the

hand of the tramp beneath the pillow, and when his finger tips reached cold metal his hand shook until he made sure that Enderby must waken. At this, he lifted the ax in his other hand and poised it, almost hopeful that the sleeping man would stir.

There was no sign of movement. Trot Enderby was sleeping soundly, and when the gun was slid out from beneath the pillow, he merely turned his head and began to snore.

The Sleeper stood up and almost laughed in the darkness. So Perseus, with winged heels and the magic sword, might have stood beside the Gorgon.

Now that he had the reassuring weight of the revolver in his hand, he was in no haste. He could afford to remember that he was wet, cold, and hungry, so first he went to the pegs along the wall and from them took down coat, vest, trousers.

He went to the bureau.

A wild cat is not more liable to screech than the varnish-stuck drawers of a bureau, but the Sleeper dared even this. It was not exactly daring, either, for he would have welcomed the wakening of his unconscious host. He had the bed well marked, and the gun was ready in his hand.

So he worked open two drawers and found the underwear and socks that he wanted. He found a pair of boots, too, standing with their toes pushed under the lower part of the bureau. He took them. He even let his touch linger until he had discovered neckties, neatly folded and stacked. Some of these he took, as well!

Then he went back to the bedside and rummaged through the clothes which hung there over the back of the chair. At the very first dip, he discovered leather, and took out a wallet slick with time and much wearing.

That was all he reasonably could hope for.

He left the bedroom, moving five times as fast as when he first approached it. In the warmth of the kitchen—the top of the stove still was hot—he undressed and afterward put on his spoils. The trousers, of course, were too short, and refused to button around his stomach. But to his utter amazement the vest and coat made for the ponderous shoulders and the long arms of Trot Enderby fitted him with a tailored smoothness. It showed the tramp to himself in a new light.

When he dressed, he opened the bread box and found good fresh pone, and in the cupboard was a high tin of plum jam. Jam and pone he devoured in great mouthfuls.

At last he was dressed and fed.

So great was his temerity that he actually considered making a fire and heating coffee, but he knew that this was sure to waken Enderby, and even if he had the power in his hand to kill, that was no reason that he should abuse the gift.

The revolver itself was an old one.

The sights had been filed off. The trigger was gone, as well, and obviously it could only be fired by fanning the hammer. He was well accustomed to this practice, for like most of his kind he had spent many an hour in shooting galleries. He had been what his friends called "a gallery crack." And to amuse himself and them, he had worked a little with the old single-actions stripped in this manner for rapid rather than accurate shooting at close quarters.

From the wall he took down a cartridge belt and fitted the weapon into its holster. The fit was good. The belt had to be lengthened a notch to fit his hips, but at last he stood ready to depart. There was only a hat to be added to his outfit. He picked a sombrero off the peg beside the door, and now his bewilderment became so great that it almost made him exclaim aloud. For that hat fitted his head with the utmost comfort and exactness!

Through the rear door he cautiously stepped out onto the porch.

The second watchdog was there, but at the sight of the tramp, he wheeled with his tail between his legs and fled in silence. The silence was what baffled the Sleeper more than all else. He could understand, possibly, the fear which the dog might feel after seeing its companion struck dead in an instant, but somehow this silent flight appeared to him an almost gruesomely unreal thing.

He went on light tiptoes up the path to the corral gate, but reaching it, he would not risk its creaking hinges. Instead, he put one of his sore hands on the top of the fence and vaulted over.

He walked on toward the barn.

There was no dawn color as yet; the stars were bright in the wind-scoured heavens; and the breeze itself had fallen, having swung around several points of the compass toward the west and south.

This fresh, open air which he breathed cleared the mind of the Sleeper at once. There was not, of course, anything in the fairy tale which he had heard from Doc about the gun which could not miss. And, no doubt, he simply had misunderstood the equally obvious interpretation which Doc wished to have placed upon his words—which was simply that the skill of Trot Enderby kept his guns from failing at a target, and not that the gun in itself had any power.

However, the careless, the childishly careless manner in which he had yielded to a first curious impulse had brought him into the greatest adventure of his life—had given to him, indeed, a new being, for such he felt that he possessed. Under his shoulders the big coat of Enderby fitted with the utmost comfort. The gun of Enderby rested on his thigh.

And yet Enderby had killed his twenty men!

One did not need to hunt for mystical or fairyland interpretations in order to understand a meaning in these comparisons and facts.

At the barn, he pulled the door back, found a lantern hanging beside that door, and, after lighting it, remembered the stolen wallet. When he opened it, he found inside the pockets two sheaves of bills. He counted out twenty-two fifties in one sheaf. The other was in smaller denominations, and made up a total of something less than four hundred.

"Two days' work," said the tramp, grinning, "at seven hundred and fifty a day, plus clothes, saddle"—here he took one down from its peg—"and horse and—"

He opened his eyes with a great start as he glanced toward the line of horses. He expected to find two or three cow-ponies. Instead, he saw five lean-legged thoroughbreds!

CHAPTER 5.

THE SLEEPER SLAYS

HE HAD SPENT his portion of time in Kentucky, and whoever so much as puts his foot inside the State of the green hills on which a blue shadow lies is bound to breathe in from the air some knowledge of horse-flesh. The tramp had some such knowledge, and he walked up and down behind the horses for a moment, forgetful of everything except their beauty. That beauty was not the sleekness of round-sided circus ponies. They had bones to show, but to his eyes there was a point with almost every bone. And such bone beneath the feel of a wisely gripping hand—such wide, flat bone, iron-hard, with none of the round and the sponginess of cold blood!

Whatever he felt about the rest, there was one which particularly caught his fancy. That was a bay mare of a peculiarly washy color, the worst in the world, and the three white stockings which are proverbially supposed to make a good horseman "deny 'em".

He did not deny this mare.

She had an ugly head with a distinctly Roman nose that spoke of a will of her own. Her eye was small, and red-rimmed with bad temper. Her hips and her withers thrust boldly out, but she looked to his keen eye like a creature of both speed and bottom, and when she tried to kick his head off, then strike him to the ground, and finally bit at him like a snapping wolf, he felt that his judgment had been reinforced rather than countered.

He gave her one sharp stroke with the cruel and supplelashed quirt. Then she stood still, though her ears were flattened with poisonous closeness. Then he saddled her, while still she failed to move, and still silently promised to explode beneath him the instant he mounted her.

At last, he had her out of the stable. In the saddle which he had picked out, there was a good fifteen-shot Winchester, loaded. Behind the same saddle a slicker was rolled. She was now ready for a long campaign, and he had not forgotten to put a twenty-pound pad of oats across her back. That would make her defy pursuit for a time, at least.

It was just the end of darkness when he got on her back, that is to say, it was that moment which appears the darkest because the very stars have lost their brilliancy, and because the mountains are black. These mountains, beaded with dark pines on the heights, and made dusky with sun-burned brush, lower down, the tramp looked on with a good deal of doubt. He had been through the mountain-desert before, but usually on freight trains. Now he was to take it with a horse, and the first thing that he saw as the dawn brightened a little in the east, was a low-swinging buzzard making round upon round, searching for some prey close to the house of Man.

Still there was no sign of the awakening of Trot Enderby.

The tramp could imagine him stretched out in his bed in the deepest dream of the poor slave who lay in the woodpile, crushed, rain-wet, and cold to the bone, shuddering and shivering, and ready for another day of torment. Of this would the dream of Enderby be.

In the meantime, the tramp swung onto the back of fifteen-two of loaded fiendishness worse than an exploding bomb.

Those pressed-back ears were not for nothing. She pitched the tramp out of the saddle with her first buck, and almost caught him with her second as he was coming down through the air.

He hit the ground flat. The dust spurted beneath him. The sound of his fall was as the clapping of hands. And he rose in time to see her tail switching through the door of the barn, which luckily he had left open.

Half stunned he went, but he went running.

This had been a bad experience, but it might have been worse. There might have been twenty-four hours of solid torture worse than this. He had just been through such a time.

Who would say that a woodpile is the nurse of Spartan patience? It was to the tramp. To be bucked from a horse was as nothing compared to being fastened by fear to the handles of a cross-cut saw.

He ran into that barn.

This time she was not tethered in a stall, and she came for him head-first. He stunned her with a stroke over the head with the loaded butt of the whip, and took her out, staggering.

He forgot the man. He forgot everything connected with escape. A cold and settled fury rose in him. He rode her forth, still staggering. The instant that her head cleared she pitched him clean over the fence, and scampered back to the barn again.

This time he climbed over the fence with the taste of his own blood running down into his mouth from ear and nose. Surely that second fall had been most crushing.

When he ran into the barn, he found her at the farther end, with her head thrown high, nodding up and down, and her upper lip thrust out, and her eyes wild with stubbornness and terror.

At this sight, the soul of the tramp was touched with pity. One might have thought that he could have saved his pity for himself, with his blood running down his face and his body so bruised and aching, and his head singing a song of its own. But he recognized dreadful terror, such as had so often possessed his soul, and he knew that no physical pain is equal to the white torture of terror.

He went up to the mare with a gentle voice and an outstretched hand which presently she noticed, pricked her ears, and then allowed herself to be led quietly from the barn.

He mounted her without trouble. She trembled and side-stepped when she felt his weight settle in the saddle. Then, as he loosed the reins, she tossed her head as though she expected to be struck over the head again.

He gentled her with quiet words. And how far better it was than the lash or the loaded butt of a whip!

The east was pink as he jogged her at last to the gate of the big corral, slid back the bar, and rode her through, and he turned her up the gully road, leaving the gate open behind him.

All was well with the tramp, so far as fresh morning, and pure air, and clear sky were concerned. His heart was high and his mind was strong; but the gait of his chosen steed was enough to topple down towers of strongest stone!

She walked with a jerk. She trotted with a heavy pounding. And her gallop was a thing to dream of, not to tell, as awkwardly did she smite the ground.

He was on the point of turning around, and, in spite of the fact that it must be near to the rising time of Trot Enderby, he would have gone back to get a second horse, when a tuft of dried weed rolled beside the trail, and the mare bolted.

She ran for a half mile like a thrown stone which knows where it is going.

She ran as though with the best of wings, and she ran, finally, like water shooting without a single riffle down a flume.

There was no more beat or jerk or strain to that wonderful flight than the flowing of the wind through the blue heavens. Like an eagle she made her rider feel. He had to throw back his head and laugh.

Half a mile she sprinted up the hill, and at the top he managed to get her under control again. After that, he noticed that she was not even breathing hard. He cared not for a heavy trot or for a clumsy gallop. He knew that her racing speed was that of a bullet, and he felt as though he had left ten thousand keen enemies behind him.

She had an ewe neck, among her other faults. He ran his hand along that uptwisted neck, now, and blessed her for her virtues. Let others have the show horses and circus performers. He was contented with the ugly lines of the mare, and that one virtue.

Then he sat her at a sharp trot for ten miles.

It nearly reduced his interior to scrambled eggs, but never once did that flawless machine stop pulling ahead on the bridle, and never once did she diminish her pace, up hill and down. It was not like sitting on a horse. It was like riding behind an engine which besides strength had the ability to pick its footing over rough as well as smooth ground.

He had no more goal than a runaway child.

He would not have been able to decide which way to go, no matter what prospects lay before him. But all that really mattered to the Sleeper was that he had found free happiness. It was not the money he had stolen, not the horse he rode, or even the mysterious gun in the holster, which filled his soul with content, though he himself would have said so. Something had happened in the Sleeper, as minute, as invisible as the germinating of the life in the seed, and the sprouting of the stalk.

He was not aware of this, except very vaguely. He knew that there was a change. He felt his manliness, for instance; but above all he was interested in the deeds which he had done during the past night. He had grown at a stroke almost rich. And he possessed a horse which seemed capable of keeping him away from any dangerous pursuit. No wonder his spirits were high. He was a thief, and now he felt a thief's joy.

A rabbit started out from behind a rock and scooted across the nearest sky line.

"Now, gun," said the Sleeper, "we'll see what

you're worth, and Doc's yarning about you!''

He pulled out the revolver, the old, clumsy, heavy gun, and fired; the rabbit ducked over the sky edge.

The thief put up the revolver with a laugh.

"Magic my eye!" he said to the sensitive ears of the mare. "I missed that rabbit a foot. If you won't kill a rabbit, just what'll you do about a man, for me?"

The trail wound down sharply, and he was busy for a quarter of an hour trying to keep in the saddle, for the mare went downhill like a mountain goat. She jumped from side to side down the gully, landing with four feet bunched together and with her head lowered. Sometimes it seemed as though she surely were bumping the rocks with her chin.

This action, with humped back and with lowered head, and this writhing from side to side at a great but an uncertain speed, made a very good imitation of bucking, and poor Sleeper bumped heavily, holding on with both hands and letting the mare find her own way and use her own tactics. He was badly frightened. He expected to be jumped from the saddle at any moment, or else that the mare as she plunged headfirst would lose her footing and that they would roll in a battered mass to the bottom of the slope.

However, neither of these things happened.

And a moment later, at the bottom of the pass, he reined the mare panting around the corner of the cliff.

In the very center of the trail at the foot of the height lay the body of a jack rabbit with a bullet-hole through the head!

CHAPTER 6.

THE SLEEPER SLIPS

HE GOT OFF THE MARE very fast and touched the body of the jack. It was still warm. And looking up, he saw the same ragged headline of rocks over which the jack had disappeared when he fired.

The gun had not missed, then. It had shot true, and the result was a dead jack rabbit.

To the Sleeper it was the greatest single fact of his life.

As has been said, he had his share of superstitions such as live on the road. But they were no stronger than the emotion which makes a man uncomfortable when he walks under a ladder, or sees a new moon over his left shoulder. That is to say, he was vaguely and mildly uncomfortable, not really moved.

Here was a different thing.

He got out the revolver and examined it carefully.

He took it to pieces. It seemed to him no different from other old guns he had seen, except that the parts were rather more worn, so that he never would have picked it out for straight shooting. While the gun was still disassembled, he remembered that Trot Enderby might at any moment come rushing up this trail. With fingers trembling he hastily put the weapon together again, and then he felt prepared, reassured, totally indifferent even to Trot Enderby, or half a dozen others like him.

There were six shots in the magic revolver!

At this, he took himself severely to task, saying grimly that this was the most total folly. He was no Christian believer. There never had been in his life a thing in which he believed, except that some fists are harder, some hands are stronger than others. To that faith he was willing to cling, because he had seen it demonstrated at his own tender expense.

On the whole, he was a cheerful, dreamy, careless, casual fellow. There never had been much evil in his nature except laziness. Stealing to him had been an almost honorable pursuit. That is to say, he approached it as children approach the stealing of sweetmeats. He was as natural, shallow, and uninspired by ambition as anything above a Hottentot.

This mystery of the revolver troubled him to the bottom of his heart.

Other things flashed upon his mind—the austere faith of religious men who certainly could not be called fools in other respects; the superstitions of Indians for which they were willing to die; and between these unreasonablenesses on the one hand and the marvels of science on the other, it seemed to the Sleeper that there well might be some peculiar property of this weapon which gave it an uncanny power.

Now that he recalled it, the very bearing of Trot Enderby had been that of a man who is contemptuous of his fellow creatures because he knows very well that it is safe to despise them. As a rule, men who respected .45-caliber Colts had to learn respect for those who wore them. Trot Enderby had not this respect. He treated humans as though they were dogs. His blazing, contemptuous eye looked through and through as though piercing souls and reading their secrets.

And why not?

Among ordinary enemies, he was a *conquistadore* sheathed in steel among the poor Indians with their weapons of brittle glass and their armor of quilted feathers.

He had spent some moments, by this time, looking at the dead rabbit. Now he climbed back onto the bay mare and started her again toward the west.

Still he had no goal, but some of the lightness of heart left him. His mind remained engrossed by the strangeness of the old Colt. He began to tell himself that a great power had been given to his hand, and why?

Because Trot Enderby was a cruel brute, for one thing, and not worthy of harboring such a treasure.

No matter what Enderby's faults were, what about the Sleeper himself, the low, degraded, bullied, lazy tramp? What right had he to such a weapon, anyway?

He could not tell. He was entering into a region of mysterious speculation which fairly made his flesh creep. At any rate, one thing was sure. There was not a human being in the world whom he needed to fear at close range.

He rode up the thicket of a canyon, among pines and willows, and coming out on the farther side, in the afternoon of that first day, he saw beneath him a flat land set in a saucer rim of sharp-sided mountains.

The ravines and the canyons of those mountains were black with trees, but the flat was smoked over with a thin purple of desert shrubbery. There he saw the cattle spotted singly and in groups, smaller than the toys for a doll's house. And beside an empty river bed, which was like a white scar across the land, he saw the roofs and the blinking windows of a village.

He rode down to it.

He knew that there might well be danger to him in a place no farther distant than this from the home of Trot Enderby, where that man and his horses might be known—his clothes, also; but he wanted a pair of trousers that fitted him, and as for the danger, did he not carry six deaths in one holster?

Alcalde was like a hundred other Western towns of its ilk. Hardly a quart of paint had been spent on its walls or roofs. Window glass was a luxury, and gardens were not. A crossroads and the river which ran full twice a year were the reasons for its being. It possessed what one expected to find—a blacksmith shop; a little hotel with a general merchandise store filling half of the first floor; two shingles of lawyers sticking out over doorways; one doctor's sign; a carpenter shop, and a scrawny straggling of houses which stood close to the street or back from it with an irregularity which showed that men were building close together not because the land was dear but because they loved company.

The Sleeper went into the general merchandise store, and there he was served by old Win Belting himself. Win had a blank pair of old gray eyes and a conciliating smile and soothing voice. He went back to the clothes department and gave the youngster his choice. Overalls and corduroys were passed over.

But a strong, neat pair of whipcords touched the fancy of Mr. Sleeper. He took them, he paid for them, and then learned that Win Belting's daughter would be able to make such alterations as would fit those trousers to the wearer as close as water.

The Sleeper hesitated, lifting his head and looking out the window. To delay here until evening was to multiply the chances of detection by ten, but the old fellow was so vague, so innocent, that he decided he would take his chance. It was true that the coat and the vest fitted him as though with a charm—a pity that the trousers should be wrong!

Young Miss Belting came in and measured him. She would have those trousers ready within two hours, at the most. The Sleeper went to the hotel, got a room, and lived up to his name. For within five minutes after he had closed the door, he was sound asleep.

When he awakened, his room was dusky, the mirror over the bureau held a dark shadow, and a hand was tapping at his door.

The Sleeper roused himself with an effort, for he had slept hard. There was in him an ocean of unexpended fatigue, and for a moment he remained on the dizzy borders of a dream. It seemed to him that he still was in a freight car, listening to the noisy engine as it shuttled the car back and forth across the switching tracks of a big yard.

Then he roused completely and bade the man at the door come in. It was the fat proprietor, with his faded flannel shirt open at the loose throat, and the single suspender strap crossing his perspiring shoulder.

"Hullo, stranger," said he.

"Hullo," said the Sleeper.

"Might you be Tom Grierson of Tucson, stranger?"

"No, I mightn't," said the Sleeper.

He yawned and stretched. Then he stood up with a shake of his head to clear his brain. It was high time that he should be on the road.

"Why?" he asked.

"Why, they's a gent downstairs heard about you comin'. Said he reckoned that you must be Tom Grierson. He'd like powerful to see you, if you don't mind."

"I don't mind," said the Sleeper. "I can give him a minute. Ask that stable boy to saddle my mare, will you, and bring her around to the front door at once?"

"Sure," said the host.

As he said this, he smiled a little, though very faintly, and chiefly on one side of his face. The Sleeper, annoyed, stared the proprietor fairly in the face.

"You don't like that horse?" he asked sharply.

"Sure, sure I do," said the hotel keeper. "She's full of points!"

He laughed a little, adding that a man had to have his joke.

"Well, she's thin, all right," admitted the Sleeper.

He went down the stairs in front of the landlord, and as he came into the lobby, which was also the sitting room of the hotel, with a stove standing in the center which made a source of heat in the winter and a doubtful ornament for the rest of the year. There had not been a soul in that lobby when the Sleeper entered the hotel.

It was fairly filled now.

Two men were lingering at the front door, rolling cigarettes and chuckling softly to one another. There were at least seven or eight others seated in the various chairs.

He blinked at them.

For the light from the open door came blindingly at him from the west, and his eyes were not yet quite accustomed to the time of day. Sleep was still lingering in them.

"All right," said he. "Which is the man that wants to speak to me?"

He turned.

To his amazement, the proprietor was no longer at his shoulder, but the double doors at the bottom of the stairs were being rapidly, and yet softly closed.

He thought, in a sudden panic, of leaping back and trying to burst those doors open, but he checked that impulse. After all, he carried deliverance in the holster.

Then he turned and scanned the crowd again.

He could see now what he had not noticed before, that though some seemed to be talking together and some to be reading their newspapers, all of them were eying him askance, and not in the most friendly manner. And if here and there he saw a smile, it was by no means a smile of cordial curiosity. It was the look of men who expect exciting action to begin at once.

Nobody spoke.

He turned farther, scanning the rest one by one with a frown of penetration, and then in the shadows of the farthest corner he saw the red head and the flaming, grim eyes of Trot Enderby!

CHAPTER 7.

THE SLEEPER DRAWS

A HAND OF ICE gripped his heart.

"Have you seen me, kid?" asked Trot Enderby.

The Sleeper mastered himself.

This was the man who had killed twenty men, but the tool of his trade was gone from him into other hands. The Sleeper thought of the old gun which he carried. Very distinctly, as he turned more squarely toward Enderby, he heard some one say in another corner of the room:

"There goes No. 21!"

It was the hush in the room which enabled him to hear this whisper. The weight of fear was in every one, and the Sleeper clearly saw death in the glittering eye of Trot Enderby.

"Well, there you are!" said the Sleeper.

A string of curses flowed from Trot Enderby's lips. Then he stopped his hand when it was halfway toward the holstered gun at his hip. He was not anxious to finish off this scene of torture, as he apparently planned it to be.

"You talk to the cur!" said Enderby. "I'd take his heart out, if I started on him even with words."

He jerked his thumb at the fat proprietor, who had appeared at the doorway with his fat, greasy smile, having gone around a back way.

"Well," said the hotel keeper, "I'll tell you how it is, stranger."

"Sleeper is his name!" barked Enderby.

"The fact is, Mr. Sleeper, that Enderby says that the coat you're standin' up in is his!"

"Does he?" asked the Sleeper.

And then it came to him, suddenly, that he was so securely trapped and among such enemies that the thing would have to come to fighting, after all.

Well, there would be Enderby, first. And after he dropped, five more. If the remainder had enough courage to rush him, then he did not understand mob psychology.

Sudden warmth flowed through his veins. He was at ease, wonderfully and perfectly at ease. He could not keep back the smile. It came naturally to his lips, and as he glanced around the room, he allowed his look to dwell the split part of a second on each pair of eyes. The smiles disappeared. Sudden gravity swept the lobby.

"That's what he claims," said the proprietor. "Maybe I'd oughta say that Trot Enderby is pretty well knowed around here—upstandin', respectable gent."

The Sleeper recalled the money in the wallet. How many respectable men carried such a sum in cash in their wallets.

"By that you imply," said the Sleeper, "that I'm the other kind?"

"Well, Mr. Sleeper, I don't imply nothin', but we're askin' if that's Enderby's coat."

"Certainly," said the Sleeper.

Every one started at this admission.

"And the trousers?"

"And the trousers," said he.

"And a wallet with fifteen hundred bucks inside of it?"

The Sleeper took out the wallet.

"Is this it?"

"You dang well know it is," declared Enderby, bursting out again.

The Sleeper put the wallet back into his pocket, though at this, he saw Enderby lurch forward a little.

"Well," said the Sleeper, "let's hear what Mr. Enderby has to say?"

"That you're a hoss thief, and need hangin'!" roared Enderby. "You—"

He paused.

"Shouting won't win," said the Sleeper. "A man's innocent till he's proved guilty. What's your story, Enderby?"

"What's yours, you rat? What hole can you sneak out at?"

The Sleeper saw a way to better his position.

He pulled a chair against the wall and sat down. "I'll tell you in time," he said. "Let's have the whole accusation first."

"Cool, too!" said Enderby. "The dog knows that he's cornered, and he's got a little sand in him. Well, boys, I'll tell you the straight of it. This young rat, he comes along and asks me for a handout—sneaking bum, all in rags. I tell him to come on in, and when he comes I put him in the woodpile and set the dogs to watching him. Hate a bum worse'n poison. Can't stand 'em!''

He made a little gesture which was oddly like a man throwing down a hand of cards.

''I put him in the woodpile,'' went on the narrator, ''and there I kept him all day, all night, all the next day, with enough chuck and water to keep him going. He was ten pounds fatter, when he came to see me! I burned some of the laziness out of him! But last night he killed one of my dogs, scared the other one off, and sneaked into my house. Swiped my clothes when I was asleep, got my wallet, saddled my best hoss, and rode off. A professional hoss thief is what I call him. Otherwise, he wouldn't 've knowed enough to pick her out from the lot. Now, there's a straight story. Raise that if you can, you bum, and afterward I'll try that coat on and show that it fits me like a glove!''

It was a pretty succinct tale. But though heads were nodded, the Sleeper merely smiled.

''I'll put down that with a better hand,'' he said. ''I was coming up from the railroad when I met this fellow. We began to talk. We hadn't been talking long, when he began yarns about cards, and in five minutes he was playing poker with me for my last twenty dollars.''

He paused and looked complacently around the room.

''Well, you ain't telling us that you beat Trot Enderby at poker, are you?'' asked the fat proprietor.

''He's a good crooked hand,'' said the Sleeper, ''but I was a little crookeder. He ran up the pack with one crimp. I ran it up with two. That was the difference.''

He leaned back in his chair and laughed a little. It was amazing to see how well a lie rang, when the teller was prepared to back mere words with action. People were grinning, and even chuckling covertly. Enderby was blank. Then his face empurpled with rage.

"The yellow dog! The yellow, lyin' dog!" was all he could gasp.

"He didn't get my twenty, boys," said the tramp. "In fact, he lost a hundred, and then five. There's fourteen hundred dollars and something in the wallet of this card sharp that he had to hand over to me, and for the last hand we made up another five hundred, with his horse, his saddle, and his clothes thrown in. And that's how I happened to come to Alcalde so well heeled."

He turned to Trot Enderby, who was fairly agape. Yet there was a white spot in either cheek, which might well have been taken as signs of guilt.

"Now, Enderby," said the tramp, "it appears that you're willing to welsh and call me a thief. Do you dare to stand up and tell the world that I haven't told the truth?"

"You—" began Enderby.

And he made a motion which has enabled many a man to shoot and be afterward liberated on the plea of self-defense. The famous hip movement! The Sleeper did not respond, except with a smile, and Enderby mastered himself. He actually turned his back in rage.

"I can't look at his crooked face!" he said. "I'd bust. Steve, take a slant at the inside of his hands, and you'll see where my ax handle rubbed off his hide! You'll see the signature of my woodpile on him, dang his heart!"

The fat proprietor, who answered to this name, went forward willingly and said: "All right, young fellow, just show me your hand, will you?"

"Here," said the Sleeper. "Can you see it well enough?"

And he thrust out his clenched fist and held it threateningly poised near the chin of the other.

The hotel keeper swayed back upon his heels so fast that he staggered. Yet he did not retreat altogether. He said, being now irritated on his own behalf:

"I tell you what, Mr. Sleeper, we gotta law around here for the handling of gents that travel with hosses that they can't show no bill of sale for!"

"Have they?" asked the Sleeper politely.

"They have, and don't you think that it takes long for that law to work, or costs much. Where's your bill of sale?"

"Here!" said the Sleeper.

And he slid out the shining length of the old Colt. It came readily and familiarly into his hand, and the flash of it sent a shudder through the bystanders.

"Do you think," said the Sleeper, "that he would have played that game down to his gun, if he hadn't meant it? I thought that he was only a crooked gambler. But I see that he's something else. I see that he's a cur who tries to take men from behind."

There came from Trot Enderby a wild cry of pain and ecstatic fury. It choked and squeaked in his throat.

"Step outside with me, you—" he began. "Step out and—"

The tramp did not even rise. But he tapped the barrel of the Colt upon his knee.

"Get out of the room yourself, Enderby," said he.
"Even if the rest don't, you know what I have. Don't
try bluffing, for the sake of your reputation. Get out. I
promise you one thing—I don't want to butcher you,
and you know, if you know anything, that you've no
more chance against this gun in my hand than a house
cat against a mountain lion. Get out of the room,
Enderby, but once you're outside, if you really want
me to come, call to me inside of three seconds, and
I'll join you!"

This he spoke without raising his voice, and so
genially that it had the tone of one speaking to a
friend.

Enderby listened as one enchanted by unworldly
things.

Then he crossed the room with a white, contorted
face, and disappeared through the doorway.

One could have heard the proverbial pin drop, so
mortal was the silence. And very audible was the
slight creaking of the belts against the labored, deep
breathing of those men.

They counted three, though not aloud. Then came
a rapid battering of hoofs against the road, and no one
needed to ask who was riding off up the trail at such
frantic speed. It was Enderby, trying to escape from
his public shame.

CHAPTER 8.

HOW IT FEELS TO BE KING

THERE WAS ONLY one person in the room who was not very greatly surprised. That was the Sleeper. Yet he, too, felt a ghostly tingle down his spine, for this was the authentication of the fable of the magic gun, of course. What other motive could have been behind the flight of the slayer of twenty men he could not imagine. It never occurred to him that the blandness of his own assurance might have had a great deal to do with this thing.

Trot Enderby had killed his "twenty" men, though as the middle-aged tramp suggested, the newspapers had something to do with that number. At least, it was well known that he had sent a good round ten or a dozen men to their last account, and some of them were celebrated ruffians. They had gone down before the gambler and his accurate shooting. But in the very boots of every gunman there lurks a feeling that one day he must meet his match. Perhaps that feeling had overcome Enderby, and as he looked into the assured and almost smiling eyes of the tramp, he must have remembered a day when he, too, was so desperately reckless that flirtations with death meant little or nothing to him. He might have thought of that, and decided that a little shame and a longer life would be welcome enough.

However, he was gone.

And to the Sleeper, it was an assurance of the greatest solemnity that the mystic legend of the revolver was the truth. It was charmed. Its owner, the great Enderby himself, when he saw that weapon, had simply thrown up the sponge and fled without more ado. Thence the thrill and the chill that passed up the spine of the Sleeper.

But the others saw this affair in a different light.

"He wanted a mob behind him," said the fat hotel keeper, with almost virtuous indignation. "He'd met his match, and he wanted backing. Otherwise, he'd 've taken the job on his own hands!"

The others did not answer, and they did not comment. But they looked upon one another with rather sick eyes, for it isn't a pleasant thing to see a great name fall, and Trot Enderby had been famous for the greater part of a generation, as generations were measured in that part of the West, in those days. He had been at the great mining camps. He had accumulated a competence and retired with it to a life of comparative inaction, only sallying out now and again from his house on the hill when he needed the stimulant of an exciting change. He was established in legend. He was established in fact. Among the tales of the great dead, one found the name of Trot Enderby mentioned. He had been there when "Duck" McGuire was shot to death by the Slawson boys. He had ridden with Doc Loftus on that famous journey from Silver City to Sonora. It was he who had ended the meteoric career of young Charlie May in Tombstone.

Now all that glory was a little altered. It could not be denied. It was the record of accomplished deeds. But instead of leaving it upon the furrowed brow of Trot Enderby, the halo was shifted at once to the young head of the tramp.

These things were in the minds of that group of eyewitnesses. And in that moment of silence, when they stared at one another, and then back at the doors, the windows, the floor, they were marking down every particular.

This was history. To have been present here had, at first, seemed a mere lark—to watch terrible Enderby discipline a young stranger. Instead, it was a Waterloo.

There was the chair in which the Sleeper had sat. Yonder was the shadowy corner in which Trot Enderby had stood. (Might they not have guessed, by the obscurity in which he shrouded himself, that there was something of fear in the mind of the gunman and gambler?)

Yonder came the Sleeper through the doorway, and the proprietor, so silently, so cleverly, had closed the doors and locked them to shut off retreat.

A thing for laughter—to dream that this terrible and casual young man ever could wish to retreat!

Here he had stood and sat down.

What was the hour?

Half a dozen heads turned and marked the big-faced clock that hung on the wall above the registry desk. Yes, those hands had told one vastly important moment.

The proprietor interrupted these profound reflections, these quiet memorizings, by walking up to the Sleeper and holding out his hand.

"Mr. Sleeper," said he, "I was wrong as the dickens. That Trot Enderby, he told me you were no good. Well, I believed him. I locked the doors behind you. As if you'd try to get away! But—dang him!— he knew the job was too big for him! He wanted to have the crowd do his work!"

At this moment, the Sleeper was sublime.

He smiled, and the smile was not an affected one. He smiled, because the delicious hidden humor of this scene ate deep into the very marrow of his bones.

He took the hand of the proprietor. Naturally, he was strong, but there was one respect in which he was beyond other men, and that was his grip. It had been developed by hanging onto beams and rods beneath passenger trains, where a weak hold is a quick death. It had been developed by jumping at the iron ladders which run up and down the ends of freight cars. You jump with your feet and your hands bunched together. If the hands catch a partial hold, then, like a sailor, every finger of the hand must be a fishhook, or he falls to death under the wheels, or to a bone-breaking drop down the steep cinders of the embankment. The Sleeper had fallen. But only once. After that, he learned to hold on.

When he saw that extended hand, he knew that a casual touch would allow the hotel keeper to feel the sore places on his palm and inside his fingers, which might be an eloquent testimonial to his own lie and to the truth of the story which Trot Enderby had told. If, on the other hand, he refused that handshake, he established himself at once as a "grouch," a most detestable characteristic in the Far West.

So he compromised by taking the hand of the proprietor in his own and gripping it with all his might,
though he smiled to make it appear a casual thing.
The bones grated in the back of the hotel man's hand.
He felt that they were being shattered.

He could not help groaning, as the Sleeper said
cordially:

"Why, Steve, anybody can make at least *one* little
mistake about a stranger!"

That was a neat bit of accent.

Steve managed to get away. Everybody was grinning broadly.

"Hello," said the Sleeper gently. "I didn't hurt
you, did I?"

"Hurt me?" cried Steve, half laughing, and still
half groaning, as he went about holding his tormented hand against his fat stomach. "Hurt me? I
don't know what you call hurt! But look at this!"

Suddenly, he displayed that hand. He held it forth
for all eyes to see—and there was a visible stain upon
it.

"You squeezed the blood out of me, that's all!"

It made something to look at—blood pressed from
a human hand by mere gripping. They were in such a
humor that it never occurred to a man of them that
this blood might have come from the stranger's hand,
but they flocked and stared. Then they looked at the
Sleeper as at a hero.

And he?

He felt like a beggar who has been made into a
king. There was the same dizzy joy, the unbelief, the
sense of impermanence.

They introduced themselves one by one, but they

excused themselves from shaking hands. They made jokes about it. They said that they had no blood to spare. That they were workingmen and needed their hands. That spare parts to a good many machines were sold in old Win's store, but that hands were hard to buy even there.

They chuckled over their own jokes and laughed at others. They put the Sleeper at home. And he found himself standing somewhat apart, as a man above the rest, outside of them and their interests, a greater force, a keener brain, a loftier personality.

"Suppose Enderby went off with the mare?" some one suggested.

At this, there was a rush for the outside, and toward the barn, but the Sleeper did not follow, for it seemed rather out of place and beneath his new dignity to show alarm or to betray curiosity even about such a peerless animal as the bay mare.

The proprietor was going with the rest, but he noticed that the new possessor of the mare had not followed the others and he checked himself at the door, turning back.

"You figger that he ain't taken the hoss, Mr. Sleeper," said he.

"I guess he hasn't," said the other.

"Well, maybe you're right. He was kind of in a hurry, all right. Now, that was a surprisin' thing, to see Enderby show yellow, that way."

The Sleeper felt a slight pang of compunction. "Well, it may not have been his day, and he felt it in his bones," he said. "He felt unlucky, that's all. I dare say that he's brave enough, Enderby is."

The other nodded and grinned. "Not his day! Oh, he felt that, all right. He knew that when he come here and talked up a lynchin'! He knows how we feel about hoss thieves in these parts since Parmenter stole Ironwood."

"I haven't heard of that."

"You mean that?"

"Yes, it's a fact. Ironwood the name of a horse?"

"Why, that's Ironwood that won the Creole stakes in New Orleans two years back."

"Ah, yes," said the Sleeper, feeling that this was a matter of town pride which it was heresy in a stranger not to know.

"You remember?"

"I've heard the name."

"I bet you have. It ain't every hoss in the world that runs for twenty-five thousand dollars and wins! Then Parmenter stole that hoss, the skunk! Now old Morice is broke. His heart is broke, too. And hoss thieves don't rate very high around here ever since."

"Well, Morice has the twenty-five thousand," said the Sleeper, feeling that that amount of money was enough to console any man for even a greater loss than that of a horse.

"He spent that tryin' to get Ironwood back. He took three parties up there into the mountains, and three times they got nothin'. The last time there was a fight. Three men laid out as good as dead, and poor old Morice been tryin' to learn the use of a wooden leg since them days. I'll take you over in the morning."

"I'll be traveling on," said the Sleeper, who felt that the more mileage he piled up the better it would be for him.

"Well, nobody would wanta be leavin' Alcalde without seein' poor old Joe Morice. You better wait for that. He's up by sunrise, anyways.''

"Well, I'll wait," said the Sleeper.

And then the flood of men came back, chattering cheerfully, and announcing complacently the last marvel, that the great Trot Enderby not only had fled, but actually had gone off without taking the horse which he claimed as his own. And that failure, as all of Alcalde agreed, was as good as a bill of sale to young Mr. Sleeper.

CHAPTER 9.

HOW ALCALDE WAS PUT ON THE MAP

NEVER DID THE SLEEPER live up to his name as upon this night. The enormous fatigue which had been accumulated during the time when he worked at the woodpile of Trot Enderby now took control of him and drugged him with a black weight. He hardly could touch his supper, but then had to stagger to his bed, and he fell upon the bed without undressing.

When he wakened he found that he had slept all through the night to the rose of the morning, and still he could have slept, except that a jackass in the hotel corral was braying louder than the conch shells of twenty Solomon Islanders.

When he got up, he found that his refitted trousers were waiting for him, laid upon a chair. The bearer must have knocked and failed to waken him.

He undressed, took a cold bath, and dressing once more, he found himself wonderfully refreshed. He could gaze about him with open eyes now, and look forward to breakfast.

What a breakfast it was! Great salty slices of ham,

and fried eggs from the hotel henyard, and piles of sour-milk biscuits with a crust like golden honey, and afterward, a stack of buckwheat flapjacks drenched with a flood of maple sirup. Three great cups of black coffee washed down this meal, and then the Sleeper attacked his first cigarette and felt equal to anything in the world.

A mild happiness flowed through him; he sat in the slant, early sunrise and stared at the morning blue of the mountains, with no desire to stir. There Steve, the hotel man, found him, and took him to see the town celebrity, old Joe Morice. They went out to the edge of Alcalde, with Steve talking all the way.

"When this here Morice showed up in Alcalde twenty year back, I remember it like yesterday. Came in driving a buckboard pulled by a runty, pot-bellied mare. He had a year-old baby. His wife was dead and left him the girl, which her name was Eve-lyn. You'll be seeing her, too."

Steve smiled a little and nodded as though he agreed with himself that this was something of an importance which only he could understand.

"He was a regular hard-handed puncher, this Morice, but he couldn't go out to work on the range because there was nobody to look after the kid. He used to work in town. He would do anything. Dig up a vegetable garden for you, wash windows, take a hand house cleaning. Got a patch of land and raised what he could. Managed somehow to get along, but that pot-bellied gray mare was where he lived.

"I says to him: 'Morice, how come that runty little mare could get you over the road all the way between San Pedro and here?'

"He gives me a crooked look.

" 'Stranger,' says he. 'This here is Iron Lady, by Martyr, out of Adamant!'

"Well, I doubted that that meant anything, but after talkin' around a while, seein' that I wasn't hankerin' for the fight which he was pretty anxious to give me, he pulls out a wallet, and in the wallet there was a couple of small bills, and then a folded official-looking paper, signed and everything, saying that the gray mare, Iron Lady, was foaled by Adamant, and that the sire was Martyr. Then he got out a small-sized stud book and started in readin' to me about their ancestors.

"Well, I'm a democrat. I says: 'All these here hosses, they all come out of one Adam-hoss, I reckon.'

"He gives me another mean look. He says: 'Hosses, stranger, is a dang sight longer in their line and better bred than humans, not leavin' out the King of England, or the first gentleman of France!'

"I didn't argue none. Argument ain't my line. I humored him. It's the best way with a crank, which I reckoned that he was. I says just nothin' and I leave him be.

"Well, he works six months, and lives on nothin', except what he feeds his kid, and then he leaves her with a neighbor's wife and starts off with the mare, and when he comes back, he's spent all the money that he could beg or borrow or save. Poker? No, sir. He says that's the stud fee of Christian, which was a fine and fancy stallion back in Kentucky. Which he'd gone and got a reduced rate, at that! He says that Christian is about the finest thing on four legs, and wants to talk breeding lines to everybody in Alcalde to prove that the foal would have to be the finest hoss ever born.

"Well, it wasn't.

"It was a runty little mare no better'n her ma. She never amounted to anything, but old Morice, he works along and saves all his money, and pretty soon off he goes with the foal, which he called her Rod-of-Iron. She was a growed-up mare, and dog-gone me if he don't spend all his savings for those years to pay *her* fee and shipping costs, and he breeds her to a stallion called Lucky Word, which he says it's a new strain and a lot more likely to do good with the Iron line. He could read you books to prove that, too.

"And yet the foal of Rod-of-Iron was no good, neither. It was another filly. Runty like the rest. Couldn't raise a gallop. An Injun pony could beat her.

" 'Endurance—that's the quality in the Iron strain,' says Morice.

"You couldn't discourage him, though. He called this one Iron Will, which was a good name for himself, if not for the mare. And when she'd growed up, he takes all his savin's again—mind you, he lives worse'n a squatter—and away he takes her again. But he says that he's got a great idea, and that all his other breeding ideas, they were no good at all. We could've told him that ourselves, mind you! The new daddy is Westminster. And he gets still another filly by name of Gray Iron, that's the worst of the whole string. Broke down in front when it was two, and not so good behind, neither.

" 'What a grand middle piece, though!' says poor Morice.

''We all figgered he was a crazy man, by this time, though.

''We felt sorry for him, and used to shake our heads over him, and then comes the time and he takes Gray Iron away to a stallion by name of Woodman, that never had done nothing on the track, but old Morice, he could talk to you for a week to show you that Woodman was the right cross for his blood. Woodman, he got still another filly, called True Iron, and I gotta say that True Iron is quite a mare. You can see her. She ain't fast enough for the track but she's got points that a blind man can see, and the old girl can gallop all day. Old Morice, he says that he's got the right strain at last, and he takes True Iron to another stallion of the same line, by name of Forester, which was another that had broke down in training. And by the jumpin' Jiminy that Forester, he gets the first colt that poor Morice had had, and the name of that colt is a name that you've heard about. It's Ironwood! He looks like something. Not that we believed in him. Morice, he'd failed so often that we couldn't believe. But a coupla the boys, they offered a good price for Ironwood, and Morice, he just laughed at them.

'' 'You can't buy history that cheap!' he used to say.

''We got kinda mad, hearin' him talk.

''He'd backed old Chris Main with a stake, and dog-gone me if Chris didn't strike it up in the hills. He struck it pretty good, and old man Morice, his share was enough for him to send Ironwood off and put him in training as a yearling. Along comes his two-year-old form. He runs eight times and gets a third out of it.

" 'Patience and time,' says Morice, 'is all that he needs.'

"We listened and we laughed.

"Then comes the three-year-old form, and that there dog-gone Ironwood, he keeps on runnin', and he never gets anything at all.

" 'The distances is too short,' says old Morice. 'He needs a mile and a half. I'm gunna enter him in the Creole Stakes.' Which he done it! Yes, sir, he sold his place, put out his girl to board, and goes back to see the big race. He had five hundred left over and he puts it down with the bookies. He gets good odds, too. Fifty to one looked easy to those bookies. What had Ironwood done? Why, one third in two years of runnin'! And when the old man gets back there, he says that he finds out the dog-gone trainer that he's trusted the hoss to ain't been doin' him right—has been short-changin' him right along for food and exercise. So he makes a switch, and signs up a cheap apprentice jockey that's a good deal overweight.

" 'Weight'll only warm up Ironwood,' says he.

"Well, sir, along comes the day of that race. And they line up for a mile and a half, and twenty-five thousand hangin' in the air for the luckiest and bestest hoss of the bunch. They had *hosses* there, mind you. They had Lucifer, all the way shipped from Saratoga. They had Irish Doctor, too, that was a champeen. They had Grievous, and a grievous hard mare she always was to beat. And in under a feather's weight.

"They spring the barrier. They go off with a roar, I reckon, at a great big track like New Orleans.

"They do the first half with Irish Doctor a coupla jumps in the lead. Then along comes Lucifer, and

Grievous close up. And who's last? Why, whacha think? Ironwood, of course!

"Ironwood last!

"They come to a mile in mighty fast time, and now Grievous and Lucifer is close up and when they turn into the stretch, there's Lucifer stickin' his head out in front. He was the favorite, and all the people, old Morice says, are yellin': 'Lucifer, Lucifer!' like to bust.

"But Lucifer, he didn't have the race in his pocket, not yet. No, sir, because that Irish Doctor, he was game, like all his race are. Show him a fight, and he loved it, and he comes again, hard under the whip, and right along with him comes Grievous on her second wind, fair wingin' it along!

"They go like lightning, sir, down that stretch, and the people, they begin to get pretty wild. They pretty nigh stand on their heads.

"Lucifer, he still has his nose out in front, still workin' hard and not givin' no tricks away, and Irish Doctor splitting himself every stride, all done up and gone, and sprawling, but his heart still lifting him along, like a good heart will. And on the outside, there's Grievous flowin' over the ground. 'In faultless style, as always,' says the writer in the paper. Now, in the span of your hand you could stretch the difference between their noses, and the wire winkin' and shinin' ahead of them, and the jockeys swingin' with their hosses and ridin' for glory and a fat bonus, when all at once they gives up a screech in the stand, and there's old Morice, a-standin' alongside of the rail and yellin': 'Baby, baby, d'you see me? Come on, baby!' Which was the kind of a fool name that he had give the colt in the pasture at home.

"Why, yes, sir. Out there, clean on the outside, they was a gray hoss that left the pack behind him like he had smelled the home barn. He'd got his second wind. He was stretchin' to his stride for the first time in his life. He was goin' so fast that the apprentice on him leaves his whip and takes a hard hold and hopes to Heaven this here streak of lightnin' won't slide out from under him.

"The longer that race went, the harder he fights for his head, the more that fool lump of a jockey holds back, and the wider Ironwood splits himself. And he comes up on the outside faster'n fire in dry stubble. And he leaves them three dog-gone high-priced thoroughbreds to study the look of his tail, and he opens up a coupla lengths of daylight, and makes it three for luck as he goes under that wire with fifteen pound overweight and chills and fever on his back. And he runs another half mile past the finish, and then bucks his jockey off to show that he ain't only beginning to fight.

"So that's how Ironwood won the Creole Stakes and put Alcalde on the map."

CHAPTER 10.

ABOUT A HORSE—AND WASHING DISHES

WHEN STEVE HAD come to this point, he paused for a moment in order that the importance of his remarks might sink in upon the other, and the tramp was duly impressed, to be sure.

"Twenty-five thousand—that's a big stake," he said. "And it must have made this Ironwood a famous horse."

"Yes, sir, that's something that it didn't do nothing else but," said the hotel man. "Them newspaper smarts, they pretty nigh to died, when it come to talkin' about that race and that dog-gone long-drawed-out gray hoss that had surprised them all and won. Yes, sir, they'd about laughed themselves to death before that race, when they talked about Ironwood entering, and they allowed that the owner of that hoss was a man with a sense of humor, because he sure didn't mind setting the world down to laugh. They'd pointed out that Ironwood didn't have no sign of a show, and a hundred to one was easy money agin' him.

"We used to read those papers out here and plumb blush for Morice makin' such a fool of himself; but we didn't blush afterward. We sat down and grinned and seen the same gents writin' long articles to explain why Ironwood had won, and how they'd always had a sneakin' suspicion that he was a champeen under the skin, because look at the blood what was in him, and couldn't a blind man pick out a colt that had Martyr and Westminster in his blood. They pointed out that everything was easy explained, and that in all his races, he had been comin' on at the end, though mostly he never come much faster than to get last. They talked about him runnin' into his true form, and a hoss that needed a lot of work, and all such rot. And they sure talked themselves sideways into a lot of new notions.

"The best of it was that Mr. Philip Hampton that owned Lucifer, he comes right out and says out loud for everybody to hear him, that he figgered before the race that Lucifer was the best dog-gone distance hoss in the country, but that he'd seen different, and he would be mighty glad to pay sixty thousand dollars for Ironwood even if he *had* only won one race, and they said that it was a pity they wasn't more races of two mile on the programs so that Ironwood really could make the others eat dust.

"All the tracks they wrote letters askin' Mr. Morice would he enter his stallion in some of their events, and they called him 'distinguished breeder,' and 'man that had made history,' and a lot more of truck just like that.

"It didn't upset old man Morice none at all. He wrote back that Ironwood was through for a little while, and was comin' back West for a rest, and then he would send him out to campaign agin' the biggest and the best hosses that was in the country, any distance from a mile and a half up.

"Then he brought Ironwood back.

"You can tell me that we turned out for him, and you'd tell me right. We swallered our smiles now, and we went and cheered for that hoss when he come down out of the box car. Ironwood, he come down the plank and he looked at us without no concern at all. He looked mighty long and low. He was fifteen three, growed up, and the way they'd fined him down for racin' hadn't made his barrel look small. I flashed my mind back to that pot-bellied Iron Lady. Here was her middle piece, all over again.

"He wasn't such a pretty hoss. His neck looked a pile like the neck of a goat, and his upper lip was long enough for two, and had a tuft of white whiskers on the end of it. They was a funny thing about him, the way that his temples sunk in like an old hoss, and we used to say that that showed the lifetime that old Morice had put in on the breedin' of this here hoss. His eyes was dull, too, more like the eye of a stall-fed ox than a champeen race hoss. Well, as I was sayin', he wasn't no picture, but when you braced up close to him you could see that he was a great machine. He had big bones, sure, but that give him a place for his runnin' muscles to hitch on. Take a look at him behind, he was as square as a box above the hocks, and those hocks was let down so low that they pretty nigh hit the dust, like the hind legs of a jack rabbit. He stood over about a quarter of a mile, but a saddle covered his whole dog-gone back. You never seen such a hoss for point. He had a good color, too, and was a dark, thickly dappled gray, going off into black points. He was iron to the knees, and his nose was dipped in soot, too, except for his whiskers on the end of his upper lip. Which Morice, he used to say that Ironwood's hair was turnin' white he worried so much about when he was gunna eat next.

"Well, they got Ironwood home to the old place, where the newspapermen they followed along and took pictures of Morice holding the halter, and Morice standin' lookin' Ironwood in the eye, and Morice settin' down, and Morice standin' up. They took pictures of Ironwood every fool way you could imagine, and then of the corral, the barn, the watering trough, the two little pastures, the house, the hitchin' post, the whole dog-gone place. They took a brigade of pictures of Evelyn Morice, which nobody blamed them none. But most of all, they got the pictures of old Iron Lady. She's thirty, now, if she's a day. The other fillies have all been sold, but old Iron Lady, she's still there. Strong as a rock, they called her, and give her full-page pictures in the supplements.

"For three whole weeks, we invested a lot of money in the newspapers, and told a lot of lies about Morice and ourselves to the special writers that stepped off to pick up new ideas.

"Then one morning we woke up and found that the stallion was gone. We couldn't believe it, but it was a fact. We went out and stared at his empty corral, and went into the barn that didn't hold him. Only old Iron Lady was there, standin' asleep in the sun, faded and white as snow, and lookin' mean when she looked at all. We fetched out the news, little by little.

"For that matter, nobody needed really to ask who had done it. Who would've dared? Only Parmenter, of course. That danged Parmenter, he sure would've been the only one; and pretty soon we heard that he'd been seen here, and then seen there, ridin' that hoss in the hills. He was ridin' Ironwood when he went into Mustang Corner and cleaned out the First National there. There was a kid in a second story window with a kodak that even took a snapshot of him. You couldn't mistake that long-bodied gray hoss, no more than you could mistake Parmenter's ugly face.

"Of course, the papers made a big write-up and fuss. But that didn't matter. They had wrote up Parmenter before, without coaxing him into a jail.

"Then old Morice made his three tries, lost his money and his leg, and here you are."

They had come to a scattered grove of trees near the bank of the draw, and through the trunks of the aspens the Sleeper could see a little unpainted shack, with a narrow veranda in front of it like the visor on a battered old cap—such a cap, say, as Civil War soldiers had worn. The rest of the house was as staggering as the veranda poles, and they were as crooked as the last front teeth of a very old man.

Behind the shack appeared a small shed, and a few little corrals, half fenced in wire, and half in poles.

Steve had paused.

"That's where the stallion was born, Mr. Sleeper," said he. "Yes, sir, he run out there in that pasture, too, and I've seen him many a time in the corral, and eatin' at the straw stack, yonder, that looks as though its backbone had been ate out and was gunna fall over. When he was a colt, he wasn't much better-lookin' than that cow that's lickin' up the straw right now. All belly he was, just like her. You ever notice a cow's stomach, Mr. Sleeper, how it looks like it was always tight enough to bust?''

"Hey, Ev!" called a shrill, nasal voice from the house.

"Hel-lo!" answered a girl from beyond the shed.

"Fetch in some more wood when you're comin', will you?"

"We'll fetch in the wood for him," said Steve.

They rounded the house, and there found a chopping block whose face had been battered and worn at the four corners and again, deeply, in the center. Beside this lay a small quantity of chopped wood.

"Look!" said Steve. "Lookit, will you?" He pointed to the marks of the ax.

"Well, what about it?" inquired the Sleeper.

"Her work!" said the hotel keeper. "You never seen a woman that could hit a mark with an ax, did you? No, they sort of chew off pieces of wood, bit by bit. And her, how could she whang through a stick with a good lick?"

He laughed a little, softly.

And the Sleeper gained an impression that a small mystery of some sort was covered by his words.

Steve it was who gathered an armful that ate up all the wood that was prepared. He led the way to the open door of the kitchen, too.

"Hullo, pop!" said he.

The Sleeper, past the shoulder of his companion, had sight of a lean man of not much more than fifty-five. It seemed odd that he should be referred to so regularly as if he were a veritable octogenarian. But at least his hair was snowy white. His face was hard and dry with time, not withered. His brown skin had a clean, firm look, and his eyes were exceedingly bright. He wore a short beard, cut away from the front part of the chin, and thereby giving a goatish touch to his appearance. It was a very old fashion that the Sleeper never had seen before except in old family portraits.

He was washing dishes, and smoking a short pipe. He turned toward them, the dishrag still in his hand, dripping over his trousers, and over the floor. He gave them no greeting, not even so much as a nod, but he began talking as though they had been with him for a long time.

"You ever notice something, Steve?"

"Yeah, I've noticed a few."

"About dishwashin', I mean."

"Yeah. I've noticed that it wrinkles the skin of your fingers, if that's what you mean."

"Nacherally, that ain't what I mean. What I mean is that dishwashing don't never leave you no extra hands. Ever notice that?"

"Yeah, I guess anybody would notice that."

"So, this pipe's been droolin' ashes for five minutes, and I can't tamp it without puttin' it out. I never took no comfort with a pipe when washin' dishes. Either the smoke stings my eyes about out, or else they's a lot of ashes spillin' into the water. Though they say that ashes are a cleansin' thing. Who's this?"

"This is Mr. Sleeper that—"

"Him that run out Enderby? You stay long enough and Enderby will run back!" he remarked to the boy with assurance. "Set down. Light me a match, Steve. It's gunna be a heck of a hot day."

CHAPTER 11.

MORICE, EVELYN, IRON LADY

OLD MORICE had finished with the dishes and come to the pans, but before he went to the washing of these, he begged Steve to refill and pack his pipe for him, which the hotel proprietor set about doing. Steve would have completed the job by doing the pans, but this the host would not permit.

"You come out here to talk, not to do pans," said he. "Where's the rag for the pans, though? I've figgered out that it takes seven days for a dishrag to turn into a pan-rag, Steve. And seven days more, it's so dog-gone black that it don't do even a pan very much good. There's a rag has lived and died in fourteen days, all service, and no complainin' but gradually turnin' dark. And that's the way with humans, Steve. They start right. They start bright. But, pretty soon, they get all kind of mixed up with wrong ideas, and they turn gray; and they turn black; and before the finish there ain't much good in 'em!"

"Hold on, pop," said Steve. "You ain't sayin' that every old man is a bad man?"

73

''Not bad, but not good.''

''Why, there's old Bulwer, He's old. But lookit the lot of good that he's always doin'?''

''He's gotta get his share of attention,'' said Morice. ''A young man gets that by makin' of money, and an old man gets it by spendin' of money, and there you are!''

''Why, come along,'' said Steve. ''Look at Mrs. Barton. Lookit her, will you?''

''I'm lookin','' said Morice.

''Ain't she a jim dandy, though? Always goin' around and doing good to folks. She ain't got any money to spend. She spends herself. She spends her time.''

''Time is just another name for money,'' declared the old man. ''And Mrs. Barton, she gets a considerable share of glory. Every time when she goes to church lookin' so meek and mild, she knows that everybody is starin' at her. You bet she knows. Or when she stops in front of the store, and the punchers run out and hold her hoss, and help her down to the street, and she inquires after their ma and pa—glory is what she's gettin'. Glory is what she's after like any Injun on a warpath, and every time that anybody notices her and takes off his hat extra high, and every time that she hears the whisper go right and left around her in a crowd, then she's gotta hold herself from whoppin' out loud, because it's another scalp that she's counted, and don't you make no mistake.

This description of virtue and the virtuous made the Sleeper stare.

Old Morice continued with his dishes.

''I guess you kinda don't like her,'' said Steve, ''poor old Mrs. Barton.''

"I like her fine, I like her fine," answered Morice, "but all that I wanta say is that nobody is so all-fired much better than nobody else, when it comes right down to the point. We're all about the same height. And there is few so low that they can't be kicked as high as the minister."

"Yeah," said Steve, laughing a little at this thought, "but I understand that when old Mrs. Barton come around and wanted to take care of you—when your leg was hurt—you wouldn't let her come into the house at all."

"No more wouldn't I," said the old man, "and who blames me? I lay in my bed wonderin' why it was that I could feel pains in a foot that I no longer was wearin', when I look over toward the front door, and there's old Molly Barton, noddin' at me, half tearful, and half bright. She was fixin' to walk right in on me.

" 'Hey, you, Molly Barton!' I hollers at her.

" 'Yes, Joe—poor fellow!' says she. 'I'm coming right in to take care of you.'

" 'Don't you dare!' says I. 'Keep right outa this house, will you? You don't get in here. There ain't an ounce of glory that I'm gunna give away to you, you old thief,' says I.

" 'Joseph Morice!' says she.

" 'Here!' says I.

" 'I dunno that I understand such language!' says she.

" 'You better start in and learn,' says I, 'because it's the only way that people with sense ever would talk to you.'

" 'You're lyin' there in pain and sufferin',' says she, 'and you're clean out of your head,' she says.

'You don't know what you're sayin' to me, poor feller,' says she.

" 'I do, though,' says I. 'I know every word. I'm a-lyin' here in pain and sufferin', but if you come an inch nearer me through that door, I'm gunna heave this here boot at you!'

"Which right then I reached down and picked me up a boot off of the floor.

"She popped her eyes at me, then, and held up her hands, but you can bet that she didn't come no closer.

" 'Oh, poor Joe Morice,' says she to me, 'have you gone and lost your wits?'

" 'Go and spread that news around the town, if you want to,' says I, 'but don't you stand there another minute botherin' me. When I'm fit and well, I'm as glad to see you as the next man, but I ain't gunna let you have my scalp, Molly. So get out of here and leave me alone.'

"It was kind of a surprisin' thing, but she got, all right. And later on, up comes the minister, pantin', and red in the face. Molly had sent him over. She'd told him that I was ravin' in the throes of death and didn't know right from wrong, no more.

" 'Well,' says I to the minister, 'even if I was as bad as all that, I wouldn't need you to steer me. I can travel by my own compass.'

"So that got rid of him. But I tell you what, Steve, this here world is gettin' so dang Christian that a man has gotta keep on the lookout all the time to keep himself from bein' patted and pitied and turned into a house dog, which is a sick dog. Now, what fetched you out here with your new gun fighter?"

"Hey?" exclaimed Steve, a little shocked.

"Did you want to show me off to him, with my wooden leg, or did you wanta show him off to me?" continued this terrible old man.

"Why, pop," said the hotel man, "I didn't want neither. But I just come out neighborly to see you."

"Nobody never made a neighborly call," said Morice, "except to gossip or to get gossiped about. I hear that Trot Enderby went off at a full gallop."

"You never seen nothin' like it," declared Steve, growing warm at the memory. "The way he's come over all of us all the time! But he pulled in his horns and got, I tell you."

"He had an idea, then," said Joe Morice. "He's a thinkin' man, that there Enderby, and everybody that thinks is dangerous. That goes for silent men, too."

"How come, pop?" asked Steve.

"If you keep the exhaust shut down, the smallest kind of a fire will some day raise the steam," answered Morice. "There's many a boy been silent because he was a fool that has growed up into a wise man, because silence got to be a habit."

"That sounds kind of funny, pop," said the other. "But whacha mean by it?"

"Well, I'll tell you. They's only one way to be right, but they's a thousand ways to be wrong. A man that won't keep still is like a hoss that won't lie down; he never wins. That's the trouble with me. Too much talk, and no action."

"Why, pop, lookit Ironwood! Didn't you do him?"

"Me? Not by a long sight. Iron Lady, she gets half the credit, and Heaven gets the rest. All that I done was to set and wait. Help yourself to some coffee, you boys, I been so busy talkin' and admirin' the sound of my voice that I've clean forgot it was my house that you walked into."

They told him that they already had eaten.

The pans were now finished, hung up in order on nails behind the stove, and the pan-rag was spread out on top of the dishpan. The old man regarded it sharply for a moment.

"There's a rag in its sixth day," said Morice. "Done its duty. Worked hard. Ain't wore out, either. But it's got spoiled and soiled and has gotta be thrown away to-morrow. You can keep your mouth shut!"

He turned on the Sleeper and pointed a sudden finger at him. The boy started, but Steve said with a grin:

"Well, then, he's gotta be a wise man, according to you, pop."

"I dunno," said Morice. "They's some are silent because they still are thinkin' and some are silent because they don't wanta get found out. Are you goin' back to town now?"

"Why, pop, you wanta send us away?"

"No, no! Glad to have you. It ain't every day that I got new ears to listen to my old ideas. Hey, Ev! Ev!"

"Hel-lo!" answered a small voice in the distance.

He stumped on the wooden leg to the door and leaned there, shouting: "C'mon in! Hey, Ev! C'mon in!" He turned and explained: "She's finished pitching hay in the back field, I reckon, or just about."

Presently she came.

She wore a dress of blue calico, so old, so faded by time and many washings, that it flashed almost white in the sun, but she passed from the sunlight to the comparative dimness of the kitchen, and then the Sleeper could see her.

She was small and slenderly made. The wind had blown her old ruffled collar against her brown throat, and knocked her hair into a tangled mist, but this did not make her ill at ease, or keep her from smiling. She was so pretty and delicate that the Sleeper wanted to touch her with his hands, and reassure her as if she were a child. His heart ached. It seemed that she understood labor and sorrow, but not how to complain about them.

"Here, Ev, come here!" said her father.

She went to him, nodding and smiling at Steve.

"Now you finished lookin' at me, Mr. Sleeper, you can start in lookin' at Ev," said Morice. "Ain't much to see, at first sight. Lightweight. Not much bone." He took her wrist in his hand, as he said this; and the girl endured this exhibition with a wonderful, childlike patience. She looked not at the two visitors but, steadily, into the face of her father.

"But pretty well balanced," said Morice. "Head fits onto her neck pretty good. Got a fair spread of jaw, too. You look down at her feet. Yes, sir, that's the trouble with her. Kind of small. But made of good hard stuff. She can go on 'em all day, and even through rough country. And—"

"Dang it, stop!" shouted Steve, tormented and furious.

"They're tired of looking at you already, Ev," said the father. "You better take 'em outside, then. I guess that they come here to see Iron Lady."

CHAPTER 12.

FATHER AND DAUGHTER

THE SLEEPER, hot of face and more than a little giddy, was glad to get out of the house into the open air. Old Morice remained behind, while Steve still was raging.

"He's getting sourer and sourer, Evelyn," said he, "but I never seen him do anything as bad as that before."

She did not answer for a moment, but absently touched the wrist which her father had held as though his grip had been over hard.

"He has all sorts of ways of making a joke, Steve," she answered. "It doesn't matter a bit to me. You mustn't be angry with him."

She had a light, high voice, sweet as the voice of a child. The Sleeper kept walking a little apart, so that he could watch her. He was growing more and more dizzy. He felt as though he had run a long distance and needed to sit down and catch his breath again. They reached a corral fence:

"Here, girl; here, girl! Come along, old lady!" called Evelyn Morice.

They heard a snort. From behind the shed an old white mare came into view. Her bones stuck out with age, but she picked up her feet without stumbling and came toward them at a good, brisk walk.

"She still can raise a gallop," said the girl. "That's Iron Lady!"

She turned directly to the Sleeper, as she said this, and the Sleeper blinked and looked hastily away toward the mare again.

Old Iron Lady came on, cocking her ears and letting them fall alternately. She looked as dumpy and battered a thing as ever he had seen, and yet he could see the big, flat bone, and the ample heart and lung room in her girth, and the ground she stood over. She had had greatness in her, or a great horse could not have come from her blood, so that the Sleeper regarded her with a touch of awe, for great horses fill the mind of a man more than any other thing in the world. A dog may be brave and devoted; or a child may be true; or a friend may be faithful; but the very essence and business of a horse is that he lay down his life for his master. Into the brave, big eyes of the old mare the Sleeper stared. And for the first time in all his lazy shiftless, worthless life it seemed that the ground had dropped away from beneath his feet. It was a breathless fall of self-respect; now at last he realized his essential unimportance, and the worth of patient labor, and the unvalued significance of the life work of poor Joe Morice, even if he had been robbed of the fruits of it before his death.

He looked at the mare again, and again.

He had felt that he knew horses very well. But no matter how young this pudgy old mare once had been, it must have taken genius to see in her the makings of a great line. To know horses is a life work. And he—at what had he ever worked at all? He had walked gayly into this little, run-down place. And he had found in it his most profound humiliation.

They went back toward the house, and the girl excused herself. She had work to do. She was glad to have met Mr. Sleeper. She hoped that they both would stay and talk to her father, because he really enjoyed talk, even if he seemed a little dry and sour, from time to time.

"He is not very happy," she confided softly to them.

So she left them, and Steve familiarly gripped the arm of the Sleeper.

"You ever see anything like her?"

"No," said the Sleeper. "No, no!"

He shook off the hand of the other impatiently, for the touch was interrupting his thoughts.

"Yeah," said Steve, still grinning, "you wanta be alone to think and wish, after you've seen her. There ain't anything like her in the world, I reckon. Well, we'll go in and talk to the old man a minute. I wanted you to see something before you left Alcalde. It ain't a bad old town, you take it all around."

Old Morice was stretched in a canvas chair on the veranda, reading a newspaper, which was time-yellowed around the edges.

He lowered it to speak to them.

"Here they tell me that they been and made a combine of the Chester Smelter and the Goodwood Co., Steve."

"Why, they done that two years ago! How old's that newspaper?"

"Reckon it must be two years old, then. It come wrapped around some groceries, yesterday. But news is news, if you don't know it," said Morice. "A hundred years from now a lot of news will be livin', and a lot will be dead, but the men will be the same, I reckon, unless they've got all combined."

"What's wrong with combinin', pop? Which I mean to say, you roll two companies into one, and they's only one boss to pay, and a mighty less lot of competition."

"Aye," said the horse breeder, "but when you come right down to it, ain't it true that what you combine is hands, and not brains; and what I claim is that ten thousand little heads workin' is better than ten big brains doin' all the thinkin' for the rest of the country. Lookit Parmenter. Now, there was a time when there was a dozen important crooks around these parts. There was Sorrell, the yegg, that busted safes as easy as walnuts. There was Harry Bell, that done murder so slick, and would give you a dead man for five hundred dollars—or cut that price, even, if he was a little down in funds. There was Dolly Chipping, that used to make counterfeit and shove the queer. There was Lefty Bullen, that done his work along the border, runnin' across chinks and greasers, and cartin' in' dope, too. There was Noll Perry, that could steal a hoss right out from under your saddle, and that rustled your cows away so swift and easy that it was like a dream. But that there outfit is all combined up with Parmenter. Lookit the difference. Lookit what it means to the newspapers. When anything's done, it's always Parmenter. Parmenter and his men done the job; and then they gotta sit down and work up old pictures of Parmenter, and tell the story of his life all over again, and people get so disgusted with reading about the same man over and over again that I tell you what, boys, they're beginning to lose interest in crime! That's what we're comin' to!"

He dropped the newspaper to the floor and refilled his pipe.

After he had lighted it, and had it drawing well, and had tamped down the first bright glow to a smudge of black, he went on:

"Well, you seen her, Mr. Sleeper?"

"A grand old mare, sir," said the Sleeper.

"I wasn't thinkin' of the filly," said the breeder.

"Filly?" echoed the Sleeper.

"He means Evelyn," said Steve dryly. "He thinks what everybody thinks. There ain't anybody like her, pop."

"Well, well," said Morice, "There ain't anybody like her, and yet I can't get me a price offered. I gotta get a combine to offer me a price on her, after all. It's gettin' so that a man can't do business exceptin' with a corporation."

"Say, pop," asked Steve. "Tell me whacha mean by a price on Evelyn. Is that a new kind of a joke?"

"Never meant nothin' more than that in my whole life," said the father calmly.

Steve reddened with anger. The Sleeper grew pale.

"I wouldn't wanta believe that you'd sell her, like them millionaires sell their daughters for to get titles into the family, pop!"

The Sleeper turned paler still.

"He doesn't mean money, Steve," he interrupted.

At this, Joe Morice turned his head slowly and looked for a moment into the white face and the hypnotized eyes of the youth.

"I don't mean money," he admitted. "But supposin' that one of them brave young men—or old men, either—that've seen my girl and wanted her so bad that they turned as yaller as jaundice—supposin' that one of them was to bring down my Ironwood out of the hills, wouldn't I give him the girl in exchange? Yes, sir, and boot, too! As much to boot as I could raise!"

"Hey, pop!" shouted Steve, outraged. "I dunno that I wanta hear you talk no more! Give up your girl for your hoss?"

"That's what I was sayin'," said the old man placidly. "Give up Evelyn. Give up the sound of her, and the sight of her. Give up the touch of her, too, which she can rub a headache offn any man's forehead. Give her all up, for Ironwood."

"I wouldn't believe you," exclaimed Steve. "Suppose that murderin' brute of a Parmenter was to make up his mind to the exchange?"

"He could have her," said Morice.

"It ain't true. You're jokin'!" cried Steve, his virtuous rage increasing.

"He means," said the Sleeper hoarsely, "that Parmenter would've turned straight, if he wanted to do such a thing."

Again the father looked askance at the boy, and then smoked his pipe in silence again.

The Sleeper stood up. His knees were weak beneath him. "We'd better start on, Steve!" said he.

"All right," said Steve. "I don't wonder that

you've heard enough. Never heard such a funny line of talk before, out of old man Morice. Pop, I'm kinda ashamed of you."

"Are you?" said Morice. "The boy ain't, though. We'll be seein' you again, Mr. Sleeper?"

"I'm riding on out of Alcalde," said the Sleeper, with determination. "I'll never see you again, Mr. Morice. Good-by."

"Good-by for a while," said Morice. "You'll be back pretty soon. So long!"

They left and went down the road toward the hotel again.

"What he mean by that talk of you coming back? The old man sounds sort of loony to-day," declared Steve.

To this, the Sleeper returned no answer. He walked along with his head fallen, and his feet scuffling through the thick, soft dust of the road. Now and again he sighed, and the other saw him shake his head once or twice.

"Aye," said Steve, interpreting. "He's pretty bad. He's turning in the brain, all right, like milk. He's getting sour. Poor old pop! Well, he's had enough happen to him to make him go wrong, before the end. They's gotta be something done about it. We gotta have a talk about it here in town. It ain't right that girl should be left out there with a gent whose brain is turning, like that!"

The Sleeper paused.

"What's the matter?" asked Steve.

"I've got to go back."

"To his house?"

"Yes."

"Forget something?"

"Yes."

"I'll go along slow, but I gotta get back to the hotel. Hurry up, Mr. Sleeper. Or you'll be startin' your ride in the heat of the day, which it sure takes the gimp out of a hoss quick."

CHAPTER 13.

A BARGAIN

IF IT TAKES the gimp out of a horse to start a long journey in the middle of the day, it also took the nerve of the Sleeper to return to the house of old Morice, for he went as the bird to the snake, or the spider to the fly. A feeling of fatality possessed him. It had come over him when he first heard Morice proclaim his selling price of the girl. It persisted in his mind now. It was as bad, to look at the emotion from another viewpoint, as the impulse of the climber to hurl himself from a height.

The Sleeper walked slowly back. Twice he paused—once at the little bridge, where the road humped its back like a swimming whale, and again at the margin of the aspen wood. But these halts were only momentory and he was driven straight back until he stood beside the veranda once more. Over to the side, he saw a jack rabbit nibbling at some greenery, and that the rabbit should expose itself so frankly to the eyes of gun-wearing men did not seem to the boy more strange than that he should have come back to the house of Morice.

The latter was in the midst of his reading of that same yellow-stained newspaper. He looked over the upper edge of it and sang out in his sharp, ringing voice:

"Hullo, Mr. Sleeper. I didn't expect you as quick as this. Leave something behind you?"

The Sleeper did not answer.

One does not hasten to reply when a question is already answered in the mind of the questioner.

But that strange old fellow went on, calling loudly:

"Hullo, Ev, Ev! Where are you, Ev?"

"Here!" she called from the distance. "Coming!"

She would be hurrying in, with her brown face flushed with haste, and her patient, gentle eyes waiting, like the eyes of a deer.

"Well, here you are back again," went on old Morice, to fill in the interim. "Set down and rest yourself. Sorry there ain't another chair, but that's the way with invalids. They never got time to look after nothin' but their own comforts. Ornery lot, invalids are. They feed on pity, and pity turns any stomach sour. I never see a one-legged beggar, or a blind one, or a poor gent without no arms at all, without tellin' myself that I know what he really needs more'n the money that he asks for!"

He paused.

"Well?" said the Sleeper.

"He needs bicarbonate of soda," said Morice sharply. "That's what he needs. Well, set yourself down on the edge of the porch. A stool is better than nothin' at all, and maybe mean conversation is better than silence."

"How old would Ironwood be?" asked the boy.

"They's two ways of looking at that," replied Morice. "Some one might say that he's six. That's one way of talkin' it. But from another way, he's six million, because it's about that long since the first hoss run between the teeth of a saber-toothed tiger and got clean away, and flicked off away from the big tree-eating lizards. I'd rather say that Ironwood is six million years, plus all the brains and the prayers of old Pop Morice, all his life long. Which age would you pick out, if you was to write a book, young feller?"

"I don't know," said the Sleeper dreamily, and only half hearing the words of his host. "I was thinking of something else."

"Ay," said the old man. "You was thinkin' of something else, and I could name the thing. She'll be here in a second. Here she is now!"

The girl at that moment came hurrying around the corner of the house, and springing lightly from the ground onto the veranda, she kissed Morice and asked him what he wished.

"Manners," said this terrible man of irony, "is come on to a might fine point, since I was young, because now folks come dashin' along and never pay no attention to young strangers, but they go and kiss ma and pa and thumb the nose at travelers. Is that right, honey?"

She saw the Sleeper, then, who had risen, and turned a fiery brick-red. He was angry enough to fight. But he felt such a fool that he wished his embarrassment would melt him into a hot mist and let him blow out of sight.

She said: "How do you do again, Mr. Sleeper."

"He's lost something here," said old Morice. "Start huntin' around for it, honey. Young Mr. Sleeper, there, he's lost something and had to come all the way back to here for it."

"What is it, Mr. Sleeper?" she asked.

"I haven't—" began the Sleeper, but Morice broke in and overrode him, like the tyrant that he was, saying:

"What would he've come back for, except that he had lost something? Something he hardly knows what to call it. You would have to read his mind to guess. Look at him, Ev."

She lifted her eyes at the Sleeper, and then let her glance drift mildly past him.

"Have you looked at him, Ev?"

"Yes," said she.

"What color is his hair, then?"

"Brown," said she.

The Sleeper wondered at her gentle self-control. Years of this strange sort of half-banter must have been endured before she could bear herself so calmly.

"What color is his eyes?"

"Gray, Daddy," said she.

"What color is his skin?"

"It's olive-brown," she replied.

"How tall is he?"

"Just a little over six feet."

"Hey! As tall as that?"

"Yes, I think so."

"Say, Ev—"

"Yes?" she asked patiently, and her eyes widened a little, and softened a little, asking the stranger's pardon for this conversation at his expense.

"You've looked him over pretty good, then?"

"Yes," she said.

"Now, Ev, would you call him a ugly, or a plain, or a handsome young feller?"

"He doesn't want us to talk about him, Daddy," said she.

"Answer me!" he roared.

She started, and caught her breath.

"Look at him again!" said the bully.

Actually, she obeyed. The Sleeper was touched to the heart.

"This is nonsense, Mr. Morice!" said he. "I won't have this sort of thing!"

"You hear him, Ev," said Morice. "He's proud, d'you see. Young, proud, strong, and a gun fighter. Now, what more would you want in a man?"

She looked patiently from him to the Sleeper and did not speak. This dignity in her surprised and touched the Sleeper. He began to think that Morice was an incarnate fiend.

"But you ain't answered me, Ev. Would you call him a handsome man? You would, of course," he went on, letting her off on that point, "and the fact is, honey, that you need to look mighty careful at him, because he's looked careful at you, and had all of your good points showed to him. Here's a man, Ev, that's lookin' for a job. A big job, and a man-sized job. Ain't I right, Mr. Sleeper?"

The Sleeper said nothing, but that made no difference to old Morice, who continued:

"Seems nacheral to call him mister. The rest are Tom, Dick, and Harry. But this is a mister. Now, Ev, when you want to ask what is the job that he'll tackle, I'll tell you. He thinks it'd about fill his hands to go yonder into the mountains and have a chat with Parmenter and get Ironwood out of him. That's the job that he hankers for.''

''Ah,'' she said, ''have you been persuading him, Daddy? We've had so many men hurt before—do you want to have a dead man on our conscience?''

Old Morice made a gesture toward the girl, half-sneering.

''You see what she thinks of you, son. A lot of good men, brave men, big men, have started out for Ironwood, but when she sees you, she knows that it'd be Ironwood or death! That's what I call a compliment. And I agree with you, Ev. It'd be Ironwood or death, for him.''

She disregarded this. She merely said to the Sleeper:

''Do you really think of such a thing?''

The Sleeper glanced from her to Morice. He was beginning to be afraid of the horse breeder and his mind-reading.

''Yes,'' he said. ''I've thought of it.''

''Do you know what it means? Do you know Parmenter?'' she asked. ''Do you know how many times the posses have tried to catch him? And that was even before he had Ironwood to take him safely away!''

''Ten men ain't got no chance,'' said Morice. ''But one man has. One man could work it where ten men would miss. Every hand has a chance to miss, and twenty hands makes twenty chances to fail. This here fellow, Ev, a gent like Trot Enderby that's been scaring us in this neck of the woods for so many years, what's Trot Enderby and his twenty dead men to Mr. Sleeper? Why, nothin' at all! He laughs at that. He takes away Trot Enderby's clothes, because he feels like a change. He takes away Trot's hoss, because he's tired of walkin'. And Trot's afraid to foller after. That's the kind of a gent that Mr. Sleeper is. Yes, sir, he'd like to have a whirl at Parmenter, and who are we to keep the young and the ambitious from havin' a chance to use their full strength? I'd be ashamed to hold him back. Only, they's another thing to look at. Suppose he does this job, how's he to be paid?''

"All that Ironwood ever won in racing afterward," she suggested. "It's only the horse himself that you want, daddy!"

"Ah, money, money!" said Morice. "That's the sauce that even the young girls think about in these days. But money don't pay for life and death. Life and death is what he risks, goin' up into the mountains, and what's the pay we'll give to him to make him have a warm heart as he stands before Parmenter? What's the most precious thing we've got in the world?"

"I don't know," she said honestly, and shook her head.

"It's you!" cried Morice.

This, like the blow of a hand, made her step back against the wall of the house, but she did not so much as catch her breath. And the Sleeper almost went to her with his hands outstretched.

"Tell her!" cried Morice suddenly. "Tell her, man, that it's her that you want, and her that you'll fight for! And tell him, Ev, that you'll give yourself to make the bargain!"

CHAPTER 14.

A LETTER TO PARMENTER

MANY LONG MINUTES before, he had guessed that old Morice had this in mind, but the sudden, brutal enunciation staggered the Sleeper. Yet he waited terrible long seconds, staring at her, and she at him.

Then courage came to the Sleeper, for he saw, suddenly, that the girl would not refuse even this, so used was she to subordinating herself in everything to her father. He said in a deliberate way:

"You don't know me, Mr. Morice, or you wouldn't suggest such a thing. I'll tell you. I'm a common tramp. I've never done an honest day's work in my life, except in prison."

He waited, after this confession. But the strange old man merely rubbed his hands and grinned at the two young people.

"That's the lover for you, Ev," said he. "Can't bear to have you keep wrong ideas about him in your head, but wants you to know everything from the start. Well, look him over and then tell me what you'll do!"

"I don't want you to answer that," said the Sleeper.

He began to be apprehensive. He looked about him, half fierce and half frightened.

"Tell me!" thundered Morice, in a way he had of changing his voice and letting it roll hugely out. "What brought you back here this morning except Evelyn's face?"

The Sleeper made a gesture of surrender, admitting the truth of this, but he wouldn't put the thing in words.

"Bashful, that's what he is," said Morice. "Why, Ev, this here is a regular angel with wings compared with the tobacco-chewin' punchers that've been hangin' around here of a Sunday afternoon, and scratching the floor all up with their dog-gone spurs. He says that he's a tramp. Why, there ain't a better way to get an education than to ride the rails for a coupla years and find out about things and people. Don't you let him talk himself down. He's worth a high price—if he brings in Ironwood!"

Suddenly he stood up and stumped into the house, merely saying: "I'm gunna leave you out here to talk it over together."

He slammed the door behind him, and the Sleeper, standing bolt upright, blinked at the sound, and saw the little lines of dust leap from the cracks in the veranda floor.

He watched that dust rise, and he watched the wind catch it and scour it away. Still, he could not lift his glance to the face of the girl.

"Well," he said, still looking down, "your father is a very great joker, isn't he?"

"Yes," said a small and breathless voice.

The Sleeper then was able to face her. She was frightened as could be, and had both her hands pressed behind her against the wall as though she were prepared to dodge to either side. At this, he put out a hand toward her, palm up.

"You don't take him seriously," he suggested.

"No," she breathed.

Her fear made him more at ease.

"You see how it is," he explained. "I was sorry about Ironwood. I wanted to help. I still want to."

"Then it wasn't on account of me that you came back?" she asked him rapidly and softly.

He tried to say no, but the word stuck in his throat. He could only gaze miserably.

He at last managed to mutter: "You'd think me a great fool, of course. It would be like something out of a book, I mean—love at first sight—" He laughed. The sound of that high-pitched, false laughter wounded his own ears.

"No, I wouldn't think it was just something out of a book," she told him. "I know what such a thing can be."

"Do you?" said the Sleeper, with a great leap of his heart.

She raised a small hand against him. By that he knew that he had been stepping toward her, and he stopped himself. There were other more beautiful women, but none to fit so exactly into his mind, gentle, true, and cherishable.

"Did you come back for me?" she asked him.

"Yes," said the Sleeper, and stood prepared for scorn, even though he knew that there could be no scorn in her.

Then she said: "I've always thought that I could

do anything for my father. But I couldn't do—I mean, I love another man.''

The Sleeper found himself grinning like a fool with what he tried to make a polite smile of assent.

''Of course,'' said he, very hoarsely. ''How could you help? Everybody's been here to worship you. How could you help? Oh, I understand that perfectly well! You know—still, a cat will look at a king!'' He shook his head to clear his stunned brain. ''It wouldn't make any difference,'' he said. ''I'd still go ahead and try my hand with Ironwood.''

''Would you?''

''Yes, I would.''

''For the sake of my father, and you don't know him, except to-day?''

''I'd feel sort of bound to do something,'' said the Sleeper.

''I'll have to tell you!'' said the girl, beginning to tremble, her voice shaking also. ''I'll have to tell who it is.''

''I've not asked to know,'' he told her.

She nodded, but went straight on:

''It was last spring. It was early spring. There was still snow on the top of Mount Loman. And I was late milking the cow, so that I saw the hills fade, and nothing was clear except the snow in the twilight. I was milking the cow, yonder in the corral.''

Here she stopped. The Sleeper stood like stone. He wanted to interrupt her and tell her that this was none of his business, but, somehow, he could not speak.

''When I had finished,'' she went on, ''I picked up the bucket and the milk stool and went to the gate. A man was there leaning on the other side of the fence. He opened the gate for me, and I walked through. He took the weight of the bucket of milk, and he took my hand with it. He wasn't very tall. He looked rather rounded and sleek, as far as I could tell. He wore short mustaches. But when he spoke to me, everything stopped in my mind to listen. He said that he was Parmenter. He said that he had been waiting for me for more than two years, and that now he was ready to take me."

"A robber—a murderer!" said the Sleeper. "A man that—" He remembered that he had been a sneak thief and stopped, biting his lip.

"I didn't seem to care what he had been," said she. "It only mattered that he was there, talking. He said that he wanted to give up his way of life and marry, and he said that he wished to marry me. He would bring back Ironwood, he said, and take me away."

She waited for comment. The Sleeper could make none.

"He told me," said she, "that I didn't need to hurry, and that he would wait until I sent word that I was ready. I've been waiting ever since, trying to think, and knowing that my father never would forgive me if I went with that man. I've never whispered this to any one before. But you had to know. Will you understand, then?"

"Aye," said the Sleeper faintly. "I understand. You cared for him, all at once."

"Yes," said she.

"I'll do more than understand," said he. "I'll help you."

"How can you do that?"

"I'll take word from you to him. To Parmenter, I mean."

"Would you do that for me?"

"Do you see?" said the Sleeper. "I want to be gone away and forget you, but I know that I can't do that. Next best is to stay and face things out. Even a gun can be faced down, sometimes. If you'll write a message, I'll carry the letter. I want to see Parmenter. I don't know why. I almost have to see him, since you've told me this."

The door of the house was wrenched open.

Old Morice flung himself out with a shout, but his leg slipped on the veranda floor, and the Sleeper had to catch him in strong arms to keep him from falling.

Straight into the face of the Sleeper old Morice was shouting insults.

"I could've known what you are by the look of your calf's eye!" he yelled. "I wish that I'd never seen you! Get out of my sight! D'you hear? Get away and stay away! You maunderin' weak-wit, you thick-headed, sleepy-eyed snake! Get out of my sight! You'll carry letters, will you? You'll be a danged go-between, will you?"

The Sleeper set him safely upright and then hastened down the path away from the house. Even the dogs of Enderby had not been more terrible to him than the wrath of the old man.

"Into the house with you!" thundered the father.

The girl already had disappeared, with a low, frightened cry.

The Sleeper, in the meantime, had hurried off under the trees, when he heard a peculiar hitching step behind him and turned to see old Morice following as fast as he could. He thought the horse breeder must have gone mad, and was already to take to his heels, when he was amazed to hear Morice call out in a guarded voice:

"Wait a minute! Sleeper! Wait a minute!"

He waited, ready to take to flight. And Morice came panting up.

He tried to take the Sleeper by the lapel of his coat, but the latter skillfully eluded this grasp.

"I don't mean you no harm," said Morice. "Stand and listen to me, will you? I've had another idea. I've thought out a different plan—"

He rested a hand against the trunk of a tree and breathed heavily, still watching the Sleeper with his fiery eye.

"Wait near here," he said. "I'm gunna go off for a short walk. You slip into the house and get the letter from my girl. Go off with it. Take it to Parmenter. I'll leave you free for that."

"What's your scheme?" asked the Sleeper curiously. "Do you want the horse at a price like that?"

Old Morice began to laugh, and the sound of that laughter was as savagely exultant as anything the Sleeper ever had heard.

"Do I want any horse at the price of everlasting fire?" he demanded. "No, young man, but I want you to carry that letter to Parmenter. You hear?"

"I don't understand. What's for you to gain in that, Morice?"

"You don't understand. Of course, you don't understand. But what'll happen when you deliver that letter?"

"Why, I don't know."

"Think again!"

"I tell you, how can I guess? I'll just see Parmenter, and that's all."

The old man laughed again, but this time through his closed teeth.

"That's all I want!" said he.

CHAPTER 15.

A WOUNDED RIDER

WHEN THE SLEEPER said good-by to Steve, the hotel proprietor, the latter showed a good deal of curiosity.

"Didn't Old Man Morice try to hook you up to his interests?" he asked. "Didn't he try to get you to throw in with him agin' Parmenter, the thief?"

But the Sleeper avoided an answer to this question. He shook hands. He waved to a group of people who had come out to watch him off, and then he took the western trail out of Alcalde. That trail he kept to until he was well outside the limits of the town. Then he swung sharply to the left and went south across the plain, pointing his course toward the Tinnio Pass, a ragged indentation in the southern mountains.

Toward this he kept the bay mare headed, and found to his great relief, after an hour on the way, that she was one of those rare animals which will hold to a course after it has been well picked out for them. She could make deviations right and left in order to get better going, but she always ended by pointing straight toward the pass again. Her bone-racking trot she maintained also, until he drew her up. There was a pounding in his brain and a pain in his stomach from her severe gait. Besides, he was in no hurry to get to the Tinnio Pass. It opened, men said, upon that upper country over which the great Parmenter was king, and he had a letter in his pocket addressed to that gentleman in the strangely bold, free-swinging handwriting of pretty Evelyn Morice.

That should be a passport for him, but still he was in no haste. It was exquisite pain to be sending her invitation to her lover. But at least he was still involved in her affairs, within her horizon, and that was an odd comfort.

He had one hope, and this was what Morice had planted in his mind—that when he met Parmenter face to face, something might happen.

What, he could not say. He did not even think. He merely set the goal dimly before himself. Somewhere in the future he was to meet Parmenter, and then—

He spent a good deal of time going over what he knew of the man and his appearance. He had found pictures of the great Parmenter. He had heard the girl's own description of him as a man not very tall, and sleek, with mustaches trimmed short. But when he returned to the hotel that day and opened the subject of Parmenter, he had various impressions given to him. For one man said that Parmenter was very tall, and that he had a raw-boned look. And another told him that Parmenter was not only fat, but he was soft and beginning to grow bald, and gray around the temples. Still a third wished to say that Parmenter was not soft at all, but was really a giant of strength. Men differed regarding his age. He was called as young as thirty and as old as fifty. But, young and old, every one agreed that there was only one Parmenter, and that when a man heard his voice, he knew it was the true Parmenter, no matter in what disguise.

These stories excited the tramp more and more. But let Parmenter have all the virtues and the strengths in the world, he had none which, in a certain sense, could be matched with the gun of Trot Enderby, now comfortably fitted to the hip of the Sleeper. It was the matching of this old Colt and its loose action, felt the present wearer, against the band, the wisdom, the experience, the cruel cunning of the outlaw.

Night found him in the foothills. The pass was just above him. It looked like a clean cleft through the heights, though as a matter of fact he had been told that it was merely the quickest way of coming in among them. This was the narrow rift which carried one to the heart of the wilderness. It was the gate to the domain of Parmenter.

He camped in a nest of stones, because he felt that these would give him a shelter sufficient to hide the light of his fire from prying eyes. He should not, perhaps, light a fire at all, but self-indulgence proved stronger than caution. He made a fire of good dry wood from the brush that grew all around him, and with it boiled some coffee—there had been a trickle of water an hour before camping from which he could fill his canteen and then let the bay drink.

After that he lay at ease, sipping the coffee, munching hard crackers, and then, as he smoked a cigarette with his head pillowed on one arm, looking up toward the stars, and with the mare lifting her fire-struck eyes from her grazing now and again, he felt that he would not have been in any other place than this, or committed to any other adventure than this ride into the mountains to find Parmenter.

For, when they met, what would happen?

He became aware that the mare, after stamping and snorting softly, had raised her head and was gazing fixedly toward some distant point in the night, behind her present master. It seemed to the Sleeper's drowsy mind that this might be a warning, and he was about to turn on his elbow, at least, to peer over his shoulder toward the darkness when the cold, round mouth of a gun dropped on the exact center of his forehead, and he glanced up the barrel of a rifle to a grim, bearded face behind the weapon. This long and heavy weapon the stranger carried like a revolver, in one hand, and used it lightly. His left arm was crudely supported in a red-stained sling that passed around his neck.

"Who are you?" pleasantly asked the stranger.

"A fool!" said the Sleeper.

"Yeah, you're that," said the other. "But what's your name?"

"They call me the Sleeper."

"Yeah, you're that, too. D'you belong? I guess not."

"To what?"

The bearded man jerked his head toward the pass.

"I don't know what you mean," said the Sleeper.

"Are you Parmenter's?"

"Parmenter's what?" asked the Sleeper. "You mean, am I one of his men?"

"That's what I've been tryin' to ask you for the last ten minutes, but I couldn't talk simple enough for you to understand. You getting my drift now? D'you belong to the boys?''

"No," said the Sleeper, "I belong to nobody."

The stranger stepped back and settled the rifle against the rock. Then he slumped to the ground.

"If you don't belong, fix me up!" he said. "I'm bleeding to death!''

The Sleeper came to his feet, agape. He could see, now, that there was a bluish tint in the temples of the man, and that he was grinning with exhaustion. He worked off the coat, cut away the sleeve, and saw that the whole side of the stranger was soaked with rapidly dripping red. He had been shot through the fleshy lower part of the shoulder by a rifle bullet that had clipped through without tearing the flesh badly; nevertheless, the wound was in such a position that he had been unable to stop the bleeding. The Sleeper made a good strong tourniquet. The oozing of the blood stopped.

This was achieved at the cost of exquisite pain, no doubt, but the bearded man uttered not an oath, not a murmur. He accepted this anguish almost gratefully, and then drank off a big tin cup of coffee and munched some hardtack with it.

"You'd better stretch out and have a sleep," suggested the tramp.

The other made the snarling beginning of a laugh, but checked it, as though the heaving of his chest hurt him too much.

"Sleep, eh?" said he. "If I don't keep moving I'll have a sleep, all right, that'll last long enough to rest me.''

He got up with a staggering lurch, and the Sleeper

steadied him on his feet.

"You're not going to try to ride, are you?" he protested, see the stranger was making toward a cow pony whose eyes showed beyond the circle of the rocks.

"Give me a hand up," said the other. "I'll stick to the saddle once I get into it."

The Sleeper obeyed. As he laid hold of this man, he could feel the tremor of weakness and of effort in all the heavy body. He lifted, and the weight shifted from his hands into the saddle with a heavy thump.

"You'll never make it," said the Sleeper. "Stay here and I'll take care of you, man."

"You stay here and you won't be able to take care of yourself, let alone me," answered the other. "Leave go the bridle, will you? I'm off!"

"You'll fall before you've gone a mile."

"I will if I stay here wastin' my strength with talk."

"What are you afraid of?"

"You fool!" cried the other, his impatience breaking out loudly. "Can't you see that I'm one of them, and that I'm bound *out*?"

He touched the pony with his spurs, and the mustang jogged off through the night.

The Sleeper watched the rider melt away into the dark. Even at the beginning of the ride the man's head was canted far to one side and then to the other, swaying with feebleness. But something about his shoulders and the grip of his knees on the sides of the horse told the watcher that this journeyer would go far before he slid to the ground.

Then the Sleeper went back to the fire in haste to put it out.

It was so securely fenced around with rocks that nothing appeared of the fire except a very, very dim glow. And yet there were eyes in those mountains so keen that even this small illumination was sufficient to catch their attention.

The Sleeper extinguished that fire as fast as he could, and leading the mare, went off to a good distance. There he made his final camp for that evening, but he found that sleep was hard to win, and that for the first time in his life he was lying warmly wrapped, but staring at the stars and seeing unpleasant pictures among them.

This man of the beard, how he clung in the mind of the Sleeper!

He looked fit for anything in the way of violent action, and yet he had failed to please the terrible Parmenter. Or was it some breach of loyalty and personal faith which had exiled him from the valley with a bullet wound that had missed the heart so narrowly? Certainly it had been fired to kill.

He found his thoughts trailing after the fugitive, but feeling exactly the same absence of hope which had appeared in the face of the bearded man himself, as though he were matched against an arm too long to be escaped. He had left them. He was bound out. And the Sleeper felt he knew what the end of that voyage would be, and at what a shadowy coast the big fellow would ultimately arrive.

At last sleep came. He dreamed that he had met Parmenter and was frozen to the bone by one glance from him. Then he wakened, and found his body chill with the morning wind off the heights.

CHAPTER 16.

A MAN IN RAGS

IF HE WAS AWAKE and cold in the morning wind, at least he was safe from the dream, and the Sleeper jumped up and swung his arms to restore his body warmth. He told himself that now was the time to show the utmost caution. It was no doubt true that his letter would make him reasonably safe in hands of the great Parmenter, but he was still far from that chief. He must use every precaution—and yet ten minutes later he was cooking his breakfast, for hunger was a force of temptation which the tramp could not resist as long as there was food at hand. Toasted bacon, hardtack and coffee, spiced with mountain air, made an excellent meal for him. And the bay mare, too, seemed to be sharpened in spirits. She had her ears pricked and her eyes bright, and when he saddled her, he was almost chucked off over her tail by her first leap forward.

He stuck on by the grace of luck and rode straight up through the hills with the fresh air growing warmer as the sun mounted, until he came into the throat of the pass itself. He readily could understand from this point of view why Parmenter chose these mountains for his headquarters, for the pass opened on a torn and ragged sea of peaks, some naked, some shadowy with forest. And in the valleys there were thickets of rather undersized sycamores, and ash, willow, walnut, and cherry which grew dense enough to make hard riding for any one who did not know the lay of the land perfectly well.

There were comfortable sights of game now and then, which proved that the region had not yet been hunted over to any great extent. He heard the note of an oriole; he heard the purring wings of quail rising in a bevy, and saw a gay cock pheasant on the edge of some brush. Best of all, on a hill-top at least half a mile away he saw the clear silhouette of an antlered stag. It made the Sleeper hungry, even so short a time after breakfast.

But the farther he invaded this country the more he felt like a navigator in an open small boat, alone in unknown seas. His familiar terrain comprised tramp jungles on the outskirts of towns whose hen yards could be invaded for supper time; and he knew railroads—all the empire of roundhouses, switching yards, big stations and small repair yards, Mexican freight-car villages on the Santa Fe, together with every detail which one needs in order to fly across the continent as a tramp royal riding blind baggage, or pursue the way more leisurely on frieghts. He could read the face of a "brakie," and tell to ten cents exactly what the fellow would ask for permission to ride across his section unmolested. He not only knew "shacks" and their kind, but he had a good nose for railroad detectives, and could outline the character of a "flatty" as far away as the deer he now saw on the hill-top.

This was the kingdom that he knew, and through which he had skulked and lingered, avoiding labor, starving rather than work. Every muscle in his body still protested against the mere thoughts of effort of any kind. And it seemed a weary distance before him and a wearier distance to return.

That was not all.

The very size of the country and its strangeness oppressed him. His loneliness grew. The mountains seemed vaster.

Then, in the midst of the pass, the ground grew more easy, for it opened out into rich, rolling grass lands, which ought to have been fattening cattle, though not a cow was in sight. It was a natural little pocket among the heights, with several thousand acres where water gushed up in springs, and the hollows stood thick with good timber, and the crowns of the hills offered sun-cured grass of the best. It was too low for the snows, and it was too high for the heat.

He was not surprised when the trail took him close to what seemed the ruins of a house, burned down, perhaps, or thrown in a heap by an earthquake. He could trace the rude rectangle which its outer walls once had covered, but all was smudged and obscured by the finger of time. And in the very center of the outline there had sprung up a small thicket.

There was a small lean-to built near the place, and in front of the lean-to a man was fitting a coyote skin on a stretcher. He had as wild a look, this mountain dweller, as the Sleeper ever had seen in any human. No tramp of the road could have been more ragged, and these rags were of home-made deerskin. He had moccasins on his feet, and a little fur cap on his head, while his long hair flowed down to his shoulders and framed a face covered to the eyes with straggling beard.

He looked up when he saw the Sleeper, then hailed him with a wave of the hand.

The Sleeper rode over to him.

"You seen a lot of wagons coming up toward the pass, loaded down?" asked the mountain man.

"No," said the Sleeper. "Wagons?" he added. "How could wagons come up over that trail?"

"How could they? Oh, they could come, all right. You ain't long in these mountains or you'd know what wagons can do!"

"No," said the tramp. "I'm new in this place."

"I've wrote and ordered two months ago," said the other, parting his beard and stroking it in thought and worry. "It oughta be here before this."

"A lot of stuff?" inquired the Sleeper curiously.

"Yeah. The whole fixings for a house. A bang-up stove, the first thing. Why, that stove would about load down a hoss all by itself."

He laughed happily at the thought.

"And chairs, tables, sinks, bathtubs. Everything! I'm gunna have a house, not a danged shack, I tell you! I had a house here before!" He gestured at the rectangular mound.

"Why do you want to build here?" asked the Sleeper. "Cattle?"

"Why, don't you see 'em?" said the other. He turned and waved his hand. "Well," he said, after staring at the empty hills in amazement. "I reckon that they've all gone down into the hollows, and that's a funny thing, at this time of day. They'd oughta be out fillin' their stomachs before the heat. But then, who could ever understand the ways of a cow in her mind? Or a steer? Anyway, there they are, fattenin', gettin' heavy for the market."

He laughed again exultantly. "When I look 'em over," he said, "I wonder that there's enough people to eat that many. It'll sure glut the market when they're turned in for slaughter."

"I don't see a one," said the Sleeper, puzzled. He looked again at the rags of the stranger. "When did the other house go? Fire?"

"Fire. Yes. I was a fool and built it of wood. It wouldn't stand. Wood won't stand. You gotta have rock. That'll stand, all right. Well, I was a fool. I built out of logs, and the fire come along with Parmenter and burned it down."

"Parmenter?"

"Yeah. He done it. Come and cleaned out my place. Drove off all of the cows and cleaned me out, and then put a match to the house. He said that he wanted to keep these here mountains clean of ranchers. So he cleaned me out, but you can't beat this country. The grass grows and the cows grow with it, and here I got me a bigger herd than I ever run before!"

He laughed again, his bright and confiding eye fixed upon the Sleeper.

"When did this happen?"

"When? Lemme see!" He fixed his eye upon space. "Well, it must 'a' been as much as a coupla months ago," said the mountain man.

"A couple of months ago that this house burned

down?" asked the Sleeper, amazed. And he stared at the grassgrown mounds.

"Yeah, about that long ago," said the other. "Made a terrible roarin' column of flame, I'll tell you. The heads of it jumped into the sky and put the stars out. Everything was black except the fire itself. You never seen a finer blaze than my house made!"

The Sleeper nodded. He was puzzled.

"But there's grass over the ruins," he said. "How could that happen in so few weeks?"

"Ah, you're a stranger to these here mountains," said the other almost pityingly. "You dunno how the grass grows. Mighty fast!"

"And a thicket in the middle of your floor?" asked the Sleeper. He pointed toward the bushes, which were several years' growth.

The ragged fellow regarded them complacently.

"Yeah. You'd think that not even weeds could grow that fast, wouldn't you?" he remarked. "But these here mountains, they're rich, I tell you. And things will grow, up here, in a way that'd surprise you."

It came suddenly home to the tramp. The mind of the man was lost. It was not only his house that had gone from him.

"Well," said the Sleeper gently, "I hope that you'll get your wagons up here soon."

"They gotta come," said the mountain man. "The skunks! They're mighty keen to get your money quick, but they ain't half so keen to deliver what you've ordered. Why? Because they get the money in the bank, working on interest for them. That's the reason, I tell you! Oh, no! They get a lot of pleasure out of the money that we pay in advance! Stoves—bathtubs, too! There ain't been a bathtub before in the whole range of these here mountains, I reckon! And a big boiler for the hot water. Gotta have them things, if you wanta have a real house. I read it once in a book," he confided at the last.

"Why did Parmenter do it?" asked the Sleeper.

"Him? Parmenter?"

"Yes. Parmenter."

"Why, he didn't have no good reason. But they's some that build and they's some that tear down. Some folks is the wood that is piled in a heap, and some is the fire that burns it."

"The everlasting scoundrel!" cried out the Sleeper.

"Well, no," answered the man of leather rags surprisingly. "The fact is that the good Lord warms His hands at a fire like that. And there ain't so often that a good heat gets clean up to heaven, if you want my idea on it!"

The cheerfulness of this poor fellow was more terrible, in the eyes of Sleeper, than fierce complaints and open hatred. He longed to be gone from a place where his hand and thought could be of no help. And, drawing a deep breath, he said to the other:

"Well, so long. Where would a man be apt to find Parmenter?"

"Ride straight on and you'll meet him," said the man of rags. "Everybody does. So long!"

He turned back to his work, and the Sleeper continued on his course.

CHAPTER 17.

A QUESTION OF LANGUAGE

HE CAME TO A VALLEY into which the trail dipped, and wound down it with many twistings and windings among the thicket of trees. He was now glad of them, however, for they gave him a shade against the increasing brightness of the sun, which grew hot with amazing speed, though it was still not the prime of the day.

At last he turned with the increasing sweep of the canyon and saw before him a hill with an old Mexican town white as chalk upon the top of it, and the trail a dim mark, zig-zagging up the side of the hill.

By the huddling houses and the whitewashed walls he knew that the place was Mexican, and by the narrowness of the streets—for he could look between the housetops and measure the width with some degree of accuracy. In Vera Cruz, which he had reached by stowing himself away in a freighter, he had learned to recognize these things in another day, just as he had learned Spanish in the Vera Cruz jail. It was the memory of the jail, perhaps, that made him shiver a little as he looked up toward this town. Or perhaps it was the icy brightness of the whitewashed walls under the sunshine.

All at once it seemed to the Sleeper that there was only one obvious and sensible thing for him to do, and this was to leave the goal he had started for, turn about, and get as fast as he could out of this country where men were driven wounded away, or where they were robbed of their wits by the cruelties of Parmenter. But the words of old Morice rang still in his mind. When he met Parmenter, something would happen. What would it be?

He loosed the rein again, and with her racking trot, the mare carried him forward to the pitch of the hill. There she was reduced to a walk, and he was sorry for it. He wanted to throw himself forward on his fate, which he felt, with an odd surety of premonition, that he was bound to find in this village with its huddle of a hundred houses and its old, moldering walls stretched snugly around it. There was an arched gateway through which the trail pointed. And the upper part of the way was so steep that the surface had been cut into steps. No wagon could enter here. In fact, there was hardly room for a single horseman to pass through without scraping his feet on either side. The archway above his head was covered with names and initials. He went slowly on, reading them. One bit of doggerel stuck in his mind afterward:

Here passed Vanderheisen Kip.
Pull your guns and let 'em rip!

He could not help smiling, but he guessed that a

good many of the same frame of mind had passed this way before him.

Then he was through the short tunnel that pierced the wall and saw the town immediately before him.

The narrow streets were built on steps, swinging crookedly here and there among the crowding houses. The walls blazed, the shadows slept in the middle heat of the day. He saw a woman squatted in a doorway, rubbing maize into a pulp for the preparation of tortillas—a sudden taste for those clammy things came back to him, a fiercer hunger than that for venison. A pair of pigs, contentedly rubbing sides, went down the street and barely divided to allow room for the legs of the mare. Here was a child puffing with straining cheeks and with outward-thrusting eyes as it labored to get music out of a very sick harmonica. And then he had a glimpse of a whole train of youngsters scampering like monkeys over a succession of roofs.

But they ran silently. And what noise there was in the town was deadened by the thin mountain air and seemed to come from a great distance. He began to feel as though he had ridden into a dream. But the central core of that dream, he kept saying to himself, was Parmenter. That memory could keep him awake.

So, fairly alert, he went on up the steps of the street, the unaccustomed hoofs of the mare slipping now and again on the stone paving, which was polished with wear in the center, and patched with moss and with stubborn gray lichens along the edges.

Then the street opened into a minute plaza, with a small church at one side, and a bell tower rising above it, with the bell in the open lantern, secured by lashings of weather-blackened ropes to a cracked and sagging bell beam above. A dog sat on the steps of the church, scratching itself. It leaped with bristling hair to bark at a stranger, and the Sleeper felt suddenly as though he had entered a private house.

There was a shoemaker cross-legged at the door of his dark little shop, putting a clumsy half sole on an equally clumsy shoe. And yet he displayed upon a bench beside him a magnificent new pair of riding boots which undoubtedly he had made with his own hands, and inlaid the tops with elaborate patterns in black and red.

He stopped his work to stare at the stranger also, and to look from him at the barking dog, as though he were curious to learn whatever the dog knew or guessed about this new fellow.

Exactly facing the church the Sleeper saw a cantina. On the sidewalk before it stood two tables, baking and warping in the sun. Within opened a narrow, cool vista, and here the Sleeper decided to stop, for he could guess that the life of the town flowed from and around this cantina, as the blood of the body flows around the heart. And if there was anything to be learned by gossip, it could be learned here.

Straightway he dismounted, tied his horse at the hitching post, and passed through the low entrance.

It was very dim inside. Darkness takes to a degree the place of coolness so that the shutters of this cantina were closed on the sunward side, though in this manner they admitted most of the heat of the day and barred out every stir of air.

It was a poverty-stricken little place. The only attempt at decoration appeared in the mirror behind the bar, for on the glass was a crude design in gilded paint, most of which had worn away, so that the original pattern could only be guessed at, and that vaguely. The floor was set out with a few little home-made tables, with square tops. Those tables looked to the Sleeper like handy imitations of clubs, if need should arise. Only one man was in the place. He looked like a muleteer, or one of some such calling, and he had in his hand a good coiled length of blacksnake, the red string of the lash dripping down to the floor like a snake's tongue, while the heavy, loaded butt was grasped in the palm of the hands and the central coils were wrapped around the fellow's wrist. He kept this whip in his right hand, using the left for drinking and for holding his cigarette, so that it was plain that he expected to use the blacksnake on higher game than mules, if there were ever a need. He wore a patch over one eye, which proverbially makes a man look a villain, and succeeded very well in this case. For he had a scowling forehead, with three deep wrinkles incised in the center, like those which are apt to be used by actors and singers for making up for the part of Mephistopheles.

This fellow, after giving the stranger a hard stare, deliberately turned his head away to indicate a sullen lack of interest.

The bartender had been sitting at the table of his single guest, but now he rose and hurried behind the bar. There he picked up a towel and began polishing off the surface, while he nodded and smiled toward the Sleeper. He was as keen, quick, and gay as a cricket. When he was sober, his broad forehead and his pinched cheeks gave him somewhat the look of a death's head, but since he was nearly always smiling and bowing and nodding, and always agreeing with every one, this silent look of his never was noticed except by the very patient and the very observant.

There was beer. And the Sleeper took a glass of it. It was homemade, and very bad and flat, with a decided flavor of resin in it. However, it was drinkable, and the tramp managed to struggle through half of his glass while he sat in a dark corner. There he looked over the dirty little shadowy cantina again, and once more fixed his attention on the muleteer. The latter had been staring brutally again; but why should one who carries a gun hesitate to meet any eye? The Sleeper deliberately looked the fellow over once more, and stared full at him, until suddenly, like a sullen animal, the Mexican swung his head to the side. He was snarling silently. He looked ready to spring from the table and rush at the stranger.

In the meantime, the keeper of the place hovered from one table to the other. The Sleeper looked like better money for the moment, but the muleteer was an old customer, so the proprietor distributed his smiles.

He asked if the Sleeper were a stranger here, and the tramp admitted the obvious fact. Had he ever been there before? No, he had not. He was traveling for pleasure, then?

"There's pleasure up here, is there?" asked the Sleeper.

"Why, there's the old town, Señor!"

"And what's in it, amigo?"

"Houses, people, rats!" said the bartender, and he laughed a little, always winding up with a chuckle, as though he made mirth for the public and also kept over something to laugh at by himself.

"What sort of rats?" said the Sleeper.

"Gray rats. They nibble your toes at night," said the keeper of the cantina.

"That must make you laugh in your sleep," said the Sleeper.

Suddenly he found that both the men were silent. They had lifted their heads at him, as a cat will do when it sees for the first time an object of interest.

"Yes, yes, we laugh a good deal," said the muleteer.

He spoke excellent English. The Sleeper was amazed!

"You don't come from this town," he suggested.

"You mean that I speak English?"

"Yes, and a certain kind."

"Well," said the muleteer, "I learned to speak it in a certain place."

He waited, obviously expecting more questions, and therefore, the Sleeper said:

"Where was that?"

"In Sing Sing," said the muleteer. "D'you know that place?"

"I've seen it," said the Sleeper, smiling in spite of himself. "It looks as though the walls would keep the wind out! Were you there long?"

"Long enough to learn English," said the muleteer. "May I ask you something?"

"I suppose so."

"Then tell me where you learned Mexican."

"In the hoosegow at Vera Cruz," said the tramp.

Suddenly both the muleteer and the barkeeper were laughing loudly.

"Drink with me," said the tramp.

"Aye," said the muleteer, "if you'll drink first with me."

"And why?"

"It's a custom of the town. We like to see a man show his throat before he shows his wallet!"

CHAPTER 18.

ONATE COMES

THE PLACID HARDNESS of this remark made the tramp smile broadly. He had met many a callous man in his travels, but some with more claims to calm brutality than this speech suggested. The frankness made him feel more at ease. The brutality sharpened his observance of all around him.

"Very well," said he, "and I'll drink with you."

He went over and sat down at the table of the muleteer. The man, in spite of his good English, looked no better close up than he had at a distance. His face was round as a ball. The eyes were apparently unprotected by brows, and this gave him an odd look, like a frog. His brown skin supported a thick stubble of unshaven beard. He looked as though he were constantly about to burst into a tantrum. However, he smiled amiably at the stranger.

Then he added to the bartender: "Bring us some of the black wine. And don't put any knock-out drops in it. We had better wait until later on for that. Get him half drunk, and then he will never be able to notice the bitter taste.''

The tramp laughed, and so did the barkeeper, but nevertheless, the Sleeper watched the hands of the proprietor with close attention. It was so easy to sprinkle a little powder into a glass, and this seemed to him the home town and chief resort of murderous tricks of all sorts. He remembered that in the wallet which he had just heard referred to he had more than fourteen hundred dollars. Certainly the memory made his head fit very loosely upon that same throat which they were so willing to see.

The black wine was brought. It puckered the gullet after swallowing, and left a taste of ashes on the root of the tongue, but it was much better than the beer, and the muleteer drank it off with a relish, and then paid the bill.

''You've come up here for something,'' said the muleteer. ''Why don't you let us know what it is? That is, if it's not too important. We both get something for the little spy work that we do up here. A dollar here, a dollar there keeps a man's whistle wet. So, if it's nothing important, tell us your business and we'll tell it to those who ought to know.''

''It's not important,'' replied the tramp, still amused by the peculiar frankness of these rascals. ''I'm here to see Señor Parmenter. I have a message for him.''

The muleteer raised a forefinger at the bartender, and the proprietor blinked and nodded at the muleteer. His smile disappeared. For that moment he looked like a death's head.

''Well, the message shall be passed along,'' said

the muleteer. "You can buy us a drink if you want to, now."

"Of course I will," replied the tramp.

Before he could order, a woman came running into the shop with a great rustling and bustling of skirts which fell around her barrellike form like corn husks around a tamale.

She leaned over the bar so far that one of her feet left the floor and cocked out behind her. Her whisper was as loud as a dog's panting as she said to the proprietor:

"Close your door and lock it! Oñate is in town again, and three or four behind him. Oñate is sure to come here! Close your door if you don't want your shop ruined again!"

She went out.

The proprietor, with his sinister and secret smiling, had appeared as a man above the ordinary care for property and money. But now he remained for a moment with fallen head and with both his hands on the edge of the bar.

He did not complain aloud. The muleteer, in a placid mutter, commented upon the silent picture of despair.

"The last time that Oñate came," said he, "my friend there had a good lot of bottles behind that bar. He had cognac, too. It did you good to drink coffee and sip cognac with it, sitting there at the two tables in the little plaza and listening to the singing in the church, maybe—it was like Paris—"

At this word, he bit his lip and wrinkled his eyes shut. One would have thought that the memory had pierced him to the heart.

He went on again: "This fiend Oñate came. You know about him?"

"I've never heard of his name," said the Sleeper.

"You're a stranger, and Louis Oñate is a local murderer. He likes to kill people in the same block. Then the others will look up to him and whisper when he goes by. He's that kind of man. He loves to give pain. Well, Oñate came here a while ago and smashed everything except the mirror. He said that he'd leave the mirror so that it could look out on the room and see the change. But now watch. He won't lock the front door to keep out that same monster, anyway. He'll stay and endure. He has Indian blood in him. So have I. That teaches us to endure. Centuries of kicks and whip strokes in our blood. To white men we look up—and show the throat!"

As he muttered this he did not look at his companion at the table, but glared with a dreadful grimace through the doorway at the white light on the plaza. Somewhere higher in the building a door slammed loudly, and a wind whistled in a corridor. It was more solemn and lonely than the approach of a storm—not a storm on dry land, either.

"You'd better lock the front door," said the muleteer to the bartender.

"No, I won't do that, amigo," replied the little man. "I'll stay here and wait. If I closed the door he might grow angry and break the door down, and then he'd probably burn the house and us in it."

They remained for two or three minutes silently looking at one another, exchanging the opinions of bitter and oppressed blood. But they did not speak. Only the proprietor filled the glasses again and brought them back to the table.

"Drink with us!" said the tramp, offering a broad-faced silver dollar.

"Keep your money," said the little man, who was a philosopher as well as a rogue. "What are three glasses compared to what they'll be spilling here in another moment?"

He raised a hand, and clearly from the street they could hear the babble of wild, laughing voices, over which roared one dominating tone.

"That Oñate," said the muleteer, nodding. "I'll be going. You'd better come, too." He nodded to the tramp.

But the Sleeper was lost in thought. He looked at the little proprietor, who was smiling, as usual.

"Was that your wife?" he said, pointing toward the door through which the fat woman had come.

"Yes," said the other. "She's always full of worry. Five children are five worries, señor. Now you had better go quickly. Oñate does not like strangers. Better go through this back door—then he won't see you. Otherwise—"

He flicked his hand outward, as though he were waving smoke away; it was a very curt suggestion that nothing more than smoke would remain of the stranger if he lingered in this place.

The muleteer stood up, stretched himself, and started for the door.

"Our friend doesn't like to interrupt his drinks," said he to the proprietor. And they both looked at one another again.

The Sleeper, in the meantime, had not stirred. He was looking at the cracked ceiling, which sagged a good deal in the center, and at the painted border which surrounded it, with a cluster of pink doves in the center. No matter how hard these fellows might be, there was a good deal of humanity in them. They were born; they would die. In the meantime, they had wives and children. That thought, for some reason, surprised him.

Still he did not stir, and he was conscious of a weight on his hip. It was the burden of the old Colt of Trot Enderby.

"What is your name?" he asked the proprietor.

"Pedro," said the man.

"What else?"

"Nothing else. But some of them call me Lontano. Pedro Lontano, if you want two names; but one is good enough to live by. Men don't give two names to burros and dogs!" He was still smiling as he spoke.

"Pedro," said the Sleeper. "I'm going to stay here. Maybe I can keep your wine from spilling."

The muleteer abruptly turned at the door and came back into the room. He sat down at the table of the Sleeper.

"I shall stay here, also," said he. "My name is Vicente. Men don't even call me Lontano!"

"I'm glad to know you, señor," said the Sleeper gravely. "My name is Sleeper."

By magic the glasses had been filled again.

"Good dreams to you, Señor the Sleeper," said the muleteer, and lifted his drink.

Then the babble of voices came loudly up the street and echoed more widely and faintly in the plaza itself.

The Sleeper could hear that dominant, brawling throat shouting:

"We'll take a look at little Lontano. I'll fix him, Lontano, the dog! I'll teach him to complain!"

The speaker came into the doorway and paused there, looking about him as a ferret might come to a dark rabbit warren and peer red-eyed into the interior. This little man with the big voice looked like a ferret even more than he acted like one. He was not more than three or four inches over five feet in height, and even for his height, his head was small and set upon a forward-jutting neck. A scar ripped across his forehead, cheek, and right eye, and the pull of the muscles kept that eyelid fluttering and winking.

"Come in, come in!" he shouted. "There's still something here to lap up! Here's Vicente, too, the gossip and mule driver! Why shouldn't mule drivers be driven? Here is a gringo, too, I think! Are you a gringo?"

He started across the room, and, dropping his fist on the table, leaned and glared into the face of the Sleeper.

He was dressed with the foolish brilliance of a begger suddenly become rich. His jacket was a bright blue. His trousers were white. He was loaded with gold and silver work more than a rich alter cloth. But the clothes were dripped and smudged over with grease and with the stains of food and of drink. He looked like a horrible little caricature of a villain, a comic-opera murderer. But there was no comedy in his overbright eyes, greedy eyes, or in his hands, which were unnaturally long, and covered with hair to the first knuckles.

The Sleeper shrank a little, and the other bawled in his face.

"A gringo, too scared to speak. Come in, amigos!"

CHAPTER 19.

A SMOKE BUBBLE

THEY HAD SPILLED into the room already—four young fellows of twenty or so, old enough to have their strength, young enough to lack their brains. They came in shouting with laughter—foolish young laughter at nothing in particular, laughter at their own strength, laughter at the ridiculousness of the world which was their oyster. They stood about the table. They yelled over their shoulders at Pedro Lontano to bring liquor, and hastily he brought a tray full of glasses.

Fear made the Sleeper tremble. Then it left him in a flash. From cold his blood turned to hot. Anger swelled in him. He kept telling himself that he must be self-controlled. But always his mind was leaping back to the weight on his hip, and the six deaths which were read in it, as he felt.

"Get up!" shouted Oñate to the mule driver. "Get up and give your place to a gentleman."

Vicente turned white, but his glance riveted upon the face of the Sleeper, and the latter made no sign.

"You too, gringo!" yelled Oñate. "Get up before you're taken up—"

He might have said more, or else there might have been an instant move for a weapon. The man was simply made, the Sleeper thought. And the four youths stood about, proud of the savagery of their leader, agape as though they were drunk with joyous, brutal expectation.

But here came little Pedro, called Lontano. He bore up the tray of filled glasses, and offered them first to Señor Oñate. The other turned like a beast, glared, and then, catching the tray, he hurled it to the floor so violently that splinters of glass and a dash of red liquid like blood spurted far off through the doorway into the glitter of the sunshine.

"You dog!" yelled Oñate. "Glasses for gentlemen? Bring us bottles, bottles, bottles! Run, you rat!"

Pedro Lontano ran, with only one glance at the ruin on the floor.

But the Sleeper leaned and looked at his boots. There was a splash on the toe of one boot. He made his voice gentle. There was even a tremor in it, so much piled-up rage was checked and restrained against the dam of his self-control.

"Señor Oñate!" said he.

"The gringo—the gringo!" exclaimed the little ferret. "He's still in his chair, and I am standing—Oñate!"

"You've spilled something on my boot," said the Sleeper. "It must be wine, señor."

"I have spilled something on his boot," said Oñate in wild mockery. "Wine now—blood next, perhaps? What shall I do about it?"

"Get down on your knees," said the Sleeper, rising from his chair. "Get down on your knees and wipe up that stain from my boot."

Oñate, in an ecstasy of excitement, actually made a dancing step or two and clasped his hands above his head.

"Listen! I am to go on my knees before the gringo. Because why? Because he is so big. See how big he is! Fool, fool, fool!" he screamed, suddenly as tense as a cat ready to spring. "Do you hear me? The bigger you are, the bigger the target. Do you know to whom you speak? I—I am Oñate!"

He smote his breast. He shook his head. He grinned at the Sleeper like a wild cat.

The Sleeper swallowed. He could taste his own fury, and it made his throat dry.

"You have called me a gringo and a fool," said he. "But listen to me, Oñate! I give you another chance to wipe my boot, and to pay my friend Pedro Lontano for the damage you've done to-day—and the last day you were here."

Oñate laughed in a shrieking note.

"He gives me another chance. Do you hear, amigos? He gives to me, Oñate, another chance! But this is a dream, and this man is mad!"

"You think that I'm like the others," replied the Sleeper. "I'm not, Oñate. I carry death with me. I cannot miss you. Get down on your knees and do as I bid you."

Even Oñate, for an instant, was staggered by this soft-spoken assurance and the steady eyes which watched him. He gave back half a step, but steadied himself there with his long, hairy fingers twitching near the two holsters which weighted down his hips.

"Who is this?" he barked at Pedro.

"Señor," said the barkeeper, "this man is dangerous!"

The four youths, sobered, had drawn back from the table and stood on the side of their leader, but they were very quiet, and they stood carefully out of the bullet path.

Only the mule driver, Vicente, remained seated at the table, sipping the red wine, and looking thoughtfully from Oñate to the stranger.

"The wine is still on my boot," said the Sleeper. "You see that I don't ask much. Only that you take off what you put on. I count to three, Oñate!"

The Mexican was stupefied.

"He counts to three," said one of the youths softly.

But in the silence of the room the voice was perfectly audible, and the head of the ferret jerked toward the youngster.

"One!" said the Sleeper.

"To me?" screeched Oñate.

He swayed a little forward on his toes and jerked out both long, heavy guns with one movement. Yet the Sleeper was in no haste. It seemed to him that his reach for his old Colt was a most leisurely thing, and that it glided casually into his fingers; neither did he try to aim the bullet, but fired the instant the muzzle of the gun was tipped up clear of the leather.

Oñate fired both his guns into the floor, his hands automatically contracting. He sat down with a thump. It looked like a bit of cheap comedy in a small theater of the old days. But then red burst from the side of his head, and he raised his hand to the wound, dazed.

He was not fatally, he was not even seriously, wounded. But the bullet had chiseled a long furrow in the bone along the side of his head, and the weight of the blow had stunned him. He sat there shaking his head, muttering, and the disregarded guns lay on the floor.

Vicente, the mule driver, quietly got up and raised them from the floor. The four young men had disappeared like the smoke of the three shots!

And then came Pedro with an old towel, of which he made a crude bandage around the head of Oñate. The latter got to his feet. He staggered toward the brilliant sunshine of the door, but Vicente, with a most evil grin, took him by the shoulder and led him back. Oñate was agape. He looked like a half-wit.

"The boots, Señor Oñate!" said Vicente, and pointed to the feet of the Sleeper.

"Ah, *Diós*!" whispered the ferret.

But he dropped on his knees, and with his hairy bands, wiped the wine away.

He stood up again. He was trembling. The red was beginning to work through the bandage. But the two Mexicans were as adamant. They pointed out the broken glassware. Poor Oñate had to pick it up, fumbling, cutting his fingers with the broken pieces.

And then he was forced to drag out his wallet.

He had to pay for the cost of replanking the floor, because little Pedro declared that the wine stains never could be scrubbed out!

He had to pay the cost of the glasses and the wine which had been in them.

He had to pay for the cost of all his last visit and the destruction which he had wrought, little Pedro estimating the items lightly.

Finally he had to pay for having broken the peace. All the other items he had satisfied.

"And how much is this last charge, señor?" he asked. The man's spirit was broken. He was like a worm.

Pedro reached across the bar and deliberately snatched the wallet away. From it he extracted the sheaf of bills. The wallet itself he flung into the face of Oñate.

"There is just enough here to pay for the damage you've done to my reputation. Now, Señor Oñate, all is well."

The little man left his wallet behind him. He went to the doorway and paused there, looking up and down, as though uncertain which way he should go. Then he slunk to the left, keeping close to the wall.

Inside the cantina, a silence ensued, with Pedro and Vicente, as so often before, looking fixedly at one another, with the broadest of grins.

Then, from the street, far away, they heard an outbreak of the sharp, high voices of boys. And a roaring protest from some man.

"Oñate!" cried Pedro. "Oñate! They have found him out. They will pull him down, too! Oh, the young rascals! They can see the soul of a man even through winter clothing. They will be able to smell his wound a mile away."

Vicente leaned back in his chair. He made a gesture of throwing something very light into the air.

"Pouf!" said he. "That is a bubble, and now it is gone."

"A smoke bubble," said Pedro Lontano. "Hai, how it went away!"

The fat woman who had brought the warning now

returned into the doorway and peered timidly into the shop.

"Pedro—my darling!" she moaned.

She absorbed the little man in her arms. He was crushed. He gasped like one drowning:

"Let me be! You fat one! You fat idiot!"

She released him partially, murmuring: "Thank Heaven there is much of me, for all there is trembles with love of you, Pedro. Who drove that black dog out?"

Pedro pointed at the Sleeper, and the wife clasped her hands as if in prayer.

"There are seven of us to remember you, señor!" she said, and she went out, waddling, bumping the door jamb on either side.

The Sleeper settled back into his chair and sighed. He made and lighted a cigarette.

"Tell me, Pedro," said he. "Will the friends of Oñate come back here and make trouble for you?"

"His friends?" echoed Pedro.

"Yes. Like the four who were here."

"They are no longer his friends. Look, Señor Sleeper. Five minutes ago we were so far beneath him that he could only see the tops of our heads to walk on. Now he is so far beneath us that we cannot see him at all. There is nothing but murder in that bubble, señor."

The Sleeper did not answer. He was disturbed by a more profound reflection. It was the center of the little man's forehead that he had had in mind, and that he had looked at. It was only the side of the other's head that the bullet had touched.

CHAPTER 20.

YOU STAND AND WAIT

NOW, TO ANOTHER MAN it would have made little difference. For his own part, the Sleeper certainly was very glad that he had not the death of the fellow upon his conscience, but the point of greatest interest was that if there was some peculiar charm connected with this weapon, some mysterious power and attraction which made it fall in line with its target, as a snake's head must invariably point at the eye of a rifle, then this power was sufficiently inaccurate to allow the bullet to swerve at least a good two or three inches from the line.

Suppose, then, that the error had been a quarter of an inch greater, and that the little tiger had been spared altogether? In that case, Oñate would not then have been shrinking out from the town, pestered by a howling cloud of boys, worse than stinging wasps. Instead, he would have been drinking wine by the bottle, free of charge, in the bar of the Lontano. And perhaps the body of the Sleeper would lie in a corner, with a sack over its face, and a spreading pool of red about it, and the increasing buzz of flies all around. For nothing was easier than to imagine the accuracy with which that little two-handed gunman, Oñate, would have driven a pair of half-inch bullets through the heart of any enemy at such short range as that.

Yes, the scene would have been very different, and how the four young men would have laughed and shouted, and clapped the tiger on the back, and how he would have swelled his chest, and perhaps taken his exercise after drinking by whipping Vicente, the recalcitrant mule driver, through the length of the crooked little village street. There would have been much noise and excitement, and that evening the hero would have departed from the town, his chest bigger than ever, and poor Pedro would have had to drag the dead body to the back of a mule, and carry it down through the darkness to the bottom of the cliff, and there bury it in the first hole, rolling some biggish stones over it.

All this was so clear to the Sleeper that it seemed to him he actually could see the coyotes prowl by moonlight near his grave.

But the important fact was that though his gun had dropped its man, it had, nevertheless, in a great measure missed the mark. Oñate lived, and certainly that was a chance on which he never had reckoned. A glancing shot on the head of Oñate—as well reckon on handling a rattlesnake safely, using nothing but thin kid gloves!

Pedro began to scrub out the cantina floor. He talked as he worked, offering to the other two anything that his bar could afford, and free of charge.

"This is a beautiful day to me, señor," he said to the Sleeper. "You see that I leave that wallet exactly as I found it, on the surface of my bar. Go to it and take everything, or else take a half, or whatever your heart desires. Because it all is yours, and never would have left the wallet from which it was born this day without the good persuasion of your gun. Hai, señor, what a lovely sight it was! Fortune give me to see such a gun play again! What is the shooting of a gun? Nothing. But the manner of the doing, that is everything. I can sing the same notes, but I cannot make the thunder of even the little church organ. And other men can draw their guns and fire, and other men have done so in the past. Aye, and in this very room. But to stand before a double danger like the two guns of that monster among men, that beast and blood drinker, that cruel, avaricious, uneasy, restless, insatiable, abhorrent tyrant and cur, Oñate—to stand so before him, careless and at rest, toying with a revolver—delaying—oh, to handle a gun like that is to be an artist, to paint a picture, to make music sing, to turn stones into men—yes, men on horseback."

The flattery came in a stream from the lips and from the heart of the Mexican. The Sleeper enjoyed it, but he changed the subject.

"Can I talk to you freely, Pedro?"

"About everything except one."

"Parmenter?"

Pedro shrugged his shoulder.

"Well, ask your questions," he said. "I'll do what I can. So will Vicente. You are safe in our hands, señor."

They looked a precious pair, capable of any crime of deceit, craft, or violence; yet the Sleeper felt that they could be trusted.

"Down in the pass of Tinnio," he said, "or just under the lip of the pass, I met a wounded man riding as fast as he could away from the mountains. That was last night. Who was the man?"

Vicente looked at Pedro, and Pedro looked back at Vicente. There was a peculiar sympathy between the pair; they seemed able to discuss and advise in silence, by glances.

Vicente answered. He looked not at the Sleeper, but at Pedro, while he was speaking, for all the world like a schoolboy who recites, studying the face of the teacher to detect his own errors before they are corrected.

"That man was Tom Gill."

"Who was Tom Gill?"

"Well, he was not one of the five."

"Who are the five?"

"The five next to Señor Parmenter."

"And what are their names?"

"Sorrell, Bell, Chipping, Bullen, and Perry. But Señor Gill was a very good rustler."

"Ah—a rustler."

"Yes, he could pass a grown steer through the eye of a needle and cut a whole herd in a waistcoat pocket."

Vicente grinned. So did Pedro.

"One day," said Pedro, taking up the story, "this Tom Gill tried to take some cows for himself. Well, he did it very well. Got the cows and shunted them off in a neat cut when he was driving back some beef to this town of Guadalupe. He sold those cows. He got more'n five hundred dollars for the flock of 'em. Nothin' was said. Then he decided that he liked the taste of that money and he made another cut, but as he was handling those cows he ran into trouble. Señor Perry is the great rustler—the greatest of all. He came on Tom Gill making that crooked cut and shot him and chased him out of the mountains.''

''And followed him?'' asked the Sleeper.

''How can I tell?'' asked Pedro.

''You don't know whether or not he escaped?''

''Well, he is dead,'' said Vicente bluntly, ''but as for who killed him, that I don't know.''

The Sleeper pressed his lips together. The pain, the courage, the Spartan endurance of that man, Tom Gill, remained strongly in his memory. Now he was gone. The invisible machine from the Tinnio Mountains had reached out and flicked him away into nothingness.

''Then I rode up into the pass itself,'' went on the Sleeper, ''and there I found an oldish fellow in rags, talking about wagons loaded with furniture about to come up to him, and about a house filled with bathtubs and stoves that he intends to build—''

''Oh, that is Hazy Pete,'' said Pedro cheerfully. ''Every one knows about Hazy.''

''Well, I never heard of him.''

''Ten years ago—that was when Señor Parmenter first came here into the mountains—ten years ago, Hazy Pete had a fine house, and he ran three thousand cattle in those hills. Every spring he grew richer and richer. He could eat venison and sell beef. There's nothing much more pleasant than that. He was getting really rich. Yes, he was rich. Then Parmenter came along and told Pete that there wasn't room for so many cows in the hills. He wouldn't have ranchers up here in the Tinnios. He offered to buy Pete out for about half the market price. Pete laughed at him. So one day Parmenter swept these hills as bare as your hand and took all the cattle away for nothing at all. He put a match to the house and let it go up in flames, together with every blessed thing that Pete owned.

"Then we all expected that Pete would either get himself killed trying to kill Parmenter, or else he would be frightened and leave the pass, but he didn't. No, his mind seemed to stop at the fire. For ten years it has always been 'two months' since the house burned down. And in the meantime, the hills are covered with cattle in bigger herds than ever. He used to have three thousand cows. Now he has thirty thousand. Night and day, when you look for them, they've gone down into the hollows and you can't see them. But when they come up to graze, the hills are red with 'em! That's poor old Hazy Pete. No harm in him. You wonder, however, why Señor Parmenter leaves him there? Well, I have heard one of his chiefs ask, and Señor Parmenter always says that it is because Hazy Pete is a boundary marker, telling strangers that they have come to a strange country, and that they have passed their bounds."

"Yes," said Vicente slowly. "I remember the day that I rode past Hazy Pete. Something told me then to turn back, but I didn't. I went on. Now I am here in the trap—"

"Can't you leave when you please, Vicente?"

"Yes. Of course. Tom Gill left last night!"

"You mean that all the passes and the ways out of

the mountains are watched so that the men can't escape from the Tinnios?"

"No, I don't mean that. Any one can escape, probably. But it isn't the dying man that runs from his dope!"

"What do you mean by that?" asked the Sleeper.

"Eh? What do I mean? Perhaps you will see, before long."

"But tell me about this town. How old is it?"

"As old as the Incas!"

"But the Incas never owned this part of the country."

"No, perhaps not. But it is very old. There were Indians. Then the Spaniards came. They built the town."

"A strange place for a town," said the Sleeper.

"Well, it is this way. There is only one good pass through the Tinnios, and here is this town, stuck in the pass like a fishbone in a throat. I suppose that is why they built Guadalupe."

"Can you tell me, my friends, where I shall find Señor Parmenter?"

"There's only one sure way. That's to go to the top of the hill."

"What's there?"

"The house where he lives."

"Well?" said the Sleeper, anxious to draw out more information.

"When you get up there, you'll find a big wall. In the wall there is a small door with a rounded top. Beside the door there is a pull wire for a bell. When you pull the wire, you will hear the bell tinkle."

"Yes," said the Sleeper.

"Then," said Vicente, taking up the tale, "you stand there and wait."

"If the door is not opened at once, it will never be opened," said Pedro. "And then you will never get inside, and you will never see the Señor Parmenter. But if it is opened at once, you go inside, and some day you will see him."

"You go inside, and you never come out," added Vicente.

"What do you mean by that?" asked the Sleeper.

"Señor," said Pedro, "you are our friend. We have told you more than we should, already. Don't ask us to say another word!"

CHAPTER 21.

A DOOR OPENS

JUST THEN, down the steep pitch of the street, the Sleeper heard the clattering hoofs of a horse—armed hoofs that rattled and banged on the paving stones, raising volleyed echoes, and sometimes the shoes slid with a screech.

He went hastily to the door of the cantina to mark what madman actually rode a horse at speed down that murderous descent, and he was in time to see a flying rider whose horse leaped and skidded along the irregular rocky steps, driven by quirt and spur. The horseman, as he shot by, jerked his head to the side, and the tramp saw the brutal square face of Trot Enderby, convulsed and red with rage. That glance of utter hatred swept over the Sleeper and the horse tethered outside the cantina, and then Enderby was gone, clattering around the next turn of the way.

The Sleeper stepped out into the brilliant heat of the sun. It dazzled him. When he laid his hand on the neck of the down-headed bay mare, the hair burned his hand like fire. He unknotted the tie rope to lead her up the street, and as he started, he looked around him.

The dog no longer barked. It sat on the church steps, watching him intently. The shoemaker, with his awl poised in midair, stared at the stranger with equal fixity. So did an unshaven fellow who stood between two loaded burros at the edge of the plaza. So did a woman who leaned on her broom at another dark entrance. None of these people either frowned or smiled, but all watched him as men will watch an eagle sailing low in the sky, intently, with unguessed-at thoughts in every mind.

Both Vicente and Pedro stood inside the doorway, smudged over by the deep shadows, and they stared with an equal gravity, and spoke not even a word of farewell as the tramp began his progress up the winding street.

The way to the top of the hill was longer than he had expected. It zig-zagged back and forth. It went as a snake goes, with many twistings, but finally it brought him into a narrow street, either end of which looked out as through the sights of a rifle into a blue, thin void of air, and beyond this arose on the one hand the crowding Tinnio Mountains, and on the other hand he was sighting through the gap of the Tinnio Pass and toward the emptiness of the plains beyond. He could guess at them by the water mist which thickened the air in that direction.

On one side of this street there was a string of wretched little one-room shacks built of dobe. The walls were so old that their knees sagged backward, and the lower bricks were turning to mud. One could feel the weight of time on the roofs, bending and sagging them. These huts stood shoulder to shoulder, but there were yards behind them. The Sleeper could hear pigs grunting, and the rattling crackle of hens as they led their broods to scratchings in the dust. Then a jackass or a donkey began to bray, and sent enormous waves of sound echoing out over the big valley on either side. The noise was loud, and yet it seemed strangely far away, as all mountain noises do.

The Sleeper turned from it, and on the other side of this street, he faced the big wall of which he had been told.

This wall was not dobe, but was all ashlar. It was at least twenty or twenty-five feet high, and the rounded top suggested its massive thickness. It was covered and dust-gray with lichens, yet in the interstices of this filmy growth he could see the innumerable chisel marks, which showed that the stone had not been sawed, but had been worked by hand. He stepped closer. He saw that the joints were not filled with mortar, but the stones were fitted together with the most exquisite nicety. A hair could not have been inserted in any crack. By this he guessed that Indians had done the work.

The little door, the only visible opening in that great wall, was exactly as had been described to him. It was not more than an inch or two over six feet in height, and was, perhaps, six feet wide. The bell pull hung down on one side. The wire ended in a copper handle in the shape of a kid hanging with four feet bound together and head trailing down, as he had seen Mexicans cruelly carry their fresh meat with them, slung over the saddle bows for long trails.

He took hold of the copper kid, which had been

thumbed and handled to a blur of its old self, and drew downward gently. He listened, and there was no sound.

All at once his heart began to race, and he looked around with a start toward the mare. He was ready to flee. Chilly terror flowed out upon him with the silence which dwelt beyond this big wall.

Then he mastered himself with a distinct effort and tugged sharply downward at the bell pull. This time, as startling as the silence, he heard the silver rattle of the bell inside.

He stepped back to wait. His one prayer was that the door would not open.

But open it did.

On the threshold appeared a *mozo* dressed in a thin black jacket like a Chinaman's shirt. He had a pale and flat face, and he was lifting his eyebrows wearily as he asked the Sleeper to come in.

"And the horse?" asked the Sleeper.

He looked back at the horse. Her ears were flattened. She appeared both angry and suspicious, and again he yearned to fling himself into the saddle and flee down the long, twisting throat of that street and so out into the pass beyond.

He remembered Tom Gill's flight and its reported ending. So he mastered himself once more.

"You lead in the horse, too," said the house *mozo*.

He turned his back and walked forward to show the way, while the Sleeper, breathing fast almost in time with his racing heart, followed. The mare came slowly behind him, pulling back hard on the reins, grunting a little with disgust or with fear, and in this fashion they both got in clear of the lip of the door. The tunnel through the wall was fifteen feet wide, a good measure of the thickness of the masonry at this point, at the least; and as they went forward, still inside the margins of the dark shaft, the outer door shut with a loud bang, and with so much force and weight that the ground beneath the Sleeper quivered perceptibly. He had a ghostly feeling that a door might close at the farther end also, and entomb him with the mare.

Anything seemed possible to the Sleeper at that moment.

However, he went on, and came out safely into a little closed court with a lofty wall all around it, and in that wall only two doors opening.

The porter clapped his hands together twice. Instantly there appeared another servant in each of the doorways. One of these took the mare, and the other offered to lead the visitor through the second door. The Sleeper preferred, he said, to see where the mare was lodged, and no objection was made to this.

They went down an incline just steep enough to make the hoofs of the mare slip a little from time to time, and entered into deeper and deeper darkness, lighted by an occasional lantern fixed against the wall. That wall was a hewing through the solid rock, and again the Sleeper was amazed when the glinting lantern light showed him how innumerable chisel strokes had eaten away the hard rock. This labor must have been done long ago, and at a time when a working man cost little more than his keep.

Then the tunnel pitched out into spacious ranges of stables. They were bright, open, and airy. Looking up, he saw a big rise of steep cliff to the right and to the left of him. That on the right was crowned by the casements of a big house. These stables were constructed of stone. They looked like small houses thrown together and arranged for animals. And passing along down the aisles, he saw many and many a vacant space, but even now he marked down twenty horses, the worst of which would have made most riders happy. There were a few mules and mustangs, besides, and he could guess that these would be eminently useful for pure mountain work. Those other long-legged speedsters were meant for the more open country beyond the uplands. The Sleeper was convinced, now, that he was looking at the central headquarters stable of Parmenter's band.

He saw the mare put up.

She had a good big stall, with plenty of sweet fresh air coming in through a high window. She was given a feed of excellent timothy hay, which he was amazed to see, and into her feed box was poured an ample measure of oats of the first quality. The stable *mozo*, having first removed her saddle; immediately started to groom her with truly professional skill, and the Sleeper was contented.

This fellow was as silent as the rest of the servants. The tramp had hardly heard a word spoken since he rang the bell at the postern gate.

The open space between the ranges of stables was fenced on one side of the cliff, and on the other by a low wall, over which he could lean. He looked down to see what became of the water, which welled up in quantities in the middle of the court, and after running through great troughs carved in the living rock, it disappeared with a long gushing whisper through a pipe at the base of the wall.

He could see its fate clearly now. The whisper was

caused by the solid stream of the water meeting the air, and breaking into soft white spray, which showered down in a long arch and then dropped sheer to a little lake far beneath.

Yet lower than the lake, and extending well over a mile up and down before it ended, or else disappeared from view around a corner of the mountain shoulder, he saw a delightful valley, like a jeweled eye in the face of a harsh idol. So rough and ragged were the mountains all around, and so surprising was the gentle rise of the valley. Through the middle of it ran a stream, dammed up and checked, here and there, to irrigate patches of ground. There was not much level soil beside the course of the water, but the sides of the valley, up to the point where naked rocks began, had been leveled into a series of rich terraces.

Here again evidence of infinite labor—Indian labor, the Sleeper could guess. He fairly ached when he thought of the work of laying those retaining walls, carrying up massive rocks, filling the artificial pockets with soil. But now the valley made a delightful picture, and undoubtedly it was to protect and use the valley that the town of Guadalupe had been built here in the throat of the pass. On these terraces and in the floor of the valley the Sleeper saw growing patches of maize, and the blue-green of wheat—so thick a stand that it glimmered in the sunshine like water; and he saw the gray haze of olive trees, and vines with luxuriant heads raised on frames, and fruit trees in well-ordered rows, with their shadows lying cool at their feet, and over the edges of the retaining walls, from terrace to terrace, cascaded peas and beans. Many workers were toiling there in that windless green pocket under the vertical rays of the sun. Sometimes their voices climbed slowly and faintly up to him, and sometimes he heard the talking of the water in the valley; but none of these sounds were so loud that they could not be extinguished by a single gust of wind, and the gushing of the water from the pipe.

CHAPTER 22.

"I'M PARMENTER"

WHEN THE SLEEPER turned from looking over this wall, he found yet a new servant at hand, and one dressed in a little better style, who greeted him with grave courtesy and called him by name.

"How do you happen to know me?" asked the Sleeper curiously.

"We have been waiting for you," said the servant.

And with no further explanation, he led the way up into the house, over several flights of stairs. It was a big old house, built in the usual Mexican style around a patio, but since this was a yard into which horses did not come, a garden had been allowed to grow. Not much attention was given to it, apparently, and, therefore, nature stepped in with a strong hand and threw up great green streamers from climbing roses and other vines. They were so old that the trunks of some of these plants had trunks like trees. They swept up in many-branched lines, the green becoming more and more dense, until finally a solid wave broke over the highest eaves of the house and washed onto the roof. Some of the limbs had grown into the shutters, so that they were forced open, and others could be pushed wide merely by the strength of arm. The Sleeper never had seen, he felt, an older place, or one that was very much pleasanter. And to crown the coolness of these shadows, a powerful fountain threw its translucent head high in the center of the court, and sent its continual voice through all the house.

At one side of the patio, an arched way led out and gave a glimpse of pale-blue sky, with naked mountain heads melting into it.

To this the Sleeper was conducted, and found a broad terrace there under the outermost face of the house, and looking down upon the valley as he had seen it before, except that now he was at a greater distance. Shadow covered the terrace. He took off his hat and sat down. He had not asked for Parmenter. It did not seem necessary. The mysterious river of events was now bearing him forward with a speed against which he could not contend. So he surrendered to it.

The chill, sweet mountain air filled his lungs. His heart swelled. He felt brave and strong, as in a happy dream.

He who came again was the first house *mozo* he had seen, carrying a pot of water, a basin, and a coarse towel. The Sleeper gratefully washed the dust from his face and hands. The sting left his eyes, and he sat down again more at ease than before.

Now appeared two men. One carried a tray of cheap brown dishes which he set out on one of the small tables that stood on the terrace. The other laid down thick-crusted bread in round loaves, and tortillas, also, and steaming beans, giving off the pungency of the peppers with which they had been stewed. Best of all was a long spit loaded with grilled bits of the flesh of a kid. And for drink, what would there be but the best of Mexican chocolate?

The Sleeper asked no questions. At the sight of the food, his hunger struck a pang through his very heart. He sat down and devoured that tray-load. He finished the last bit of meat and bread, the last swallow of chocolate. Only a few mouthfuls of the fiery beans escaped him. Then he sat back like a gorged snake and smoked a cigarette—that supreme moment of contentment.

None of these servants had said a word to him. They went about their work not sourly, but always with a gravity which seemed to forbid question.

One of them, however, had hair coarse as that of a horse, and thickly strewn with white. He had a wide mouth and shining eyes that seemed to betray a mixture of Negro blood, and, therefore, he should prove talkative under a small temptation.

"People up here," said the Sleeper to him, as he started to pile the dishes onto the tray, "if they eat like this must grow pretty fat."

"Fat?" said the other.

He passed a hand over his face, which certainly was lean enough.

"Mountain air, señor, is a fire that burns up fat. The winters are sometimes so cold that they burn the very marrow out of one's bones, and then there is a job eating the rest of the year to put back the fat lost from your insides, to say nothing of adding any layers to the outside."

The Sleeper grinned at this idea. He leaned farther

back in his chair, and laid his legs across the seat of another.

"How long have you been here, friend?" said he.

"I have been here long enough," said the other, "to learn how to ride a horse, and a mule, too."

"And how long does that take?"

"That depends on the man," said the servant. "You can't tell how long it will take a bird to learn to fly, either." He was adroit enough in turning questions. Now he pointed over the heavy stone wall which rimmed the terrace.

"A man could use wings if he had to climb over that wall, señor!"

He picked up a small fragment of bread and tossed it over the rail, while the eye of the Sleeper followed it with interest as it dropped down and down, and grew smaller and smaller, until finally it seemed to dissolve in a rising wind, which was blowing up the valley.

That valley he could see better, now. It looked much smaller. It was hardly more than an ornamental garden, on a big scale. And the water flashed under the direct rays of the sun, in some places, and in others ran under shadow with a tarnished silver shimmer.

"From here," said the servant, "they used to chuck out the bodies, in the old days."

"What bodies?"

"Well, men that they were tired of. They made a good drop, and the screech of a big man could be heard all the way up, and the thud of him as he hit the rock. You see it? He bounced off that into the water, and the river rolled him away. A pretty good way, though. Not any longer than hanging."

He stiffened.

The Sleeper looked past him, and then saw a man crossing the patio with an active, long stride, the stride of a fast walker, with a deep flexion at the knee. He was quite short, and heavily built. One could not tell whether his bulk was muscle or fat. There was a big head, a rather long, large face, and a short mustache. Altogether, he was a sleek-looking man, so sleek-looking that one wondered, seeing him walking so fast.

He came straight out onto the terrace, out of the sun, into the shadow. He was dressed like any puncher, with leather chaps, heavily scarred and cut by riding through stiff mountain brush. He wore no gun, but the looseness of his coat suggested to the Sleeper that a weapon might be slung in a patent spring holster under the pit of either arm.

He came straight on up to the Sleeper. And the latter stood up, with his hair lifting.

The Sleeper never had seen such a face in his life. Not that there was anything extraordinary about its features, with one exception. That exception was more than enough to chill the blood of the tramp. For the eyes of this man were as pale and luminous as a bit of the sun-flooded mountain sky.

He shook hands, an abrupt, strong grip.

"You're Mr. Sleeper?" he said.

"Yes. That's my name."

"I'm Parmenter. Sit down again."

He gave an example, taking a chair by the wall, and tapping rapidly upon it with his fingers as he eyed the Sleeper. One might have thought that the face of the tramp was a page out of a book, so minutely did the other scan it, and with progressing eyes that traveled across and across, and up and down. This movement of the glance was all that kept it from being a fixed stare.

He made trivial talk, in the meantime.

"How was the trip up?"

"Well enough."

"Cold sleeping, last night?"

"Well, I had a chill before I went to sleep."

"You met Tom Gill?"

"Yes."

"I heard of that."

"Just what became of him, afterward?"

The other pointed unconcernedly upward, and the Sleeper looked and saw half a dozen black specks circling high in the air. He could understand what that meant. This horrible manner of referring to a human death, this utterly casual brutality, made him wince.

He snatched his gaze from the sky and fixed it hurriedly upon his host, again.

Parmenter was nodding, agreeing with himself. He seemed to have reached some conclusion about his visitor, but whether the opinion was flattering or the reverse, the youth could not tell. He could only guess that it must be the latter.

In the meantime, his own brain was spinning. He had come up here regretting the chivalrous necessity which compelled him to carry the girl's letter to an outlawed man. And now, in a flash, he knew what old Morice had meant when he said that something would happen when he met the great Parmenter. Something assuredly had. His blood was still running iced in his veins. He could not meet that pale, bright eye.

Then, suddenly, he remembered the gun.

As the strange flower of the moly, white blossom and black root, had saved Odysseus, so the thought of the gun and its equal magic saved the tramp.

He saw nothing. He was only the Sleeper, in the beginning, those few days ago. But now he had in his possession a strong and fatal charm. The thought of it restored the warmth to his blood. He sat up in his chair: And then he could lift his gaze and meet the pale, luminous eyes of the other steadily. He could look into and read the man at ease.

So much had the unwilling gift of Trot Enderby done for him.

"Enderby has been up here, I saw?" he suggested, as a new channel for conversation.

"Enderby's dead. You killed him," said the outlaw calmly, as though he were referring to a bit of ancient history. Then he waited.

The Sleeper took from his pocket the little white envelope which he had brought so far.

"Is that for me?" asked Parmenter.

The Sleeper hesitated.

"Well," he said, still keeping his eyes upon the face of the other, but retaining the address turned toward himself, lest the outlaw should recognize the handwriting, "well, in a sense it was meant for you."

"Ah?" said Parmenter, and he held out his hand.

"But after all, it's not worth giving to you," said the Sleeper.

And he tore the envelope squarely across.

CHAPTER 23.

TWO MEN TALK

AT THIS, PARMENTER leaned a little forward, and his hand stiffened. But the Sleeper maintained his glance upon the steady pale eyes of the man, and ripped the letter across again.

"Was it addressed to me?" asked Parmenter.

"Yes," said the Sleeper, and threw the fragments over the wall. He heard them rattle in the wind; they were gone, and the decisive step had been made.

"Ah?" said Parmenter again.

"It was what you might call a letter of introduction," said the Sleeper. "But after I met you, Parmenter, I see that there's no use in that kind of an introduction."

"Who was it from?" asked the mountain man.

"From a hotel man," said the Sleeper, lying smoothly. "He thought that I might fit in up here; but, after all, you wouldn't be helped by his advice."

"You mean Steve, in Alcalde?"

The Sleeper hesitated half a second. He did not wish to pin any trouble on the shoulders of Steve, but for the moment he could think of no one else.

"Well," he said, "it was Steve, as a matter of fact. Does his word go for much with you?"

"Steve knows more than you think about me and about other men," said Parmenter in his rapid, decisive voice. "Yes, I would have taken his opinion for some worth. Did he recommend you to me?"

"Yes."

"How long did he know you?"

"One day."

"But he saw you smash Enderby. That was something. More in five minutes than in a whole life of most men. Yes, a good deal more.

"Naturally," said Parmenter, not waiting for any comment, "he would recommend you to me. Steve is a good fellow. I like him. But you didn't want to show me his letter?"

"I read that letter," said the Sleeper. "It seemed silly. That's why I didn't show it to you."

"Silly? What did it say?"

"It talked about me as a gun fighter. I could see that wasn't chiefly what you wanted, when I got up here."

"No? And what do I want, then?"

"Men you can trust. Gun fighters usually are not."

"Go on," said Parmenter. "Gun fighters are not to be trusted, eh?"

"No. I take it they're not."

"And by throwing the letter away what have you gained?"

"Well, a fellow who comes without any recommendation hasn't a name to live up to. I'd rather start small."

"I take it that you want to join me, Sleeper?"

"That's my idea."

"Why?"

The tramp hesitated, and then the truth of his nature asserted itself.

"Because I take it to be an easy life. And a fat life, too, judging by the meal that they've just given me."

"It's not an easy life though, and it's not a fat life. I look fat but I'm not. I'm hard. Is that a real name you wear?"

"No."

"Where did you get it?"

"On the road," said the Sleeper.

"You mean really on the road?"

"Yes."

"On the tramp?"

"Yes."

"Where have you tramped?"

"From Montreal to Havana, and from Frisco to New York. A dip into Mexico, too."

"Tramp royal?"

"I never was a bindle stiff. I never had the energy to carry a pack, to tell you the truth."

"Listen to me, Sleeper!"

"Well?"

"D'you think it's a recommendation—that amount of laziness?"

"No, but I wouldn't try to pull the wool over your eyes. I wouldn't be any good at hard rides, and long marches, and that sort of thing."

"That's what our life is made up of, here."

"No, I don't think so."

"Don't you? Why not?"

"Because you have this place here."

"Well, what about that?"

"You need a housekeeper. When you're all away, you wonder what may happen up here."

The unusual eyes of Parmenter gleamed at him.

"What could happen?" he asked.

"Well, you might have twenty enemies call when you're not at home."

"How could they come in? Excuse me a moment!"

Parmenter jumped up and hurried into the inner court. He returned after a minute or two carrying a field glass, which he fixed on a distant mountain top. Then he handed the glass to the Sleeper and waved in that direction.

At first, into the strong field of the glass, nothing swam but the sunlit mist of distant clouds, and sometimes the rocky heads of the nearer mountains bumped up dark and clear in the field of vision; but presently, in the distance, filmed over with the horizon blue, he saw three smokes rising, close together.

"You see?" said Parmenter.

"Yes. I see three signal smokes, as I suppose."

"Those smokes have a definite meaning to us in this house. When people try to cross into the mountains, some of our outlying scouts spot them and send in word. Those signals have nothing to do with enemies, at present, but in case of need we get accurate information by fire, heliograph, or smoke, telling up the direction from which the enemy approaches and the number, approximately. They've never surprised me here, and they never will. Do you doubt that, now?"

"Yes, I doubt it. I think you do, also."

"What makes you think so, Sleeper?"

The tramp gestured toward the wide-ranging mountains.

"Too many doors and windows looking on your house. I'll wager that you're never away from this place without worrying."

Parmenter smiled faintly.

"Suppose I say that you're right?"

"Than that means you need a housekeeper, as I said before."

"Are you qualified? A good marketer? Know how to handle servants?"

"Not very well."

"What's your idea, then?"

"I'd simply be a lock on the door."

"I have locks."

"None that money won't open."

Parmenter took the glasses back and with them idly scanned the floor of the valley. As he did this, he said:

"Money doesn't mean much to you, man?"

The Sleeper considered this gradually, without hurry. He had mixed in a large proportion of lies with what he told of the truth, but he felt that the truth itself must predominate, or else he surely would be seen through. He examined his own mind, and when he spoke aloud, he was telling his own discoveries about himself:

"No, money doesn't mean much to me, except as a thing to dream about. Not even then as dollars and cents, but what it will buy. A fine house—fine horses—good servants—a garden—and that's what I'd have up here."

"It wouldn't be yours."

"As much mine as anybody's."

"Even as much as mine?"

"Well, you'd be called the master. But I don't care who owns the view as long as I can look at it when I please, and I don't care who owns the ground so long as I can watch the flowers grow."

"What would you do with your time? What's your ambition?"

"To eat three meals, sleep, and fill my head with things worth looking at. You and your men would come in with yarns about your long riding. I'd as soon listen to wild yarns as to do wild things."

"What about those other men of mine? Would they want to make a fair split with you, they doing the riding, and you doing the sitting still?"

"Well," said the Sleeper, "what's the use cutting hay unless you have a safe barn to store it?"

"And what's your main qualification?"

"I can be honest."

"You've never had to bother about the police?"

"Yes, plenty. That was when I was stealing to eat, as you might say."

"And now what's the difference?"

"Now I'm shooting," said the Sleeper gently, and looked away from his companion across the mountain heads.

"How long have you been on the road?"

"Well, about four years."

"You've had an education?"

"Yes."

"Family living?"

The Sleeper frowned and raised his hand quickly.

"No, no!" said he. "They are all dead!"

"Not even an uncle or an aunt that might be interested in having the wandering boy home again?"

"No, no," said the Sleeper more warmly than ever. "Nobody. There's no past for me. Nothing to go to. Don't ever think that. Nothing to call me back. You could depend on me staying with you, if ever I took the job."

"You wouldn't be taking it now, if I offered it to you?"

"No, I'd want a few days to look around and grow acclimated."

"Suppose, at the end of that time, when you've mapped every detail in your head, you decided not to stay and went back to report to some sheriff or marshal?"

"Ah, well," said the Sleeper, "there would always be a chance of that, you'd feel. But really no chance at all. I can walk a straight line. Do you doubt that?"

He looked back from the mountains toward his host and saw that Parmenter was smiling faintly again, with an inward mirth or derision.

"What do you expect me to say?" asked the great man.

"I expect you to say that you'll think me over."

"Do you?"

"Yes, but you'll be feeling more than you say."

"What shall I be feeling?"

"You'll be saying to yourself: 'Thank fortune for this man! He rounds off the picture and makes the feed box safe!' "

"Come with me," said Parmenter, "and I'll show you what I think!"

CHAPTER 24.

LOCKS AND BARS

HE LED THE WAY across the court, called for a lantern, and when it was brought and lighted—a strange thing in the middle of the day—he turned to an iron-barred door set flush with the patio wall, and showered over by drooping arms of the climbing vines. Into this, he fitted a key, turned it several times in the surprisingly small lock, and then pushed the door open. It groaned deeply; then ended on a thin, high note of complaint that went echoing far off down an inside corridor of darkness.

Parmenter led the way in, shut and locked the door behind him, and then marched ahead down the hallway. This dipped down in a long flight of steps barred by another door, as massive as the first one. And when this was opened, in a short distance they encountered a third and a fourth, all of which Parmenter unlocked, and then locked again behind them.

Now four strong doors lay between the Sleeper

and his liberty, and accumulated chills went up his spine.

Those bright sky-blue eyes, he could guess, were capable of looking on any sort of treachery and cruelty. He was no safer in the hands of this man than in the hands of a legion of fiends. And now he had marched into the center of a dark donjon with no other company than Parmenter himself!

"And here we are!" said Parmenter suddenly.

He turned sharply as he spoke, and flashed the light of his lantern into the eyes of his companion; then, with a grunt that might have meant anything, he unlocked a fifth door and led the way into a small, high-ceilinged room.

There was no furniture. There was only one object of interest in the place, and that was the face of a big steel safe which filled the whole end of the apartment.

Parmenter raised the lantern and flickered its light again and again over the front of the monster.

"Imagine five hundred mules and oxen pulling at one load!" he said. "Imagine steeps where even five hundred mules and oxen could not turn the trick, but where big purchases had to be rigged, or windlasses! I've heard the groaning of a windlass that filled the mountains with thunder. However, patience built the pyramids, and here it is!"

Going to the combination, he handed the lantern to the tramp and worked for a moment. Distinctly, the Sleeper at last heard the tumblers fall with a light click. It was a strange thing. It was like listening to a living, buried voice. A spirit, say, which dwelt here in the steel, on watch!

Then the ponderous door sagged ajar without a

sound of grating, so well-poised was it, and fitted on its hinges with such an exquisite, watchmaker's nicety. It revealed the broad interior, furnished with steel drawers, and each of these supplied with a small lock.

"Here is our stuff," said Parmenter in a very cheerful voice. "Here we keep the stuff that's worth saving. And each of us knows the combination and has a master key. By each, I mean my five chiefs— Sorrell, Bell, Chipping, Bullen, and Perry. What's your favorite color, Sleeper?"

"Green," said the tramp.

"Well, that's easy on the eyes. Look at this."

He unlocked a drawer and pulled it out. Inside, it was fitted with trays, and from those trays, uncovered by chamois or any cloth, there sparkled a wealth of blue-green light.

"Look at them," said Parmenter, holding the lantern at exactly the right height.

As he did so, the contents of the trays began to sparkle. Each separate jewel held its own mysterious depth of light, concentrated to a point, looking back at the startled face of the Sleeper like so many eyes.

"Go on and take some of them into your hands," said Parmenter.

The Sleeper, entranced, obeyed. And the first thing that his thumb and fore-finger closed upon was a monster more than a half inch across, very deep, and the flat face of it incised with a winged snake.

"That has a story," said Parmenter, in a voice of much interest. "Juan Lorredo got that from a cacique at the time of the conquest. He got it by braining the chief with his mace. Juan was a good freehitter. He didn't bother with axes and swords.

He preferred a solid club when it came to cracking skulls, here and there. Swords and axes stick, but a mace will bounce halfway back for the second stroke, if you hit hard enough. That jewel stuck in the Lorredo family for centuries. It caused three or four more murders for the possession of it, and finally it landed in the hands of Francisco Lorredo, who lived in the old house and kept up the old style regardless of expense. He was proud. That emerald, at last, had to be pawned; the news came to me. And when I heard that the Lorredos were putting their best old possessions in danger, I thought I might as well have the thing. So I called on the pawnbroker one day—there's another worth seeing''—he broke off, touching a big luminous gem with the tip of his finger.

The tramp lifted a huge table-cut emerald of the deepest color—that color of the sea where it leaves the shallows, and before it reaches to the full darkness of the deep ocean blue.

It shone, it glimmered in the palm of his hand. In its depths there was a changing point of green fire.

"Put that in your pocket to look at by the daylight," suggested Parmenter.

The Sleeper lifted his head slowly, and looked the outlaw in the face. Then he dropped the emerald back into the tray from which it had just come.

"When I was telling you about myself," he explained, "I should have said that I have a pretty good imagination and a good memory, too. No, I can keep that emerald in mind."

Parmenter smiled back at him, and the boy thought of the face of a cat.

"Well," said Parmenter, "what's your next best color?"

"I've seen enough already," said the Sleeper.

And he raised his eyes along the ranges of drawers, one by one. There were twenty in all, of varying sizes.

"Don't use too much imagination," said Parmenter. "Some of those drawers simply have papers on file, and even letters, and such things. Interesting records of Guadalupe and the life here, from one point of view or another. But, on the whole, there are a good many trinkets worth seeing in those drawers. Hard cash, too. Nothing like a nest egg in the shape of greenbacks and yellowbacks, when you come down to that! To make the total less interesting, you have to imagine it split into seven parts—one for each of the others, and two for me. Now, Sleeper, splitting it in seven parts is a sad thing, of course, but each of those parts is worth a good deal!"

The Sleeper remembered the heaped jewels in that single drawer and said not a word. A seventh part of that treasure alone would have been worth many murders from the viewpoint of ordinary criminals.

"And, as a matter of fact," went on Parmenter, as he closed the door and spun the combination disk again—softly the tumblers clicked inside—"as a matter of fact, I'm willing to make another split and divide into eight instead of seven. Sleeper, will you make the seventh man among us?"

As he spoke, he held out the master key which had unlocked the five doors and opened the tray as well.

The whole body of the Sleeper lurched forward, and his hand went out to grasp that symbol of wealth. Then he checked himself and stepped back.

"I've been in Guadalupe a couple of hours," he said. "I want to be here for a week. That's not a comment on you, Parmenter, either.''

He looked straight into the pale eyes of the other and saw that the man was smiling again.

''Not a bit. I don't take it that way. I wanted you before you said this. I want you ten times more, now. But let's go up!''

They climbed from the damp, cold chamber to the upper air; they sat again on the terrace. It seemed to the Sleeper as though they had been gone many hours and yet the shadows had hardly crawled an inch or two across the pavement.

''They all have keys, and they trust one another as well as you?'' asked the Sleeper, more amazed the more he thought of it.

''Well,'' said the other, ''let me tell you that doubt never enters our minds about one another. No man trusts himself as much as he will trust five others. And if one of us is tempted to clean out the safe of its best wealth and scamper, he can't help remembering the other five, and always it is just in the nick of time! For my part, I'd take a chance against two or three, perhaps, but not against five. Not for such men as I have with me up here. Make no mistake, my friend. I'm the leader of the pack, up to this time, but all the rest are wolves!''

The Sleeper swallowed hard. He could feel his eyes grow big, for suddenly he knew that the outlaw was telling him the pure truth in this part of the matter, at least.

''There's no nonsense preached up here,'' went on Parmenter, ''about such things as honor among thieves, and trust of one another. We simply look the facts in the face, and they stare so dashed hard at one that only a fool would miss their significance.''

"Suppose," said the Sleeper, "that any one wants to withdraw from the band?"

"We've agreed on what to do, in that case. If you joined us to-day, you could leave us to-morrow, if you choose. You would lose exactly one half of your share. That would be the penalty, unless by special vote the rest of us decide that you should get your full part."

"Has any one ever left?"

"Yes, I'm glad to say," said Parmenter. "I'm glad to say that there was one of the party strong-minded enough to break away from Guadalupe, and the valley, and the mountains. We voted him a full share, too, though he'd only been among us for a comparatively short time. Two years, I think it was. But he proved his worth. We gave him a clean bill, and escorted him to the edge of the mountains. He's living in France, now, in a fine old château on the Loire, and he's writing a long book about the wines of Anjou."

Parmenter smiled again, and he passed the tip of his tongue over his lips and swallowed, yet the Sleeper knew that it was not of wine that the outlaw was thinking.

"A fine life, a simple life," said Parmenter. "You being a fellow of a delicate sense of honor, you would not be asked to ride out. You'd simply be expected to keep the house for us, here, and act, as you suggested, as a lock on the gates. But think it all over, Sleeper. You'll have seven days to decide."

CHAPTER 25.

A MAN AFRAID OF HIMSELF

HE CLAPPED HIS HANDS. A *mozo* came running.

"Get Ricardo at once," said Parmenter.

He turned back to the Sleeper.

"You saw old Morice in Alcalde?"

"Yes, I saw him."

"Then they've told you about Ironwood?"

"Yes."

"You'll be seeing him, one of these days. He's worth a look, and a trial, too. But he's the one thing that I'm jealous about. I won't endure another man on the back of Ironwood. We all have our touchy points."

Here he laughed, and the Sleeper was amazed by the high-pitched, almost feminine sound of his voice.

"Did you see the old mare?"

"Yes."

"Grand points. But it took old Morice to understand them. A great old man that Morice. The greatest, in fact, that I've ever met. Now, I'll let you understand a bit about that. I stole Ironwood. But after I'd ridden him, I decided that I'd like to pay. I went to see Morice and offered him his own price for the stallion.

" 'A hundred thousand dollars,' said he.

" 'You shall have it,' said I.

" 'For the trouble you've already given to me,' said he. 'Bring back the gray safe and sound, and pay down a hundred thousand, and we'll call it square. I wouldn't compromise as far as that,' says he, 'only that I have to think about my girl's future.'

"Oh, a grand old man, that Morice, eh?"

"Yes," said the Sleeper carefully. "I suppose he is."

"And you saw his daughter?" asked Parmenter.

"His daughter?" said the Sleeper dreamily. "Yes, I saw her, I imagine. A girl bringing in a pail of milk. I suppose that was she."

Parmenter had tilted back in his chair. Now he let the front feet come down with a jar.

"Barely a look at her?" he said.

"Why?" said the Sleeper.

"Well, I'm asking you."

"She wore a wide-brimmed hat," said the Sleeper. He felt more uneasy than he had since this odd interview began. But he mastered himself and made his eyes lazily meet those of the bandit.

"You mean her face was in shadow?"

"Yes."

Parmenter sighed.

"Well, I'm glad of that," said he.

"Glad that she was wearing a hat?" smiled the Sleeper. "Is she as bad to see as all that?"

Parmenter drummed his fingers on the top of the wall.

"Some people like the violin better than a singing voice. Some prefer the cello. Well, I would travel across the continent just to hear her speak two words."

The Sleeper looked down. He could have said "Amen!" to that.

"That was a bad business for me," went on Parmenter, with his new and amazing frankness. "Before that, I had a reputation, of a sort. Men rather looked up to me, as they look up to the mountains, do you see."

"Well?" asked the Sleeper.

"I mean to say, that they almost enjoyed having me up here—the neighbors, I should qualify. It was a grand thing, something to talk about, something worth knowing about. I never bothered them. I slid out far afield. They heard of me in Mexico, for instance, and as far north as Denver. But the lightning never struck among them. There wasn't a man in Alcalde, I dare say, who wouldn't have been glad to see me keep on escaping from trouble. There wasn't one who wouldn't have frowned if he heard that I was captured or dead. They had reasons for that attitude. They got good prices for beef, and wheat, and such things, if they cared to cart it to the foot of the pass. I bought stuff from them even when I didn't need it, and paid double the market price, because it paid me to establish a neutral belt around the mountains, if not one of actual friendliness.

"When some of my boys ran amuck and did damage around Alcalde, or some of the other near-by towns, I saw that the damage was paid for to the hilt, and something more—for nerve shock, say! Yes, I paid for the thefts and I also paid for the worry. But I couldn't pay Morice. And after riding Ironwood, I couldn't part with him. He's not a horse. He's a wonderful machine. But that theft from the old man has done me a good deal of harm. They think I'm a snake, now. That I've stepped on an old man who couldn't strike back! And yet—''

He paused, and suddenly those pale, bright eyes looked into the core of the Sleeper's soul.

''And yet I sometimes feel,'' went on the outlaw slowly, ''that in spite of the hard pass, and the rough mountains, and all these poeple living and breathing to please me, and all the gunmen and hard fighters who work for me and ride with me, that old man off yonder in the plain may still prove more than a match for me and all the rest! I may wake up some morning and find that Ironwood is gone!''

''I'd like to see him,'' said the Sleeper.

''One of these days,'' answered the other frowning. ''I'm never in a hurry to show off Ironwood! Hello, Ricardo! I thought that you'd never get here. You old frosty-head, where have you been all this while?''

''I have been in the church praying for your soul,'' said Ricardo.

He was a very old man, with white hair that glittered like spun glass in the slant rays of the sun. He was erect, tall, dignified. Under the white brush of his brows, his eyes looked out with the brightness of a boy's—or a hawk's. Now he confronted the master of Guadalupe with a serene air, giving away nothing in humility.

''You impertinent, iron-tongued, lying scoundrel,'' said Parmenter, ''you have been in the cellar trying that cognac.''

"True," said Ricardo, amazingly unabashed, "I have been in the cellar tasting the cognac."

Parmenter uttered an exclamation of impatience.

"Now I can't tell," he said aside to the Sleeper, in English, "whether he means what he says, or whether he's simply too proud to argue with me. Ricardo," he went on, "you are the father of liars."

"Of only one, señor," said the old man. "My other child died before he had a chance to speak. However, he may have grown up in heaven."

Parmenter stared at Ricardo without a smile.

"There," he said to Sleeper in another comment, "is a heart hard enough to scratch glass. Look at him man. I've known him for years, and never have learned a kind, gentle, faithful, trustworthy, careless thing about him. He's compact and boiled-down, earthquake-proof. He's the only man in the world who's not afraid to die, in spite of the fact that he believes in another life. He's not afraid because he doesn't find it possible to feel fear. Ricardo!"

"Señor?" said the old man.

"Do you see my friend here?" asked Parmenter.

"I see a man beside you," said Ricardo.

"Tell me about him," said Parmenter. He explained aside to the Sleeper: "We always do it. We always let Ricardo try his hand at reading the character of a new man. It's an old game with us. You won't mind it."

Yet he leaned in such a way that the Sleeper knew perfectly well that his host intended to place a great deal of trust in what the old man said.

Ricardo, when he received this last order, advanced a few steps and looked at the Sleeper with a glittering eye.

"The señor is a man to sit," said he.

Parmenter chuckled softly.

"You've admitted that you like an easy life, Sleeper, but old Ricardo can't know what you've said. Listen to him!"

"The señor is not very brave," went on Ricardo.

"Hold on!" said Parmenter. "No insults, Ricardo!"

But the Sleeper could see his eyes glittering with excitement.

Ricardo raised a hand, to indicate that he had been interrupted in the middle of a sentence.

"But he is not afraid of men," concluded Ricardo.

"Not very brave, but not afraid of men! What's he afraid of, then? The dark?"

"He is more afraid of me than of you, señor," said Ricardo.

The Sleeper started. It was true that he began to feel a little chilly under the probing of this bright eye.

"Every one is!" said Parmenter.

"Except you, señor. You are more afraid of yourself than of me."

"What the deuce do you mean by that?" asked Parmenter.

Ricardo merely smiled. It could be seen that he had enjoyed the last thrust he delivered.

"You're getting old and talking through your hat," declared Parmenter. "Now, my friend, Señor Sleeper, is going to stay here in Guadalupe, and I want you to make him comfortable."

Ricardo nodded.

"Give him the best room you can fix up for him— our quarters are not very luxuriously furnished, Sleeper!" he explained aside to the latter.

Ricardo bowed again.

"If he asks for anything, see that he has it."

"I understand, señor."

"He is," said Parmenter slowly, "as if he were one of us. One of your masters, here."

"Yes, señor."

"When he speaks to you, it is as if I myself were speaking to you. Is that clear?"

"Yes, señor."

"Get out of my sight, then, and tell the rest of the *mozos* that they're to treat him with gloves on their hands and run when he looks at them."

Ricardo withdrew without a word, and Parmenter stared after him.

"He's growing old!" he said gloomily. "Afraid of myself? What sense does that make? Well, Sleeper," he went on more cheerfully, "you'll have service here, from now on. I hope that'll make up for a life that's sure to be pretty dull, in a good many ways."

"Will you answer one question?"

"I'll try to."

"Why are you willing to trust me, and why do you want me so much on my own terms?"

"I can answer that. I knew what Enderby was; and I saw to-day what he is. Besides, Oñate was a famous man. Or wild cat, more than man. Does that answer you?"

"Partly."

"The other part you'll have to guess." Parmenter stood up. "I'm busy," said he. "Make yourself at home, and ask for your room when you want it."

He left the terrace at once, with his long, rather rolling stride.

CHAPTER 26.

RICARDO KEEPS THE SCORE

THE SLEEPER SPENT another hour or so on the terrace.

He had need of an intermission of lonely thought while he tried to find exactly what was in his mind. Which is what most of us rarely do, blundering ahead with nothing more definite than vague emotions and indefinite conceptions of what we desire.

The Sleeper, like some old sophist, proposed questions to himself, and staring across the mountain faces, derived answers, as it were, from them.

Why had he come here?

To serve Evelyn Morice.

What was his immediate object?

To deliver a letter to the great Parmenter.

Why had he not done so, after arriving at his goal through very considerable peril and strange adventures?

Because at the first glimpse of those brilliant sky-blue eyes of Parmenter, he knew that no woman should be condemned to life with him.

Therefore, the letter had been destroyed undelivered—an act of perfidy, perhaps, and yet he did not find it on his conscience.

What was Parmenter's present reaction toward him?

The great outlaw was mastered by enormous curiosity.

Did he trust the Sleeper?

Yes, the Sleeper thought so.

Had that been merely a trick to tempt him, the visit to the communal treasure chamber?

No, it was probably a mixed desire to tempt the Sleeper and also to show that the new man was trusted from the beginning.

Now that he was here, what would he do?

It was the first question to which he could not return a quick answer.

He told himself that he would merely relax here for a day or two, and then he would leave Guadalupe and ride away. He told himself that he was not tempted by an opportunity to throw in his lot with the bandits. And yet as he looked over the lofty wall of the house, opened by big casements, and then looked down to the streams in the valley, running currents of sparkling emeralds, he knew that such a statement to himself was a lie. He was tempted to the bottom of his soul. This was the leisure he had always wanted. This was the ease of which he had dreamed. This was the power placed in his hand, the good position with many beneath him, the respect of his fellows—

Why, then, should he not yield to it?

Because of a girl?

She already loved another man, and had confessed her love simply and frankly to him.

Because of that doddering old cynic, Morice?

What? Could that one-legged old reprobate exercise any claim upon him?

He swore that this could not be. It was not the thought of Morice that deterred him. It was rather that he had witnessed some of the crimes of the great Parmenter on his way up to the valley. That was what held him back.

So he said to himself, and yet he could not help feeling that this was self-deception. For constantly his mind reverted to the old horse breeder in his shack, yonder on the plain, his lifework gloriously completed—and then snatched from him by the arch-thief. Every man alive, honest or dishonest, must fervently desire to see the stallion returned to old Morice. That was the emotion which made even Parmenter frown and grow thoughtful here in his inaccessible fortress.

The tramp began to sigh.

Conscience was a new disease, with him. He did not even know how to take its temperature or consider its symptoms. He only knew that a vague unrest possessed him.

At last, deciding that he would flow with the current for a day or two, and then make up his mind—to leave, undoubtedly—he rose, and sauntered back into the patio.

The sun was far to the west. Shadows covered the inner court. And, dressed with them and the climbing vines, the walls appeared more loftily romantic than ever.

A *mozo* crossed the patio. He bowed to the stranger.

"My friend," said the Sleeper, "can you find out where my room is?"

"Señor, I shall bring Ricardo. He will take you to it."

He disappeared.

The tall, spare form of Ricardo immediately stepped from a dark doorway and approached the Sleeper.

"You wish your room, señor?"

"If you please."

"Kindly come with me."

He led the way, half a step in advance.

"See how the wisteria has grown!" said Ricardo.

He pointed to one of the great vines. It rose with mighty trunk and with outflung arms. Its finger tips were straining to the upper eaves.

"This good sun and this delightful air will make things grow," said Ricardo. "Only a year or two ago I put the slip in the ground. I dug out the hole and placed manure there to enrich the place. I put it in tenderly. There where it caught not even the eastern sun of the morning—only a little warmth and light in the middle of the day, I did not think that it could live, very well. I thought it would be a stunted thing. That was only a year or two ago, and now you see!"

"A year or two?" said the Sleeper, amazed and incredulous.

"Or was it ten or twelve?" murmured Ricardo. "One forgets. As one grows old, the nearer years are blended together like the voices of a waterfall. Only in the distance the stream is clear and the pictures stand in the water like faces—a tree here, a house there— You are still young, señor, but believe me that you will understand, one day!''

"I hope so," said the youth.

They passed into the house through a gloomy arched doorway, and then up a flight of stairs, with deep, shallow steps. There was a faint odor of cookery in the air.

"They have left the kitchen door open again. That cook will have to be flogged," said Ricardo thoughtfully.

He led on up to the floor above, and then to the story still higher. Here he turned down a hall just as a door opened and they were passed in the half light of the corridor by a girl whose beauty was brilliant even in that gloom. The heart of the young Sleeper leaped.

"Who is that?" he asked softly.

Ricardo halted and whirled around. He smote his hands together.

"Señorita!" he called.

"No, no!" said the Sleeper. "Don't disturb the lady. Confound it, man, I simply asked you—"

"Yes, Ricardo?" said the loveliest of all voices, in the softest of Mexican accents, which in all the world can be the most dulcet tongue. "Yes, Ricardo?"

"I called you," said Ricardo. "Come here."

"I come," said she, without surliness.

It amazed and angered the Sleeper to see such a beauty obedient to this old man, servant as he was.

"I have nothing to say to her," said the Sleeper. "Let's go on. You embarrass me—"

It seemed that Ricardo did not hear.

"This is your new master," said Ricardo in his

dry, harsh voice. "This is Señor Sleeper."

Behold, she curtsied before him as if he were a great lord!

"That is Francesca Gomez," said Ricardo. "She sews on buttons, takes care of the flower garden, and sings with a guitar in the evening, as you please, or is silent, if you disapprove of such caterwauling."

"Willing, señor," said the girl.

Her eyes were on the floor, which was the last place that the Sleeper wished them.

"Have you placed flowers in the señor's room?" asked the harsh Ricardo.

"I have, Ricardo. Shall I go with you to—"

"Go your own way, and come when you're asked!" said Ricardo more severely than before.

She bowed again, curtsied once more to the Sleeper, and withdrew.

"Notice a woman once a week and she thinks that she's an essential in the house," growled Ricardo, passing on down the hall. "This is your room, Señor Sleeper."

It was big enough for five beds. It held only one. Two great casements opened to the brilliant west, with the green of the vine flooding in through them. The furnishings were simple. The bed itself was long and wide, and built up from the floor not with legs, but with heaped mattresses, and covers. There were half a dozen chairs. All were of different makes, and all were handmade. Yonder was a goatskin with an Indian painted backrest behind it, for reclining at any angle. There were a couple of deep easy-chairs, piled with cushions, and on the whole it seemed as though many people could be made comfortable here. In the corner, near one of the windows, there was a crude little wooden table, with an inkstand upon it. A washstand was in the opposite nook with the inevitable goatskin in front of it upon the floor. In fact, newly cleaned goatskins were used in such numbers on the floor, on the bed, on the chairs, that the prevailing note of the room was clean white. But in the center of the floor lay the rich dapplings of a jaguar's hide, with its head mounted, and its mask showing an ominous grin. The hand of Francesca could be traced, here and there. It appeared in the three or four big earthenware vases, overflowing with flowers, burning bright in the shafts of westering sunshine, or glowing more dimly through the shadow. For evening light, there appeared a pair of good big lamps, one on a stand by the bed's head, and one on the writing table.

"There were a dozen others you could have had," said Ricardo, waving to the features of the chamber, "but this will please your taste the most."

"How do you know my taste?" asked the Sleeper.

"It looks west toward Alcalde," said the old man gruffly. "Is there anything more the señor wishes of me?"

The Sleeper was too staggered by the first part of this remark to answer at once, and Ricardo instantly withdrew, leaving the Sleeper to wonder what magic insight was in old Ricardo that he should be able to read a man's mind to such an effect. It was true. The windows looked down the Tinnio Pass, and he could dream of the plains beyond.

Dream of them he did, standing with his hands resting on the deep sill, and the tendrils of the vines rustling about his face. Then he heard a loud yelling bubbling up from far beneath, and leaning out in concern, he was horrified to see a man in a white cap and apron held firmly by several fierce-looking *mozos* while one wielded a long-lashed whip and applied it liberally to the back of the shrieking, dancing cook. Old Ricardo stood by, keeping calm score of the number of strokes with a pencil and a piece of paper!

CHAPTER 27.

A PLEASANT EXPERIENCE

HE LAY DOWN to rest for a time, thinking that he would be able to sleep, but his favorite talent, which had given him his nickname, seemed to have deserted him at this moment. His brain was spinning, and as on a revolving wheel, he saw the faces of Evelyn Morice and Francesca.

Then he got up, swearing softly to himself, and pulled at a bell cord. A hand instantly tapped on the door and then opened it.

"A bath?" said the Sleeper. "Can I get some hot water for a bath? Or is there a bathroom in this place?"

"Señor, the bath is waiting for you," said the *mozo*.

The Sleeper blinked. This little touch, more than all the rest, made him feel as though he had stepped into the center of a fairy tale.

He stripped off his clothes, threw his slicker about him, and followed the *mozo* across the hall to a quite large room which looked west like his own chamber, and, therefore, was drowsily warmed by the afternoon sun.

Sunk in the floor of this apartment there was a bath of green stone into which one descended by three steps. It was big enough and deep enough to accommodate a swimmer. The Sleeper fairly yawned with luxurious pleasure.

"I call José, who understands how to rub down," said the *mozo*. "Señor Parmenter himself taught him, and even if he had the skin of a wild boar, José would not have been able to forget those floggings!"

He chuckled a little, softly, as he spoke, and disappeared through the doorway, while the Sleeper dived into the bath and floated there, soaking the unspeakable fatigue of a long ride out of his back and his legs.

When he climbed out of the bath, José waited.

He was built like a wrestler. He had the strength of a gorilla, and the touch of a juggler. He knew anatomy like a doctor, and he picked out, and worked, and stripped the big, sinewy muscles of the Sleeper until they ached with bruising pain. Then that passed, and the flesh blood leaped through the body of the tramp, and fatigue disappeared. When he stood up from the rubbing table, he was ready for a journey as long as he already had made that day, he thought. His very brain was soothed and at ease, while José stood back perspiring much, his chest heaving with his labor.

"Hai, Señor Sleeper!" said he. "To knead your muscles is like handling Indian rubber. You could have been a wrestler, señor!" He spoke with a flattering smile, as though he were paying the highest possible compliment.

So the Sleeper went back to his room and dressed. It was a big room, and a comfortable one, but he could not stay in it.

The dusk was coming. His appetite for supper was that of a tiger. He craved food, and with that craving, he pulled the bell cord. Again, instantly, the tap came at his door. It was opened. The *mozo* looked in.

"What's the supper hour?" the Sleeper asked.

"The supper hour is your hour, señor," said the *mozo*.

"I mean to say, man, at what time will the supper be served?"

"At your convenience, señor."

"But there are other people in this house."

"There are no other masters, señor."

"Not even Parmenter? Has he left?"

"He was called away. He has left a message for you. I think, señor, that Ricardo has it."

"Then where do people dine, here?"

"Wherever you wish, señor. The masters often have supper in the patio, with lanterns lighted. It is not too cool tonight, perhaps."

"Let it be in the patio, then. And as soon as possible."

He half expected the man to laugh in his face; but no, there was the usual bow, and the dark face of the Mexican withdrew.

So the Sleeper waited only long enough to knot his necktie, after he had shaken the dust from it, and then he followed slowly down the stairs. He paused for a moment, to be sure, at the first landing, in order to lean out of the narrow casement there, and look down. Beneath him, on this side, was the valley. And the light was still sufficiently bright to enable him to distinguish the workers climbing up the steep steps in the side of the valley, rising from the lower shadows as if through water, and working up and up toward the level of the big house. Even the braying of a jackass was softened to a sort of laughing, drawing music by the distance and the thin mountain air.

Then the Sleeper went down to the patio.

To his amazement, he found that even these few delays on his part had been enough. A number of lights in iron lantern frames of a very old period were burning here and there, throwing a soft radiance over the court. The lower part of the fountain was lost in dimness; but the head mounted to a silver spray and, nodding and rising, showered back into the pool with a subdued sound of coolness. Just opposite the arch which led to the terrace, and giving from his chair a view of the night-blue mountains in a curving frame, a little table was set out with a single place, and opposite to this table stood the formidable Ricardo, erect as a ramrod, unyielding as stone.

He went to the chair and drew it back for the Sleeper, and seated him in state. He waved his hand. Instantly came one carrying a whole capon boiled in butter; there were greens from which a thin perfume of good vinegar arose; and rich old red wine poured out into the glass for the new master. He had tortillas with beans, of course. There were the same little loaves of crisp bread again, and again, to his amazement, he found them freshly baked. He ate chicken. He devoured chile con carne. He discovered a whole nest of little pastry cones, filled with spiced meats and brimming with juices. Fruit appeared before him—purple-blue figs, amber grapes bursting with wine and fragrance, red apples, pears freckled with brown and gold.

"Ricardo!"

"Yes, señor?"

"This is like a hotel."

"This is much better than a hotel," said the terrible old man, "because here it is pleasantly possible to hang the waiter and burn the cook alive."

"The poor man you flogged?" asked the Sleeper.

"Ah, you heard that?"

The Sleeper looked narrowly at him.

"You knew that I would hear it," he surmised aloud, "and that was the reason that you had him whipped."

"Señor, a new master always wishes to feel his authority."

"I hadn't ordered it," said the Sleeper. "How do you excuse cruelty like that?"

"Easily," said the old Ricardo. "If I let them have their way, the whole house would soon be reeking like a wayside tavern. Would you prefer that, señor?"

"But how do you think that you have pleased me by whipping the poor man?"

"If you are cruel," said Ricardo, "you will be glad to see the sight. In that way you will be pleased. If you are not cruel, you will forbid such things to happen again. In that way also, you will be pleased. Every man who holds the reins wants to feel out a new horse."

The Sleeper could not help laughing at this naïve explanation. Then he said:

"Well, Ricardo, have I the power to bid and forbid?"

"You have, señor, until I receive word from Señor Parmenter to the contrary. Until he gives a new order, you are the master of the house. If you command that we should tear it to the ground, we would have to obey you."

"So?" said the Sleeper.

"It is true."

"Then never flog a man again—until I give orders for it."

Ricardo bowed. He was so skillful in the matter of lowering his eyes that he had only to move his head an inch or two in order to give the sense of quite a deep bow.

The Sleeper sat back, with a cup of coffee in his hand.

"Who made this coffee, Ricardo?"

"I made it with my own hands, señor, if it is good."

The Sleeper laughed again.

"What if it's bad?"

"Then the detestable scoundrel of a second cook should be flogged."

"It is so bad," said the Sleeper, "that he really ought to be flogged!"

"Good!" said Ricardo. "A whip stroke in the morning makes a quiet horse all day!"

"Don't let the man be touched," said the Sleeper. "Nevertheless, the coffee is bad. Tell him so."

"I shall tell him," said Ricardo, "if I have your permission, that the new master does not believe in floggings, and that he usually gives two warnings before the things he *does* believe in, happen. Shall I tell them that?"

"What would you have the thing I believe in be?" asked the Sleeper.

"That is a thing that you and I could talk over," said Ricardo. "I have a good many ideas. I am half Indian. The better half, señor!"

He made one of his small, solemn bows, as he spoke.

"Will you tell something about yourself?" asked the Sleeper.

"Gladly, señor. I wish to have no secrets. What shall I tell you?"

"What have you done?"

"I began," said Ricardo, "as a sneak thief, when I was a boy. I went from that into highway robbery, and graduated from that to smuggling, which was an excellent business. However, safe-cracking was better still, and when that grew dull, I graduated again, and became a hired murderer."

"Ah?" said the Sleeper.

"Not a common one," said Ricardo. "I used to charge never less than five hundred dollars. It was a pleasant life. The life of a gentleman."

"What made you leave it? The danger?"

"No, but the monotony. I graduated again, therefore, and embraced the opportunity, many years ago, of coming to Guadalupe."

"Where you are—"

"The housekeeper, señor," said Ricardo, and made another of those ceremonial little bows. "That singing I was speaking of, shall I command it for you, señor?"

CHAPTER 28.

IN THE GLOOM

"CATERWAULING YOU CALLED it then," said the Sleeper.

"That was when the sun was up," said Ricardo. "Every cat has a right to change its mind at night, and, therefore, why not the men, as well?"

"Well, why not?" murmured the Sleeper. "You're a rare fellow, Ricardo. Yes, let's have the singing, if I'm free to ask for it."

"There is nothing in Guadalupe," sand Ricardo, "that you cannot ask for. You have the key to every man's house in your hand. All that you see is yours."

"For the moment," said the Sleeper, "you make me feel rich. But I should think that at your age you'd want to retire, Ricardo."

"I am too old to retire," said Ricardo. "That is to say, I have not enough time left to enjoy a new life!"

He clapped his hands twice, as he spoke, and instantly, as though showering out of the central sky above him, the Sleeper heard the murmur of a guitar and the sweet, distant singing of a girl.

"If you wish to continue talking—" explained Ricardo.

"No, let me hear the whole voice, if you can."

Ricardo made a single gesture. Instantly, the strong, pure voice flooded the court. It might have been as simple a thing as the opening of a door or a shutter, but it was like a touch of magic to the Sleeper, so much enchantment was already in the air.

The song ended.

"She will also dance here in the courtyard for you," said Ricardo. "Or another song, as you please."

"Neither," said the Sleeper.

Ricardo made another little gesture.

"I, also, if the señor permits," said he, "prefer to drink good wine slowly. Has the señor any other wish?"

"To be left alone, here," said the tramp.

The table was taken instantly. He sat in the dim solitude of the patio, while Ricardo held before him a box of excellent Havanas, slender, folded in dark wrappers, oily and rich to the touch, and fragrant with all the perfection of well-cured tobacco leaf when lighted.

On this, the Sleeper puffed slowly, luxuriously, his head fallen back against the top of the chair, and his eyes drifting and wandering slowly among the stars. Above the rough margin of the walls, there was fenced in a great rectangle, and there burned the beautiful triangle of Vega, Deneb, and Altair, clustered around by lesser myriads. Brightly they shone to the tramp, and suddenly his mind flew off to other places and to other times when he had seen that same triangle blazing in the heavens, high or low—as when he had been stretched on the jolting surface of a flat car, with a cold wind off the St. Lawrence River biting him to the bone, and no more cover than his own unhappy and hungry thoughts—for at that time he had been three days without food. And he thought of a night when he had toiled through the Tennessee mountains up a steep, twisting, muddy road, with huge rain clouds flying across the sky, but with a gap broken open through which he had seen these three peerless stars in their heaven. And he had thought suddenly, at that time, of their purity, and of his own defiled and muddy life, without true hope, without real honor, with no more golden goal than steak and eggs, and with no more glorious reward that a stolen hen roasted over a small fire in a tramp jungle.

Here, for whatever reason, he was free from hunger, and free from weariness and dirt. Clean clothes fitted a clean body. His thoughts were free. And though he lived in a sort of Castle Perilous, yet he was sensible on his hip of the constant pressure and weight of the old single-action Colt which was his shield and his safeguard.

So he dreamed away his time.

At last, the cigar was burned to a butt.

A whole box, filled almost to the top, was ready to his hand. The watchful Ricardo came forward and offered another smoke. But he waved them away.

"Yes," said Ricardo, speaking softly, as though he would fit his voice into the evening calm, "the truth is that, like beer, the first cigar is the best, Señor, I am glad to see that you are a man of taste, which is something hard to find among those who often have gone hungry."

"Have I often been hungry?" said the tramp.

"Yes," said Ricardo, "you often have been hungry."

"And how could you tell that?"

"By a certain welcome, señor, that I saw in your eye when it fell upon the boiled chicken, as though it was a face that you had seen before but hardly expected to make a constant familiar of. That was one sign."

"Other signs, then, Ricardo?"

"Well, señor, for another thing, I don't know of a man who has ever come to Guadalupe except after having fasted, and that not once but many times."

The Sleeper smiled. He enjoyed listening to the worldly wisdom of this hard old man.

"I thought, Ricardo," said he, "that I told you I wished to be alone."

"I did not speak, señor."

"However, you were standing here."

"You could not see my face, señor, which is the quickest way to forget a man."

"Do you think so?"

"Señor, many a man has stood all his life, and in crowds, too, and yet never been noticed more than a lamp-post. Yes, less than that, for a lamp-post must by its nature hold up a lighted face!"

"Ricardo, you were standing there in the shadows not to serve me but to watch me."

"However, I could not see all your thoughts, señor."

"Could you see any of them?"

"Why, I could guess."

"Such as what?"

"That you had not often seen stars through cigar smoke, señor."

"By that you suggest that I've rarely had the price to buy cigars, Ricardo?"

"By that I suggest that you've gone to bed early when you can, señor."

The Sleeper stood up.

"I shall take that for a hint and go to bed now," said he. "I'll have another bath in the morning. And since I go to bed early, I'll be up by dawn. Do you hear, Ricardo?"

"Señor, everything shall be done as you desire."

"Good night, Ricardo."

"Good night, señor."

"Those murders, Ricardo—"

"Yes, señor?"

"Real murders, Ricardo?"

"Well, señor, I was paid for them!"

The Sleeper went up to his room. He did not find the way obscure, for a *mozo*, unbidden, came out and lighted him to his door with a lantern, and then went in and touched a match to the two lamps, and stood by until he had turned the wicks to the correct height. Then he stood by the door and waited.

"Nothing more," said the tramp. "Good night!"

The *mozo* bowed and departed. All these men moved with the silence of the hair-winged owls in the dusky evening air.

But the Sleeper, standing again at the window, found that he was not looking far off to the wedgelike passage through the Tinnio Pass, and that he was no longer thinking of the plains beyond, of Alcalde, and old Morice, and Evelyn Morice; but instead, he was looking sheer down at the dark court where he had seen the cook being flogged, and then over the outer wall toward the little huddled town of Guadalupe itself, with its serpentining street that wound up the hillside and led the flocking houses to the high and unhospitable wall of the house of Parmenter. He would have given a good deal to know the true history of that house before it had fallen into the hands of the bandit. But, for some reason, he could not imagine it ever in law-abiding hands. It was too much like an eagle's spy-rock, or the site of a hawk's nest in the air.

And an inexplicable melancholy came over the mind and the soul of the tramp.

It was not that he had been troubled by pangs of conscience. It was the reverse. He began to wonder what he could have been in life if he had been surrounded all his days by this loftiness of position. To be virtuous—well, that was another matter. But, at least, when men live as in a castle on a rock, it must be simple to be lofty of spirit and high of soul, temperate, contented with the taste rather than the glut of what is pleasant. Otherwise, how could he, so easily, have waved away the box of Havanas? And how could he have refused to hear a second song or to see the girl dance? Why was it that one cigar was enough? Why was it that he preferred to sit with the thought of the beautiful girl drifting somewhere between him and the stars?

The Sleeper sighed.

Many good things were easy in this robber's nest! Virtue? well, that was, no doubt, a different matter. And yet he did not feel closer to evil, here in the heart of banditry, than he had done when he lay drowsily on the floor of that box car, with the old tramp and the middle-aged one beside him.

He paced the floor.

There seemed too much light from two lamps, and therefore, he put out one. He continued his walking. A moon rose. The stars grew dimmer. Still, he paced softly back and forth, and all the while the melancholy deepened in him; yet, something was lifting his heart higher and higher, until it seemed chilled by the altitude.

He was telling himself that he should go to bed, now, but bed was still far from his thoughts when he suddenly heard at the door of his room the softest tapping.

He listened.

The sound was repeated, and going to the door, he drew it cautiously wide.

Then he saw in the gloom of the hallway the black-mantled head and shoulders of the girl, and even in that dimness enough light reached her from the single lamp in his room, and again by her own radiance she shone.

It was Francesca Gomez. She shrank a little from him. She made a sound like the rustling of half-heard wings.

"What is it you wish of me, señorita?" he asked kindly.

"One small minute to hear me, señor!" said she.

"As long as you will," said the Sleeper.

He stepped back. And she came in with a quick step and closed the door quickly, silently behind her, and stood there with both her hands still gripping the knob, and her eyes fixed great and still upon his face.

CHAPTER 29.

FRANCESCA'S STORY

THE SLEEPER, for he knew, somehow, that it would make her more at ease, drew still farther back toward the big windows.

"There's something ahead, or else something that's following you," said he. "But you needn't have any fear here, I think. Will you tell me what is wrong, señorita?"

She turned the key in the lock; he heard the bolt go home through its wards. Now, as though there actually were some danger silent but breathing behind her in the hall from which the locking of the door shielded her, but as though she still dreaded the man inside the room, and fear and weakness had broken her down, she slipped on her knees against the wall with a hand yet raised to the knob, and with her face buried in the crook of her other arm.

There she sobbed, silently, but he could tell the vibration of her body by the light, quick chattering of the bolt against its steel chamber in the wall.

The heart of the Sleeper was touched. What young

man can resist beauty in distress? He went to her quickly. She protested. The touch of her hand was like ice on his face, but the Sleeper raised her in his powerful arms, though with some surprise. She was graceful as a cat, but she was made round and strong, and passed his expectation by some fifteen or twenty pounds.

The Sleeper carried her to a chair where the moon would just touch her face, and there he deposited her without finding much to say on the journey except to tell her, many times over, that there was nothing to be afraid of. He would have left her there, but she clung to him.

"You are true and good!" said Francesca Gomez, her voice still shuddering with tears. "I knew that you were by your gentle voice when I first heard you. I knew again, tonight, I can trust you, señor!"

She had her face turned up to his, and at the sight of the wet tears on her cheeks and loading her lashes, the Sleeper was almost overwhelmed with a desire to kiss her.

He told himself that he was a brute, and managed to straighten a little. He patted her head; he could not think of what else to do, except to tell her mechanically, that there was nothing for her to be afraid of.

"Ah, señor, ah, señor," said she, "how can you say such a thing in Guadalupe? Who lives here without fear? Not even the master of them all! Not even the master! Not even that Señor Parmenter!"

She released him and clapped her hands over her face. Her dusky, olive skin made those hands like shadows against shadows, but the light of a jewel trembled on one finger, and the childish slenderness of the round wrists disturbed the Sleeper.

He went back a little farther to the casement, and was glad of the good, cool wind that blew in upon him and made breathing easier. For the Sleeper felt as though he had walked up a long hill. Yet he had only carried a beauty the width of a room.

She continued to sob. She could curl up in an amazingly small compass, and she lay now in the chair with her head down on both her hands. The Sleeper went a little closer. The moonlight touched the glossy round of her head and the nape of her neck. He touched her head also.

"Has some one been unkind to you?" he asked her.

"Unkind?" cried she. "Oh, what is unkindness to me? I could be a slave—I could be a worker in the fields. Oh, I would gladly do that, but not—but not—"

The Sleeper said nothing. His diaphragm had grown icy and rose higher and higher in his breast. He trembled, as it were, on the verge of falling to his knees and gathering her closer in his arms. It would have been a far more dangerous position for telling her that he, at least, would be a shield between her and danger.

Then the Sleeper told himself that he was a scoundrel, to take advantage of a lady in distress, and that he was undoubtedly a worthless creature, for was it not another whom he loved so tenderly, so devotedly, with such a lost and fatal love?

He tried to conjure up the vision of the gentle, pure face of Evelyn Morice. It refused to rise! He told himself that he was a man, and strong; that she was a woman, and weak; but somehow all of his words fell upon deaf ears—his own!

"Señorita," he heard himself saying, with almost a tremor in his voice, "won't you please tell me why you are here in Guadalupe?"

"Oh, Heaven forgive him!" sobbed the girl. "I am here because I was brought here."

"Against your will?"

"Who in the whole world would stay here of free will?" she asked. "Except murderers, robbers, traitors, plunderers of churches, fiends in the shapes and voices of men, scoundrels—oh!"

Now, as she said this with a growing heat, she came suddenly upon a stopping point that made her lift her tearful face and made her eyes shine big with fear, while she clasped her hands beneath her chin.

"I have offended you!" she cried to him softly. "I have stabbed you with my words!"

Her voice was like the crooning of a dove at sunset above a blue and golden standing water.

"You haven't offended me," said the Sleeper, "because, as a matter of fact, I haven't joined them—as yet—"

"You've not yet joined them?"

"No, not yet!"

"Then in the name of Heaven, run away from them and save yourself, señor! Flee from them while there still is time—"

"For that matter," said he, "I suppose nobody can run away unless it's the pleasure of Parmenter."

"He is a great and a terrible man," she admitted, "but after all, there are ways. There are people in whom he has to trust who cannot be trusted. Señor, señor, there are ladders over every wall, or holes under it, and you can save yourself. Believe me, for I know of ways! If I had the strength and the courage of a man, do you think that these big stones would keep me inside? No, no, not for a moment!''

She sat up straight. Her head was high. Such was the contrast between her now and as she had been the moment before, that the Sleeper could hardly believe his eyes. Yes, if she were a man, there undoubtedly was very little that she would not attempt. Even as a woman, she seemed at that instant capable of everything.

''Señorita,'' said he, ''who brought you here?''

''I was brought by the worst of them all!'' she declared. ''That long-throated, black-eyed snake of a man, Bullen. The smuggler brought me!''

''Will you tell me how?'' asked the Sleeper gently. ''I don't want to hurt you. But can you tell me?''

She laid a hand over her heart, as though asking of it what her strength might be and how far it could extend. Then she said:

''I cannot tell you everything—but if you had seen our dear, sleepy, careless life in the old village in Mexico, Señor Sleeper, and the patio with the dobe pillars all crooked, and the arches all sagging, and the rose vines everywhere, climbing like children! Well, if you had seen that, and the good, simple face of my father—and his brave, gentle eyes that would trust every man. Strange dogs came to his hand. Horses loved him. But there were men who would betray him! Well, the American trader came to buy from our little ranch, and that was Señor Bullen—a curse on the day when I first saw his face, and he saw mine! Look, my dear friend, and see that I have a pretty face, and that I am young. And when he saw me as he was crossing the patio, he stopped in mid-stride and fixed me with his eye. I had seen that look before, when he saw my father's best horse. The horse was gone that instant. Yes, the very next moment a price was on it too big for my father to resist, and as I felt his eye, I wondered what price would be put on me!''

"Horrible!" said the Sleeper. "A beast, and not a man!"

"Yes," said the girl, rather thoughtfully than with her former wild emotion. "But there was no price. A thief will never buy except what he can get so cheap that the price is robbery itself. And Señor Bullen knew that I never could be taken with my father's will. What could he do, then?''

"I don't know," said the Sleeper. "Except that he stole you, señorita?"

"Yes," said the girl quietly. "And I heard the shot fired. I ran out and found my father lying in the moonlight.

" 'A terrible accident,' said the smuggler.

"He was dead," she ended.

"Ah?" said the Sleeper faintly.

"He could not leave me alone in the house, he said," continued Francesca. "His men would watch over the body, and I should go with him to my uncle's house, which was fifteen miles nearer to the border. But I must not stay alone in that house. We were too poor to have servants, señor. It was I who took care of the little place, and my dear father—so happily—I went back and threw myself on his body. They lifted me. The poor dead arms could not hold me, señor. They were helpless, now! Even I had more strength!

"They carried me to the carriage. We drove hard for the border. Señor Bullen was with me, his beady little eyes looking ahead at the moonlight on the road, never speaking. I was too sick and weak from weep-ing. I could not watch, I could not doubt, until I saw the heads of the mountains around me, and knew that we had been on the way too long. Then I jumped up, but he caught me and dragged me down beside him.

"I asked him what he was doing, where he was taking me.

" 'Into a new life, my little beauty,' said he.

"It was true. Into a new life, a life of horror, he carried me, and I am here!"

She caught her breath and then went on:

"He gave me a week to consent to marry him, but before the week was up, he had to go away on one of his smuggling trips. I have been here ever since, counting the sacred days of freedom from him, like beads on a rosary, praying for death from Heaven before he comes back—and death I shall have!" she ended sternly. "I am thoroughly prepared, for I carry it with me always, now!"

And suddenly, in her hand, there lay a short, bulldog revolver with a grim, gaping muzzle.

The Sleeper stared at it.

He would have thought, in all this world, that her hand would be the last to find such a weapon. He could imagine her taking sudden poison, or the stroke of a stiletto, sharp as a fine-drawn icicle. But this was far different. There was something brutal, savage, bluntly Northern in the weapon and in the grip in which she held it, familiarly.

He found himself saying the thing that before had been on his lips:

"Would you trust yourself in my hands, then, to try and escape?"

CHAPTER 30.

A LADY'S AID

DESERT FLOWERS do not bloom so quickly after rain as Francesca did, then. It was as though the sun were shining in the room, the presence of her joy before him.

Would she go? Aye, it was the vague hope of that offer had drawn her to him, she declared. Go with him? Yes, trust him to the end of time!

He made her sit down again. In her impatience she teetered on the edge of the chair like a child.

"We have to be thoughtful and calm," said the Sleeper, his heart beating fast.

"Thoughtful," she said, "and calm. Yes, yes!"

"Now, then, you think you know a safe way out of the house?"

"Yes. One where not even a mouse will see us go!"

"We'll hardly have much luck if we start away on foot, Francesca. You realize that? Not that I'm unwilling to try anything that—"

"But I'm going to take you to the finest horse in the world. You're to ride Ironwood!"

"By Heaven!" said the Sleeper, his mind rushing back to old Morice. "Do you mean that?"

"Yes, yes! And I've in mind the very mount for me. He's a roan gelding. He can run all day. He's a mountain goat in sureness of foot!"

"And the way from the house?"

"Simply out of the stables—"

"But are not the grooms on duty there?"

"None at this time of night. They sleep near the horses, but not actually in the stable. They have to be rung out of bed at this hour."

"And then?"

"Simply down the slant way to the bottom of the valley. And still down the valley. There is one man there on guard—"

"He is dead, then," said the Sleeper slowly.

She caught a hand to her lips, and stared at him.

"We'll have to pay for this exit," said he. "That's all. They've taken your father's life, Francesca!"

She nodded. She could not speak.

"Whatever we do, we mustn't waste any more time tonight," said he. And he stood up.

She was before him at the door. Her excited whisper trembled back at him. She flung herself suddenly into his arms and kissed him.

"Ah, how good, how brave!" said Francesca Gomez.

He, in a haze of enchantment, followed her down the hall, and down the winding stairs, with their deep and shallow steps. They entered the lower regions of the house, and the lights dripped from iron lantern frames down the moist walls and down the moldy steps. She, still hurrying in advance, pushed open a heavy door, at last, and the stable was before them.

The moonlight dropped a steady torrent of silver upon the open court. The sound of the gushing water was to him like a paean of escape. Still she went unhesitatingly forward, and unlatched the door of a little shed, apart from the rest. She found with a ready hand a lantern beside the door. The moment that she lighted it, the Sleeper saw before him Ironwood, at last.

Built long and low, with the shoulders and the girth of a lion, with the bone to carry a house and the quarters to lift it, ewe-necked, and his long upper lip foolishly fringed with a white mustache, he was as far from a picture horse as the work of a great draftsman is from the pretty idealisms of an amateur. Even with the knowledge of what that stallion was, and the story of the Creole Stakes still ringing in his mind, yet the Sleeper could not feel, at first, that the gray horse belonged anywhere except in front of a plow, or jogging between the shafts of a buckboard, dragging home the week's supplies to the ranch house on a Saturday night. He had to look again, and yet again, before he saw the running points. Not that he could feel convinced of real speed. No, he could understand why the experts had slipped over this as a necessarily sluggish performer. But a hunter would have picked out this as a model to carry weight across country, plugging doggedly along. Given any foot at all, certain it was that Ironwood never would lose heart or wind.

The girl already was throwing a saddle on the back of a roan, explaining in a gasping whisper:

"These two are specially Parmenter's. Thank heavens he left them both behind, this time!"

He took down the saddle from behind the stallion,

and as he did so, he saw the girl whip into the saddle which already she had cinched upon the back of the roan.

The Sleeper put his own saddle back on its peg.

"What's wrong?" she breathed at him. "Hurry, hurry! The night's our chance!"

But he stared at her, with two pictures bright in his mind's eye.

One was the bulldog revolver, familiarly at home in her grip; the other was her leap into that saddle.

"Francesca, my dear," said the Sleeper, "before we start on the out-trail, suppose you tell me your real name?"

"Real name?" she said, amazed.

"Yes. Is it Rose or May, or Myrtle or Lily, or Sally or Minnie, or Dorothy or Ruth? When you're at home, I mean, what's your name then, Francesca?"

She slid rather limply from the saddle.

"Do you doubt me, señor?" said she.

"I have no more strength to doubt you," said the Sleeper dryly, "than your poor father had in his dead arms. I was simply asking a few questions that popped up into my mind."

The answer of Francesca was a most unpoetic and unladylike grunt. She turned about and took the roan back to the stall. She stripped the saddle from its back, and rejoined him.

Then she stared straight into his eyes. Her own were as bold as brass, sullen, gloomy.

"I thought you were a real flathead, all angles," finally said Francesca, in English. "But you saw through me at last!"

"At last?" said the Sleeper. He felt that he could afford some prevarication, now, seeing how nearly he had fallen victim to this trickster.

"Well," said the girl, stamping impatiently, "don't tell me that you tumbled right away?"

"Didn't I?" said the Sleeper, smiling with assumed knowledge.

"You were woozy," said the girl. "You'd better confess that. Honor bright, Sleeper, you were a little groggy when I pulled the sob stuff, and all that?"

"You've overlooked something," said the Sleeper. "A good actress always inspires the ham-and-eggers. I simply tried to do my little bit, and you were always a help."

"Was I?" said the girl, tilting her pretty head to one side and regarding him critically. "Well, I'm still dizzy. I thought you were as easy as they come, but you turn out hard-boiled. You're a new kind, Sleeper. Why did you let me drift so long?"

"I didn't want to bother you when you were dreaming so sweetly," said he. "Besides, I wanted to see how close you'd bring me to the guns."

He thought that she winced a little, at this.

"Well," she said, "if you were as much of a sap as they told me, and as I guessed, it wouldn't have made any difference. One sucker less in the world lets the strong trees grow, Sleeper! But," she continued, irritated more and more, "it stops me to think how you put it over. No arm waving, either. Standing like a marble-faced boy while I kiss the stony lips. It beats me still, when I think about it! Actor? You're all by yourself!"

Still she was gloomy.

He looked at her with an amazement that he hardly could subdue and master. She would have taken him under the guns of indifferent marksmen without turning a hair.

"Do you think I've been a fool not to follow the stage, Francesca?" he asked her.

"Drop that. I'm Pat Lawlor," said she. "You've heard about me, big boy. I'm the one they call the Lawloress. You've heard about me, eh?"

"Not a whisper," said he. "This is pretty far southwest, for me."

"Yeah?" she drawled. Then, returning to her spirit of wonder, she added: "You're the little child that I was gunna lead by the hand! You're the drowsy baby that I was gunna hush to sleep! Sleeper, it kind of takes away my self-respect to think what a fool you've made of me!"

"Well," said he, "I'll make a concession."

"I don't believe it," said the girl. "What is it?"

"I'll never tell Parmenter."

She laughed harshly. Her very voice had changed with her new manner.

"Do you have to tell the Old Nick what happens?" she asked him. "no more do you Parmenter. He'll know everything, by this. He's up there, dragging at a cigar and laughing to himself, thinking you into kingdom come. But in another minute, he'll know everything. Say, Sleeper, where'd you get it?"

"What?" he asked.

"The baby look," said she.

"I didn't know I had it," said he.

"Yeah?" she asked cynically; "I guess you ain't studied yourself from every angle. Oh, I guess you ain't! I tell you, handsome, when you put on that woozy look up there in your room, I pretty near had a change of heart. I pretty near busted out laughing and told you to grow a while before you mingled with real men like run around up here! You had me done up. Yeah, I pretty near pitied you. And I'm the Lawloress, at that! C'mon back. I'm dead for a smoke."

She led the way from the stable, while the Sleeper, still fairly dizzy in the brain, followed her slowly.

Outside in the moonlight, as she closed and latched the door of the little stable behind her, she called out:

"Hullo, boys!"

There was no answer.

"Aw, c'mon out," said the Lawloress. "C'mon out and meet one of yourselves. Can't you see that I've pulled a dud?"

At this, there was still a moment of delay, and then from around the corner of the nearest shed, there appeared three men, like steps of a ladder, one extremely tall and gawky, carrying a rifle loosely swinging in his hand; one of middle size similarly armed, and one much shorter with the double barrels of a sawed-off shot gun laid carefully across his arm.

CHAPTER 31.

THREE OR FOUR MEN

"PRETTY, AIN'T THEY?" asked the girl.

She waved at the three.

"Lookit the honor that the big chief he paid to you, will you? Lookit three of the big guns laid down here side by side to blow you out of your happy home. Which is your skin, I take it?"

"It was," said the Sleeper, "but now I think Guadalupe will do for me. I grow to like the atmosphere better and better."

"Said the dog as he choked the cat," she commented. "But I'll believe you. I'll believe anything you say, because it looks like I can't help myself. Listen, boys, he's had the low-down from the start. This is Lefty Bullen, Sleeper. I been tellin' him about your long neck and your snaky eye, Lefty. You've been a kidnaper to-night, you'll be interested to know."

"What did I kidnap?" asked Bullen, in a bass as profound as his body was slight.

"Me, handsome," said the girl.

"Not while I had my fingers crossed," said Lefty. "Hullo, Sleeper. Glad to meetcha."

"This is Brick Sorrell, our pet yegg. He could break open a mountain and not make no more sound than a bird floppin' its wings. Couldn't you, Brick?"

"Aw, shut up," said Brick. "I've heard your line longer'n the rest of 'em, remember."

"Somebody knock him down for me, the ruffian," said the girl lightly.

She turned to him of middle size, a man of forty years, perhaps, with a very pale, thoughtful face beneath the moon.

"And this here is Dolly," said the girl. "Smile, Dolly, and show your pretty teeth for the gentleman. This is Dolly, all right, Sleeper. I've saved our best for the last. Dolly Chipping is our pet gunman. He shoots the eyes out of needles without half tryin', and unties a silk knot at a hundred yards. Don'tcha, Dolly?"

"How are you?" said Dolly Chipping. "You'll excuse my left hand," he went on in his courteous, gentle voice. "I've hurt my right."

"Yeah, his right hand is achin'," said the Lawloress. "It always is. Achin' for a kill and near dyin' now that he's missed his chance to gun for you. Be patient, Dolly. You might have a chance later on. But this mustard is likely to burn the roof right off the top of your soft palate, honey!"

"I'm very glad that you're still with us," said Dolly Chipping. "A moment ago I thought you were outward bound, but I see that you were only dropping into the station to read the time-table and—"

"Listen at him!" said the girl, with loud laughter. "Ain't he got a cute line, though? Little old Dolly, he's all by himself, too. Gimme your arm, honey, and help Patty up the steep stairs. She's all one ache, after workin' over this lowlifer. I cried real tears, Dolly. You oughta seen me weep. Whatcha say, Sleeper? Was it good? It *was* good. I clung a good deal, too, and developed a kidnapin' and a dead daddy, and all on the spur of the moment without any coaching from Big Grand.''

"Aw, shut up!" said Brick Sorrell again. "You got no idea the way you make me tired, Pat. Shut up. I'm gunna go to bed.''

"All right, honey," said the Lawloress. "I'll come and tuck you all in later on. Kiss Patty good night before you go to—''

"Yeah!" snarled Sorrell. "Keep off of me, will you? Rather have a cat clawin' at me, you poison-brained—''

"Why, Brick," came the gentle voice of Chipping, the gunman, "haven't you made enough of a speech all in one place?''

It seemed to the Sleeper, for a moment that the shortest of the three would fling the double load of buckshot in his gun into the body of Chipping, but after an instant of hesitation, Sorrell turned on his heel and strode off.

"He's tired, that's all," explained the soft voice of Dolly Chipping. "He didn't really mean what he said.''

Sorrell wheeled sharply. "Didn't I?" said he.

"No," said Chipping, more subdued than ever, "I hope you didn't, Sorrell.''

Again the yegg hesitated, but discretion proved stronger than the impulse to fight. He turned once more and was presently gone from sight.

"You oughtn't to do it, Dolly," said the girl, with a touch of real anxiety in her tone. "You oughtn't to rub him the wrong way so often. One of these days—"

"I wonder," drawled Dolly. "I'm beginning to be afraid not."

Through the spinal marrow of the Sleeper, a chill mounted numbly to his brain.

"His wife and child," said Dolly, "we'd provide for—"

"Quit it, will yuh?" demanded Pat Lawlor. "You're givin' the Sleeper the shakes. Ain't he, big boy?"

"Yes," said the Sleeper, "he is."

At this, Dolly Chipping turned his head sharply and looked straight at the face of the Sleeper. The man was a basilisk. With his quiet voice he thinly masked what even on this short acquaintance the Sleeper could recognize as a savage, continual desire for battle—not battle, perhaps, so much as the sheer desire for slaughter. He was glad of the shadow from the moon that covered his face, he felt fairly well.

But why need he fear?

He carried on his hip the charmed weight of the old single-action Colt which could not fail to conquer in any single battle. So he turned his head and looked steadily at Chipping, as they crossed the courtyard.

The soft, chill hand of the girl reached up and gently pushed against his cheek.

"Don't you look at Dolly that way, big boy," said she. "Dolly doesn't mean any harm. He's carnivorous, that's all. And when we've had him here for a while, livin' on vegetables, and tortillas, and such, you can't wonder that old Dolly gets a gnawing in the

222

middle of the stomach. Ain't that right, Dolly dear? I
tell you what, Dolly, I've heard some good news for
you. Over yonder in the mountain they've found a
nice new puma caved up in a nice new cave. Eleven
foot of him waitin' over there for Dolly to come and
shoot his eyes out. Don't that make you feel better,
Dolly? Couldn't you go to bed and have a nice, sweet
dream on that?

Dolly Chipping answered, in his mellow tone:

"Are you making a joke of me, Patty? It's quite all
right. I don't mind being the target. We all have to
serve when Patty wants to shoot. Your turn may
come one of these days, Sleeper!"

"Now you see how nice he is?" said the Lawloress, reaching out and patting the head of the gunman. "He can purr, and everything. It's only now
and then that he gets to ragin' around for raw meat.
Ain't it, Dolly dear?"

"Leave him be!" said tall Lefty Bullen in his
ominous rumble. "You done enough talkin' already
to last you a week."

"It won't, though," said the girl in her careless,
impertinent way. "He's our stage manager, big
boy," she confided. "He makes the thunder off
stage. Sometimes it's so real that you pretty near
have to jump, but then you remember that it's just old
silly Lefty, that never meant no *real* harm in his life!"

She went on with her banter, which for Lefty apparently was barbed.

"Old Lefty," she said, "he just works along in his
quiet little way pickin' up a band of sheep here and a
flock of goats there, and runnin' his iron on a stray
cow, here and there. Sometimes he floats over the
river and brings in some dope. That quiets people's

nerves, says Lefty. And then sometimes, he'll slant off and run in a bunch of chinks, which is what keeps down the price of laundry work all over the country. Lefty is a kind of philanthropist, and a public bene-factor, and he really ought to be up there in Con-gress, teaching them what's good for the country. Because Lefty, he knows. Don't you, you great big beautiful thing, you?"

"Oh, Jiminy!" sighed Lefty Bullen. "Wouldn't I like to wring your neck one of these days, Patty?"

"Maybe you will, too, Lefty," suggested she. "Such a nice soft neck, too, Lefty. Poor little throat," said she, laying a hand upon it, "filled with music all summer long, and kind words, and gentle-ness, Lefty will wring you dry, one of these days."

"Bah!" said Lefty Bullen, and his rage was so extreme that he strode away from them—they were going up the stairs, at that moment—two and three steps at a time, and immediately disappeared around a bend.

"Well," said Dolly Chipping, always gentle, "you've badgered two of them into running away. I suppose it will be my turn, next?"

"No," said she, "I wanted to get them away so that I could talk to the pair of you."

She halted under a lantern, and pulling on their arms, made them face one another.

"You got off on the wrong foot, boys," said she, speaking rapidly. "Listen, Dolly—don't try to eat this meat. It's poison. Listen, Sleeper—don't work up trouble with Dolly, because he's self-rising! D'you hear me both?"

The Sleeper had grown cold, to the core of his being, not with fear, but with deep, invincible dislike.

"You have me wrong, Patty. I'm willing to be friends, always," Dolly Chipping was saying, with a faint smile on his intellectual face; and his gray eyes dwelt steadily—steadily on the Sleeper.

"Chipping," said the tramp, "the other two were hired hands, one might say. But you're an artist with a gun. You get your living by murder, I can gather. And to-night you waited around a corner in the moonlight to sink a bullet in my skull. And—"

The small hand of the girl closed over his lips, but he brushed her strongly aside—with his left hand.

"I think you're a rat," said the Sleeper. "A snake is a kitchen pet, compared to you. This job you started on—there's plenty of moonlight for it still, outside. Will you come?"

The glance of the other did not falter. It seemed that his smile widened. Then suddenly it went out.

"This boy is, indeed, very young," he said easily. "I'll leave you to soothe him, Patty!"

And Dolly Chipping went, lazily, slowly, up the steps before them. And the Sleeper, staring after him, heard the words that he himself had just spoken ringing in his ears, as though they had come from the lips of another. He was amazed.

"You don't understand," he heard the girl whisper. "Neither do I! Every minute of your life here is going to be danger, from now on—but I never knew how many yards of man could be wrapped up in one package, before to-night!"

CHAPTER 32.

THE MAN IN CHARGE

THE LAST WORDS of the girl, that night, were to bid the Sleeper be strictly on his guard and before he went to bed, he braced a chair in front of the door, after locking it, and then placed across the window sills the only silent sentinels which he could think of—thumb tacks face upward, from a paper of them which he found on his writing table, though for what purpose put there he could not think.

Then he went to bed to trust to his ears and luck.

When he wakened, nothing had been disturbed. The tacks remained as they had been put in order on the sills, and the lock of the door had not been turned.

He was up in the pink of the dawn, with the wind blowing keenly through the windows. He called for another bath, was rubbed down by the strong hands of the wrestler, and forthwith went down to the court with the appetite of a lion and the step of a wild deer.

The deeper he advanced in this adventure, the more intrigued he was by the very dangers around him, and he smiled and waved to old Ricardo, who was gruffly giving orders to some servants in the patio. He dismissed them and stood near the chair of the Sleeper while the latter rubbed the morning chill out of his hands and looked cheerfully forth across the valley.

"You didn't expect to see me again this morning, when I left you last night, Ricardo?" said he.

"No," said Ricardo with the utmost frankness. "But a young heart and a steady nerve will do great things even in Guadalupe. You slept well, señor, as I can see in your face. May you have many more good nights with us!"

"My friend, Mr. Murderer Chipping," said the Sleeper, "is he up now?"

"No," said Ricardo. "He will not be up till noon. He sleeps badly. Some people say that he has dreams until daylight."

Breakfast arrived, and with it came Parmenter, slowly sauntering down with an early-morning cigarette between his fingers. He waved it at the Sleeper.

"Well done, Sleeper!" said he.

The latter eyed him with peculiar attention. This man had laid a murder trap for him, the night before. Yet somehow it was difficult to fly into a temper about it.

"I almost turned the corner," he said, "but you see that I changed my mind in time."

"Did you change your mind, Sleeper?" asked Parmenter curiously. "Or didn't you see through the sham from the beginning? Well, I haven't a right to ask that. But, of course, you see that no man is any good to us until he's been through the fire. After that, we can tell pretty well what sort of steel is in him."

"How many survive?" asked the Sleeper.

"Nearly all," said the other. "We don't let them in until we're nearly sure. But I admit that none of them have had the sort of a testing that you got."

"It was Chipping's idea, wasn't it?"

"What makes you accuse him?"

"Because he had something against me."

"Oñate. Chipping liked that blood-thirsty brute, I don't know why. However, it's over and done with. Chipping has pocketed his grudge, and you'll do the same if you stay with us. I'm away with Bullen and Sorrell. That leaves you in charge here, for the day. Chipping is likely to sleep most of the time, you see. He's been out on a long trip, and that's one reason his nerves were edgy last night. I've simply stopped to ask if you've come to a decision, as yet?"

"No," said the Sleeper. "Not yet. When you say that I'm in charge, what do you mean?"

"That it's as though I were here. You're my representative. Is that clear?"

"I'll try to make it clear."

"So long, then, Sleeper!"

"So long, Parmenter!"

The other walked off as calmly as he had come, with the same long-stepping, rather rolling gait which made the Sleeper think of a sailor on shore.

This touch of conversation made him thoughtful for some time. He finished his breakfast, and fell to dreaming on the mountains, which were changing rapidly as the light of the day grew stronger and stronger.

Every moment he told himself that he would go down to the valley for a walk, but there was something enchanting in the pure, keen air that kept him in his place. The faces of those mountains looked across at him like friends, and he wondered what others they had seen lounging here on the terrace. Mostly his thoughts changed slowly between Parmenter and "the Lawloress," as she permitted herself to be called. And now and then he found himself sitting stiffly erect, with a sudden remembrance of Chipping.

The casual way in which Parmenter confessed the murder plan was enough to have taken his breath; but he knew, suddenly and completely, that such schemes could not be new in Guadalupe. In the machine of Parmenter, men were simply cogs, to be fitted in or thrown away according to their peculiar quality. It might be that other tests lay before him, but he had an idea that murder would never again be the answer.

He had passed into the inner stronghold. He wondered what would happen to him next, and sat there on the terrace in a chilly state of expectation, and almost pleasant fear.

The sun grew warm. A flight of birds showered over the top of the big house and fell like fluttering dead leaves, in swirls and clutters, to the center of the valley, then steadied, and shot down it with a wonderful speed.

Then he heard a clamor break out in the inner court.

Three or four *mozos* came toward him, hustling along among them a tall young fellow with a crimsoned rag tied around his head and his clothes in tatters. A little apart from this group came another youth, with a battered mouth and a swollen eye. Ricardo marched before all.

When he had come near to the Sleeper, he halted the others with a gesture and stepped before his new master.

"Señor," said he, "this is Leon Giberto—this one with the big eye. The man with the broken head is his younger brother José! Leon asserts that José attacked him and nearly murdered him this morning. He has come to complain. I did not dare to waken Señor Chipping. You must give a judgment for us, Señor Sleeper! You, Leon, tell him in two words what is wrong."

These villagers stood as still as mice, while Leon made a half step forward, and got a good grip with both hands upon the hat which he carried.

He said, in a shaken voice: "When my father died, señor, he left his land to me—we live just outside the town. He left the house and the mules to José. In this way he thought that we would have to live peacefully together. But no! José will not drive the mules. He will not plow the ground. I must do all this. He lolls at home all day, or else goes out and shoots squirrels, and then he goes down to Guadalupe and drinks mescal, and comes home drunk and strikes me. Last night he was out all night. He came home as you see him, and rushed at me. I fled. My neighbors, as you see, saved me. They brought him here. He is the son of my father and my mother, señor, but to live with him is to live with a tiger!"

"You—the rest of you. What do you witness?" asked Ricardo.

"It is all true," said several voices.

"You, José?" asked Ricardo.

José was sullenly silent.

"Answer!" said Ricardo, letting his voice boom.

José flung up his head. His lip curled with contempt. He answered not a word.

And the mind of the Sleeper went back to his school days, where in the school yard he had seen one young savage surrounded by half a dozen enemies, bleeding, but dauntless before them all, surly, savage with the savagery of a beast.

"Set his arms free!" said the Sleeper.

There was a murmur.

"Obey, you fools!" exclaimed Ricardo.

José was freed. He blinked once or twice at the Sleeper; then folded his arms.

"You, José!" said the Sleeper, "answer me as man to man. Where were you last night?"

José did not speak. His whole soul blazed up with revolt and shone from his eyes.

"Are you ashamed?" asked the Sleeper.

"Shamed?" cried José. "No! I am not shamed. I went to the cantina of Pedro. I drank bad mescal. After a while, my money was gone, and I went out and stood in the street and asked if any of the people who were passing, wanted to fight for half a dollar, or twenty-five cents, or ten cents, at least. I offered them the first blow. Nobody would fight. Then I offered to fight any two of them for a dollar, for half a dollar, for ten cents. I offered to fight three at once, and let one of them stand behind me. I gave up my knife for security that I would do as I said. Three of them came. They were three brothers. You know them, señor, if they are men. They are as big as I. They live at the foot of the hill. Their name is Costa. We began to fight. The man behind struck me on the head so that I was dizzy. I ran forward and butted one of them in the stomach. He rolled in the street and gasped for air. This shock cleared my head and I turned on another, but the coward when he saw me come, picked up a large rock and threw it and hit me on the head, here.

"I took this scoundrel by the hair of the head and bashed his face against the stones, but while I was doing this, the third brother ran away as hard as he could.

"After that, I took the dollar I had won and went back and drank more mescal at Pedro's. Then it began to grow light with the dawn. Pedro locked the doors. I went home, and when I came inside it, I began to dance and to tell my brother, who is a dog, how I had fought. He would not listen. He has no heart. He wanted me to go out and harness the mules, but the mescal was growing cold in my head and it told me to go to sleep at once. My brother insisted. He swore that he would live no more with me if I did not work.

"Señor, it angered me. I told him that I would let him go live with the evil one, if he preferred, and that I would send him there at once. He ran away screaming like a girl. I followed him, and caught him once for a couple of blows, but then came the neighbors and poured over us like water over a mill wheel. That is why I am here, señor, and every word is true, or may my right hand wither!"

He ended, and holding his right hand out in front of him, he watched it with a defiant scowl, as though half expecting that it *might* change beneath his eyes.

CHAPTER 33.

TWO SENTENCES

AS JOSÉ ENDED, the others, his neighbors, looked meaningly to one another, then smiled expectantly back at the Sleeper.

"You do not like to work?" said he to the burly youth.

"No, señor. I hate death less than I hate work."

"What is it that you love to do the best?"

"To hunt deer, when I can buy food for my rifle."

"It is my rifle, señor," said the older brother.

José glanced aside at him, like a dog about to bite.

"Hunting deer through these mountains is work," said the Sleeper.

"It pleases me. That is all that I know," said the other.

"What else pleases you, José?"

"A good fight, señor, is much better than hunting deer."

"What sort of a fight do you prefer, José?"

"Clubs are very good," said José. "And a knife is a pleasant thing, too, because it makes a man twist up his face as though he had swallowed vinegar, when he feels the steel cutting into his flesh. But for me by far, the best is bare hands, señor."

He held out his hands and, with a grin, invited the Sleeper to regard them closely. They were big enough for two. And behind them were the wrists of a gorilla.

"Do you love your father's land, José?" asked the Sleeper.

"The sight of plowed ground makes my stomach turn like sour milk," said José.

"And your father's house?"

"It is no better than a horse shed. Why should I love it?"

"Is it true that you have beaten your brother?"

"Yes, and I shall beat him again, if I can. He is a coward, and all cowards deserve beatings."

"Is it true that you would not work?"

"Why should I work," said José, "so long as I could make him work for two?"

"Is there nothing on the farm or in the house that you love, José?"

He rubbed his head thoughtfully, and made a wry face as his hand touched the wound in his scalp.

"There is an old picture of my mother on the wall," said José. "It is faded, but it has a kind look. That is all that I love."

The Sleeper folded his arms.

"Tell me, Ricardo, am I free to give a judgment?"

"You're free to hang him from the outer wall, or throw him over the terrace, if you wish," said Ricardo.

"Do you hear me, José?"

"I hear you, señor."

"Do you think that you deserve punishment?"

"There are enough men here to punish me," said José calmly, "so I suppose I deserve it."

"What sort of punishment do you suggest?"

José screwed up his eyes in thought.

"Anything but the whip," said he.

"Are you afraid of the pain?"

"No, but if I lived, I would murder the men who tied and flogged me."

"Listen to me again."

"I hear you, señor."

"You are to be put in a cell every night; and every day you are to work hard."

José groaned. There was a murmur of applause from the citizens.

"As for the house and the land, you have forfeited all right to them, and they revert to your brother, who is an honest working man."

Here the applause grew quite noisy. The face of José was black as night. But though he ground his teeth, he said nothing.

"If," went on the Sleeper, "you touch another man, woman, or child while you are employed, you will be whipped in the plaza till your back is raw, and then you will be thrown from this terrace and turned into good pulverized fertilizer for the valley soil. Do you hear what I say?"

"I hear you, señor," said José bitterly.

"Your first day's work begins this moment," said the Sleeper. "Ricardo, get him a good rifle. José, you will take that rifle and go out into the mountains, and return before night with the meat of a deer. It must be a buck, and the horns to show for it. Be back by sunset, and if you come without venison, may your

favorite saints protect you! Now, off with you! Take
him, Ricardo!''

The Sleeper delivered this judgment with a scowl,
adding briefly at the end:

''If he brings back venison, let him have a good
bed, Ricardo. If he comes with empty hands, put him
on a naked rock floor. That is all. Be off!''

José had listened to the whole speech with his head
turned one way, and then the other, as though he
were hearkening against the wind. At last, joy began
to dawn in his eyes. It flared up. It reached his lips in
a tremendous grin. He was about to speak, but the
waved hand of the Sleeper silenced him. And he went
off beside Ricardo, stumbling, for his head was still
turned to enable him to stare at this singular judge.

The Sleeper himself had stood before judges who
delivered no such whimsical sentences as this. He
watched the departing backs of the entire group; he
saw them chattering; and realized that every one was
pleased—most of all the criminal who, for a minor
offense, had literally been stripped of his birthright
and condemned to march, hunting through the hot
mountains all day long.

The taste of power was in the soul of the Sleeper,
and he relished it more than wine. The day grew older
and warmer. He threw off his coat, and lolling in his
chair, he asked himself what more could man ask of
life than this rare valley, this enchanted town and
houses of Guadalupe offered to him? For here was
total leisure, and here was also adventure enough to
spice any man's days.

So the plains grew far away, and dim in his mind
was the face of old Morice. Somewhere in his heart

there was a memory of the old man's daughter, but he closed it out.

Patty Lawlor came in with Ricardo. She had been out riding, and she was swinging a quirt in very mannish style, slapping the lash against her boots. She waved a gloved hand at the Sleeper and came up to him with the old servitor beside her.

"Now, Ricardo," said she, "when you look at him he doesn't appear so wild, does he? Looks like a good, quiet boy, just taking his little nap in the sun, and too lazy to budge. But you should have seen him with Mr. Gun-eater Chipping. Has he had a good breakfast?"

"Yes, señorita."

"Keep him amused. Better let him have a little fight, now and then, for exercise, and see that he gets to bed early at night. We must take great care of him, Ricardo."

"Señorita," said the old man, "I have been a carpenter, and I know very well that one must be most careful of edged tools."

She waved Ricardo away and slumped into a chair.

"How is it, Sleeper?" she asked.

"Sleepy and comfortable," said he. "I've been playing judge."

"Yeah, I heard about that."

She lolled in her chair and stared at him with bold, gloomy, half-desperate eyes.

"It's a game with you, Sleeper. It was with me, when I first came up. But a girl ain't like a man."

"In what way, Patty?"

"Oh, a man's off by himself, anyway. Kids— wife—that kind of thing, it don't matter to him much.

Me—I'm a girl, and that's different. I've seen too much. I know too much!"

"About men, eh?"

"About myself, Sleeper. I know that I'm absolutely no good, and I can't help caring."

"Why don't you get away, then?"

"Yeah. I've gone away. Parmenter leaves me free. But you see how it is, up here. It's a grand life—for me. You can just sit, here, and have more things happen than in the middle of any city street. Yeah, I can't keep away. But I miss everything. Kids—home—husband—kids, mostly."

"You've never been married?"

"No. Maybe that's why it bothers me so much. A saddle looks mighty pretty, till you've had to carry it. But I go around prospecting the young men. Bullen, even Sorrell, and that snow-white demon Chipping—I've considered 'em all. You, too, I would've budged you if I could, big boy, last night when I was doing the crying. You're so new," she confessed casually, "and you seem kind of straight, compared to the rest of 'em. But you wouldn't be had. Who is she, big boy? I don't mean her name, but what's her color? Blue eyes, I'll lay my money, and the tender vine clings to the big manly oak, eh? Yeah, I bet that's it!"

Her eyes, looking past the Sleeper toward the mountains, grew so absent that he knew she did not expect an answer, and he remained silent, watching her. Her beauty and her gloom amazed him.

She rose suddenly.

"I'm going in," said she, but instead, she went to the Sleeper, and dropping a hand on his shoulder she said: "Be kind to me, big boy. Be friendly, and return good for evil, like they do in the Good Book. I'm so darned lonely I could bust, and the more quieter you keep the more dizzier I get about you. Just talk to me a little, Sleeper, and then maybe I'll see through you. Oh, it's nothing serious," she went on. "It's like the morning blues that wear off by noon, but it's hard to think of midday when you're yawning your head off at dawn. So long, for a while."

She got as far as the entrance to the patio, but pausing there in the shadow, one hand plucking at the tendril of a vine, she half turned, and looked back to him.

"Suppose you were judge on me, Sleeper? What about the sentence?"

"Home for life," said he.

She began to laugh softly, and he watched the flash of her eyes and her teeth with a curious detachment.

"Young and trusting is what the Sleeper really is!" said she. "Poor old boy!"

She went on, at that. He saw her pause again and half expected that she would turn once more, but she did not, resuming her way across the patio until she was out of sight.

The Sleeper fell into profound thought.

No doubt, a catalogue of her sins would make a long list, but he could not help feeling that there were infinite possibilities of good in her. He thought of his own grim past, and suddenly he began to wonder if he, also, might not grow into something better than he had been. Stronger he certainly was—better he might become. And then perhaps the taste of virtue would make a life of crime seem a dull thing indeed!

CHAPTER 34.

HANGING BY A THREAD

AT NOON JOSÉ killed his buck and had the venison at the big house three hours later. He stood before his judge, panting and grinning. He had walked and climbed and run enough to make ten days of labor, but he looked fit for an equal amount again. He had come for further orders.

"Is the rifle clean, José?" asked the Sleeper.

"As a wolf's tooth!" said José and his own white teeth flashed as he spoke.

"Then Ricardo will send you to a room. Go to sleep. Tomorrow you will have more work."

José fingered his hat, crushing it with his powerful grip.

"May I hope, señor, on some day to—"

"What?" asked the Sleeper sharply. "To leave prison?"

"No, but to spend all my life here!"

The Sleeper could not help smiling.

"We'll see," said he. "And, in the meantime, if you lift a hand against any human being—"

"If I do that, you may flay me alive, señor, and use my skin to cover saddles!"

He turned to leave, and at that instant the great Parmenter himself came into the court, whistling, and flicking a letter with one hand back and forth against his leg.

"Hello, José!" said he.

José stood at attention like a soldier before this overlord.

"I thought that you'd wind up on the end of a rope, José," said Parmenter frankly, "but Señor Sleeper has found something else for you to do. You can thank him, José. I promised you that the next trouble you made would be your last, but I'm willing to forget my threat to you. Remember Señor Sleeper. He has been a great friend to you, my lad."

"I shall pray for him every Sunday," said José.

"You scoundrel!" said Parmenter. "Do you know how to pray?"

José shook his head.

"I shall learn," said he.

Parmenter dismissed him and came on to the Sleeper.

"I thought that he had stuff in him that could be used," said the Sleeper, apologizing.

"Why not? Except that it doesn't occur to most people to use man-eating tigers for watchdogs. But I think you're right. That fellow may be worth more than gold and diamonds, before the end. The townspeople are calling Señor Sleeper a second Daniel. Leon Giberto is in a seventh heaven because he has everything that his grubby soul desires, beginning with assured peace, and poor José is ready to die for you! Altogether, it was a good stroke! I should have had you here before, Sleeper!" He added quickly: "You haven't made up your mind to stay, man?"

"Not yet," said the Sleeper.

"Well," said the other, "let it go for a little while. In the meantime, here's proof that the needle can be found in the haystack. Look here, Sleeper, at your letter of introduction!"

He held it out, and the tramp saw, with bewilderment and horror, that it was the handwriting of Evelyn Morice, the paper having been patched together with translucent tape.

The glance that saw the brief note read it to the end.

DEAR CHARLES: If you are ready to come, I am waiting. A good friend is carrying this note to you, and I hope you will see that he's safe.

EVELYN

The unforgotten beauty and calm of the girl came over the Sleeper again out of this note. He sat back. He was both frightened and confused, but he attempted to look merely thoughtful.

"Well," said Parmenter, "why didn't you give me the letter that you brought along?"

"Because," said the Sleeper slowly, feeling his way from word to word, "I took a good look at you and decided that it wouldn't be the right thing."

"I wasn't worthy of her?"

"Who would be?" asked the Sleeper.

"Tell me," said Parmenter, who had not changed color a particle, "if you're not a little fond of Evelyn Morice yourself?"

"Yes," said the Sleeper instantly. "I am."

"Perhaps that's why Patty couldn't make any headway with you, eh?"

"Perhaps," said the Sleeper.

Parmenter lighted a cigar and began to smoke it with care, his eyes wrinkling with a critical appreciation.

"You're an extraordinary fellow, Sleeper," said he. "You came up here into the hot middle of trouble in order to carry a note from the girl you care about to the man she's picked out. You came up intending to deliver the note, and then changed your mind. You tore the letter up before my eyes and gave it to the wind. I guessed that there was something in it. Steve at Alcalde never would have the brass to send me a letter of introduction in favor of any one. So when I went into the patio that day, I gave directions to comb the valley for the section of that letter. It was in my hands before the evening."

"That was why I was to eat lead?" suggested the tramp.

"Yes. I was going to have them slaughter you. I sent Patty to bait the trap. I composed the trap itself of three of the best men in the world. But you broke through in spite of everything, and here you sit at ease reading that letter which you tore up!"

"I sit here, but not at ease," said the Sleeper.

"Tell me, Sleeper, if your flesh is beginning to creep a little?"

"I'm not afraid of this moment, Parmenter. I'm afraid of to-morrow, though."

"I really think you're not afraid of the moment," agreed Parmenter thoughtfully.

He turned his pale, bright eyes upon the tramp.

"You act, man, as though you had me in the palm of your hand."

"I think I have," said the Sleeper.

"Suppose I were to snatch out a gun?"

"You mean that you might be quicker than I?"

"Yes."

"Well," said the Sleeper, "perhaps you might be, but I'd live long enough to bring you after me, I think. As a matter of fact, Parmenter, if you had twice the reputation that you've piled up, I tell you without vanity, that I'd meet you without any fear. You think that's a mystery. It *is* a mystery. It's a thing that I can't attempt to explain. It's a thing that I don't understand myself, and that you never could do anything but laugh at. I'll tell you that, a month ago, I might have run from the gun of any man. I won't tell you what happened, but you can see for yourself that there's been a change."

"I can see that," said Parmenter. "It's because of that that I want to keep you with us if I can. I'm going to overlook and forget the letter trouble. As a matter of fact, you did the manly thing. But let me tell you that it's not as easy for some of the others to accept you as it is for me. I understand that I can't expect to have you with us in a subordinate rôle. I'm willing to let you in on the higher level. But some of the others don't feel that way about it, rather naturally. They certainly, for one thing, don't appreciate your proposed place as housekeeper!"

He smiled as he said this, and then went on:

"Look here, Sleeper. You've had a chance, by this time, to see a good deal and guess at a good deal more. Why not take the chance and give me your hand now, and promise that you'll be one of us?"

The Sleeper stared at him, and hesitated.

"Otherwise, I can't answer for what may happen. Think it over for ten seconds, Sleeper!"

As he spoke, he extended his hand.

And the Sleeper turned pale with a desperate effort of mind. For here was his ideal turned into fact. Here was his endless leisure, good food, prompt service, the lift of a lord of the land. Shivering nights in box cars, or sleeping under bridges, hungry days of prowling, the prison, and the prison bars, were to be exchanged for this golden opportunity.

But it seemed to the Sleeper that at this juncture he could see little, old Morice with his wooden leg, as clearly as though the horse breeder were standing on the terrace at that moment. He remembered again what he had felt before—that the old man, in spite of years and poverty, was almost a match in strength of will for Parmenter himself.

Then he looked out of the depths of his thought back at Parmenter and shook his head.

"No," said he. "I can't do it, Parmenter. Not yet, at least."

Visibly the face of Parmenter darkened.

He stood up, saying: "I'm sorry for this. I hope that you won't be sorry too, before the end."

He walked away, and the Sleeper saw no more of him that day. The others did not show their faces, either, and even Patty Lawlor failed to appear.

So he spent his time idling, and dined on the terrace with old Ricardo near by, straight as a ramrod, stiffened rather than weakened by his eighty years or more.

For a time, the Sleeper remained there, smoking, and watching the eastern stars grow in the horizon mist like moonflowers, opening as they mounted to the clear sky above.

Then he went to bed.

He took the same rather childish precautions that he had adopted the night before, and wakened, at last, with the moon in his windows, and a light tapping sounding irregularly. He sat up at once, wide awake, startled he knew not why, and looking across at the door, he saw that the chair was no longer in place before it!

That got him out of bed with a start.

He hurried to the door, but the tapping did not come from that. And now he heard it at the first casement, and saw, the next instant, something small and white dangling against the moonshine.

He went closer, his heart commencing to beat wildly.

It was a small square of paper, suspended from a slender thread and weighted so that it had tapped with a light noise against the stone of the sill.

The moment that he took hold of the thing, the thread was released from above and fell in a sinewy line, like the ghost of a snake.

He gathered it in hastily, then opened the folded paper, which turned out to be a writing sheet, and on it the first words he read were:

DEAR SLEEPER: They've voted you dead—

CHAPTER 35.

A CHANCE AT FREEDOM

HE RECOVERED A LITTLE from the first shock of this, and then went carefully through the letter once more. It read:

DEAR SLEEPER: They've voted you dead.

They were all there, and Chipping and Sorrell were particularly hard on you. They swore that you never would fit in because you're too close to an honest man. Chipping, of course, hates you.

I was surprised to hear the chief hold out for you. He talked in grand style. You would have been proud of yourself to hear how he fought for you for a long time. He suggested that they take a longer time, and think the thing over. He suggested that Sorrell go and pull your teeth, and then they could afford to take their leisure at it. So Sorrell went to your room and stole the old revolver—

Here the blood of the Sleeper froze.

Dizzy, half blind with fear, he went back to the bed, and fumbling beneath the pillow, he found that the revolver was indeed gone!

The gun of Trot Enderby, the mysterious old single-action weapon which could not miss, as he twice had proved it!

He sat down on the edge of the bed, breathless, weak, with uncertain words forming on his lips. So the magic wand had disappeared at the very moment when he needed it most, and when even its powers might have been overtaxed.

Then it seemed to him, suddenly, that a curse had come to him with the old Colt. It had led him into a wild series of adventures. It had accumulated a hundred enmities focused upon his head, and now at last he was to be overwhelmed beneath the pile of disaster which he had rashly heaped up.

Looked at in this manner, he could see that his journey to Guadalupe, like a voyage to fairyland, was one from which he never could hope to return. He moistened his dry lips, and straining his eyes, he made out the rest of the letter.

So Sorrell went to your room and stole the old revolver, and when he came back, we all stared at it, and Sorrell shook his head over it. He said that nobody but a fool would keep such a crazy old weapon, and Chipping bit his lips, and smiled his pale, deadly smile, and declared that he wished he had known that this was the kind of gun you carried. I think he meant that he would have fought the other night, if he had guessed it.

Sorrell said it would have been better if he had

blown off the top of your head, while he was there. Chipping said that that privilege was due to him. If he had endured your tongue, you should have to taste his bullets. The rest seemed to think that this brutality was exactly in order.

They were hotter than ever against you. I think Parmenter was afraid that he'd lose authority and reputation if he defended you any longer, for suddenly he said: "Do as you please. You boys decide. That man is valuable, but perhaps not valuable for Guadalupe."

The moment that restraint was gone, they jumped at your name like wolves.

I got up and started to speak for you, believe it or not, but old Ricardo pulled me back into my chair.

(A strange thing, thought the Sleeper, that Ricardo, the majordomo, should be a member of the chief cabinet of the thieves as well!)

Ricardo leaned over me and said at my ear, "No man is dead until his time comes."

That comforted me a good deal. I don't know why. It still comforts me. I had to do something, however. I couldn't sit quiet and let you be shot down! So I'm writing this note of warning to you. They still were talking after I left. They've put a pair of men on guard at your door. They still were undecided as to whether they should finish you off to-night or in the morning. Five minutes after you've read this, I'm going to swing down a revolver, loaded, through your window. You'll find it a better gun, by a lot, than the old one they stole from you.

Then you must try to get away.

I don't know how. It's one chance in a hundred, I suppose. But if you stay here, you're a dead man, I tell you. No hope will be left for you, if the dawn sees you inside of Guadalupe.

The climbing vines are big and strong outside your window. Could you lower yourself down them? I don't see what else you can do. I can't get you a rope. They know that I'm your friend, and I'm locked into my room and can't get out.

Heaven help you, poor Sleeper!

Whether you live or die, I'll know that I've met one real man and white man in my life.

Yours to the wind-up, Patty Lawlor.

The Sleeper looked up.

On the very sill of his window glistened the promised weapon, and he went hastily to it, and took it in his hand. Again the thread supporting it was dropped.

He loosed the thread and examined the gun. It was a six-shot, double-action Smith & Wesson, a make he knew and liked, and yet he could have laughed bitterly, as he remembered what the girl had written: "A better gun, by a lot, than the old one they stole from you!"

A loud tap came at his door.

He turned toward it with his eyes bulging, and his lips strained back over his teeth, like a cornered rat.

Then he retreated to the bed, with a new idea. The knock was repeated.

"Hello!" said the Sleeper, yawning loudly.

"Hello!" came the voice of Bullen, heavy and deep. "The chief wants to see you, Sleeper."

"Dang the chief," said the Sleeper. "Tell him that sleep wants me more than he wants the Sleeper. Run along, you!"

Bullen shook the doorknob impatiently.

"You'd better come along. It's important," he said.

"Let me alone," said the Sleeper. "I've had enough of this business. I want sleep, and I'm going to have it. I'll see Parmenter in the morning."

"You'll have sleep, too, I guess," said Bullen.

Footfalls retreated.

Apparently, they had decided that it was as well to wait. The day might do as well as the night.

And as they departed, the Sleeper could hear the rumble of subdued chuckling in the hallway. They were very sure. And their hushed laughter enabled him to see them with a clear, strong light.

Actually, he had dreamed of wishing to join these murderers! And then he remembered Parmenter's offer of that day. If he had accepted, no voting of the band could put him down afterward! Instead, he had to run for his life, and hope that this stone-built fairyland would vanish like a dream behind him.

He went to the window which the greatest masses of the vine approached, but when he parted the leaves and looked at the trunk, it seemed perilously thin, and weakly twisted.

He looked down.

Even if that hard-paved court had been water, the fall would have been a perilous thing.

When he had taken note of the facts, he prepared to descend in spite of danger.

There was no other thing for him to do.

He clambered out on the window sill, and scanning

the courtyard first, he made sure that nothing was visible there except the silver-white of the moonshine on the stones, and the incredible black of the shadow which met the light in a sharp line.

Then he looked up, and straight above him, he saw the Lawloress leaning from her casement. She kissed her hand to him and instantly disappeared, while down through the air dropped a bit of white, like a scrap of smoke. He caught it from the air, a lacy little handkerchief, daintily scented with perfume, and the Sleeper, with an odd tremor of the heart, put it away in a pocket.

What would happen to the girl? Would she not be accused of having supplied him with a revolver when they shot him down and took the weapon from his body, together with that tell-tale handkerchief?

And yet he would not throw it from him, for he had an odd feeling that the girl had confided to him the best of a lost soul, and that he must keep it with him all his days.

Gingerly, he lowered himself over the sill, and trusted his weight to the vine.

He had dressed hastily but purposely left off his boots, both for climbing and for silence in running over the stones. Now these stockinged feet helped him enormously as he reached for several supports, so as to distribute his burden more carefully and widely.

He moved with the utmost caution. Not only a fall, but noise he must eschew. Yet he had not descended his own length when a whole arm of the vine ripped free from the stone of the wall and he lurched down ten or twelve feet, with a breath-taking impact at the end of the fall.

There was a huge rattling of leaves. Yet the rest of the big vine kept its hold on the wall and supported him, swinging like a hanged body at the end of a rope.

He looked dizzily about him. No one as yet had run into the court or looked out of a window, so far as he could tell, to examine into the cause of the noise, and the Sleeper climbed down hastily from fork to fork, always with a greater ease and security as the trunk grew in dimensions.

He was not ten feet from the bottom when a *mozo* came into the court carrying a bucket, and humming to himself. He had half crossed the court when his eyes fell straight upon those of the Sleeper.

"*Por Diós!*" gasped the frightened servant, and fled.

He did not drop the bucket. In his flight, he instinctively clung to it, and the Sleeper, the next moment, had dropped to the hard stones and was running for his life.

He never had doubted the way he must take. The figure of old Morice dominated him still out of the great distance. He must try to get to Ironwood and seize the stallion for his escape. No other horse could carry him well or fast enough for a possible chance at freedom. So he ran down the slanting way into the bowels of the old house.

CHAPTER 36.

IN THE SADDLE AT LAST

HE CAME WITH ALL his might down the way to the stables, and approaching them more closely, he slackened his pace, and listened eagerly to hear the least sound behind him to signify that an alarm had been given and that the big house was waking. But no sound reached his ears.

He did not take that as a token that he was by any means safe. Rather, he could envision craftily sneaking men who would be jumping into their clothes, and seizing weapons to pursue him. They would come upon him without sound, those panthers.

And he, to meet them, had only this new and untried weapon—so much better than the old Colt!

He could have groaned aloud at the thought.

As he came to the stable inclosure, a donkey began to bray, and the sound stopped him short and made him lean against the wall, a very miserably frozen and shaking figure of a man. For it seemed to him that that uproar was like a bright light cast upon him in his flight. They must see him by it. All of Guadalupe must know and waken, reaching for rifles, clubs, and knives, according to the individual talent of the fighters. But all could fight. They would not have been living in Guadalupe, otherwise.

Crouched there by the entrance to the inclosure, he saw a stable *mozo* with a saddle over his arm pass out of a stable door and go into the moonlight. He, like that fellow who had been frightened in the court above, was singing softly to himself.

He was a big man, with the bulbous lips of a Negro, and the bulging eyes of a Boston terrier. The Sleeper watched him cross the clearing—with how leisurely a pace—every heartbeat of the Sleeper was bringing him closer to death.

Yet he could afford to notice, in that interim, the flitter of the water as it ran into the trough, and he heard the whispering of the water spray as it gushed out from the conduit beyond the wall.

The moonlight which he so often had enjoyed in his life was now more dangerous to him than a brigade of hostile eyes.

It was after the saddle-bearing *mozo* had passed out of sight through a swinging door that the Sleeper heard the first noise of the alarm behind him; and this was no stealthy whisper, but a loud braying of men's voices, and of women yelling, though in the distance.

One would have said that these were people wakened by an alarm of fire, but the Sleeper knew, somehow, that the only cause for their noise was his own movements.

The instant the big Mexican *mozo* had disappeared, the Sleeper started forward again, and ran straight to the little separate stable where the gray stallion was kept. He got to the door and was about to rush through it when he heard voices inside.

"Give me three," said the voice of Bullen.

And the voice of Chipping answered: "I suppose you have aces again?"

Two of them ensconced within, and such a two! He saw them in the merciless sunshine of his memory, every feature and every line of body.

Bullen and Chipping! He would rather have had two basilisks in his way. And then he stopped, cold with wonder. For with the household rising behind him, as he could guess, and with these two expert fighters inside the little stable, he knew that he would not turn back. He had come for Ironwood as for his fate, and nothing could turn him back. With any other horse beneath him, Ironwood himself would be used to run him down.

He did not pause longer to question. He drew his revolver, and pushing the door swiftly in, he stepped like lightning into the lantern-lit gloom of the little barn.

There he stood by the door, holding his breath. He himself saw the flame leap in the lantern as he pushed the door shut behind him, and by the same light he saw the two poker players lift their ears.

"What's that?" sharply demanded Chipping.

The Sleeper dropped to his knees behind the feed box. He had sight of Ironwood, saddled and bridled. He had sight of the roan gelding which the girl had pretended to choose as a mount, now with raised head, and gleaming, big eyes, looking straight at him.

"Nothing," said Bullen. "Gimme them three!"

"Something came in, then!" exclaimed Chipping.

"Sure. The wind."

Would the wind close the door behind it?"

"Aw, of course it would. Don't the wind do as it dang pleases up here in the mountains? G'wan with the game, Chipping. You've lost your nerve since that outsider came up here."

"He'll be an insider, before noon to-morrow," said Chipping, slowly settling back to the cards again.

"I didn't make him out," said Bullen. "He looked like nothin' much to me, outside of his shoulders. I don't figger Oñate droppin' to that boy's gun play."

"Well, but he did."

"He did. But it don't seem nacheral to me. I'll bet five."

"Here's your five. And twenty more."

"You caught, did you?"

"It looks that way, my son. Doesn't it?"

"You're a grand bluffer, Chipping, but thank fortune, a pack of cards isn't a Colt. I'm going to take that money away from you, Chipping."

"How do you go about it?"

"Well, by shoving in twenty, and just hoisting you a little raise of fifty bucks, my boy."

"A great, big, bold, bad gambler," sneered Chipping. "That fifty is in, for you, and another fifty to try your nerve."

Bullen chuckled. "You and me down here," he said, his mind apparently flying away from the poker game, "to watch for a hoss, partner!"

"Well, Ironwood is worth watching."

"But how's he think—the chief, I mean—that that fellow Sleeper can get out of his room to steal a hoss? Fly, maybe?"

"I don't know," said Bullen. "If he comes, we're here for him, I suppose. Parmenter's getting old, I tell you! Here's your fifty, and another ten to tickle you along.''

The Sleeper rose and stepped lightly into the stall of Ironwood.

At last his hand touched the shoulder of the stallion, and Ironwood sniffed mildly at him, and did not plunge back.

Saddled and bridled for pursuit, but what if this were Fate taking a hand for the tramp to make this horse the means of his escape? The Sleeper found himself trembling with excitement.

Then, from the mass of the house beyond, he heard distinctly a clattering of voices.

''You're weakening, I see,'' said Bullen. ''Only ten up. A bluff, and you're weakening, Chipping!''

''All right, then have a look.''

''I'll see you higher. I'll see you where you're dizzy, on this lay out. Another fifty up to talk to me, beautiful.''

''What's that?'' demanded Chipping.

He started to his feet, and the Sleeper, with leveled gun across the back of the stallion, picked out the man, and drew an easy bead on the heart of the gun fighter. It meant merely the pulling of the trigger. Magic was not needed at such a range as this—and then a quick change of aim and a bullet for Bullen.

That would clear the first stage of his flight.

''What's what?'' asked Bullen, looking up with a scowl, while the lantern flickered up and down his face.

''They're waking up the house. Something has happened.''

''Somebody's had a dream. That's all. Don't try to back out of this hand, Chipping.''

"You talk like a simpleton. That Sleeper—"

"He must be a wonder, the way that you talk about him!"

"He's a wonder that I'm going to scalp," said Chipping. "You can take that for granted, old son. But—listen!"

Loudly, the noise came brawling down upon them, like the croaking of sea birds on a storm wind. And now Bullen rose in turn.

They were such easy targets!

If he were half blind and a child, the Sleeper knew that he could not miss such marks as these, and yet he found that his finger was not able to pull the trigger. "Murder!" he kept saying to himself and no matter how often they had deserved no better end than this, murder he could not do.

He changed his aim.

There was the lantern hanging on the wall, throwing up an uncertain, yellow flame.

What would happen if that light went out unexpectedly?

He changed his aim, and pulled the trigger, hearing at the report the crash of the glass.

Darkness followed, except where the moonshine, on one side, leaked like water through a small port. And through the darkness, he heard the two guards cursing and groaning with fear and with rage.

"He's in here!" he heard Bullen roar. "You were right, Chipping. The door, the door! Get to the door for Heaven's sake!"

But the Sleeper was already there, pulling the gray stallion behind him.

He heard some one coming with a rush. He could see nothing, but he heard a grunt, and the stallion shook his head, but without kicking. That impact had been against the hips of Ironwood, and one of the pair was down for the moment.

Then the Sleeper got to the door. That was the most perilous moment. For when he passed through it, the silhouette of himself and the horse was bound to show up clearly against the moonlight night outside.

Yet he flung the door wide, and striking Ironwood sharply in the ribs with his fist, the leap of the stallion forward jerked them both through and into the open moonlight beyond, more blinding bright than the sun ever had shone, it seemed to the tramp.

A gun barked twice behind him, its thunder closed off for the moment by the shutting of the door. And then the Sleeper, naked gun in hand, was in the saddle.

He saw, at the same moment, a rout of half a dozen people pouring out of the house entrance on the other side of the stableyard, and he fired straight in among them. He heard a piercing scream, not from one, but from two voices, and knew that the slug must have passed through two bodies.

Behind him, he heard the creaking of the opened stable door, but he did not wait to fire again at what might issue. He made straight for the low valley wall.

CHAPTER 37.

"CLEAR THE WAY!"

AS HE CAME TOWARD IT, the gray stallion, checking, thrust out his long neck and sniffed at the risk. There was a seven- or eight-foot drop on the farther side to a narrow path. Even for a man to jump into such a landing place would have been hard, let alone the bulk of horse and rider. But when the Sleeper asked him, with a pinch of the knees, Ironwood rose and softly floated over the wall, and dropped feather-like upon the path beneath.

Such an exultation came to the Sleeper as he never had known before. The possession of the mysterious gun of Trot Enderby had not been so great a thrill, nor the crushing of Oñate in Pedro's *cantina*, for here was power to lift a mountain, and the docility and grace of a cat.

Once on the path, Ironwood struck out at a reaching trot which he modified for the turns and twists going down, and every instant made the pair safer.

Certainly, there had been time for those keen marksmen above to reach the wall and open fire long

before, but though the noise of voices washed to and
fro across the courtyard like water on a deck, no one
as yet seemed to have discovered the course the
fugitive had taken. Then it occurred to the Sleeper
that the two gunmen had been driven back into the
stable, and that the crowd in the passageway had
recoiled from his single shot. Still, he could hear the
low tingling voice of one of the wounded!

Perhaps his exit had not been marked, and was not
believed, so steep was the descent of the mountainside, with the wall to shut off observance at the
beginning.

But now, as he reached a long slanting path, spotted with moonlight and shadow, he heard a loud
wailing yell above him, followed by a rifle shot that
sent a wasplike buzzing past his ear.

Other shots followed, pouring over the edge of the
wall. Firing from rests, they aimed at him, but the
light was against them, patched as it was. And nothing is more difficult than to shoot accurately down
hill.

He dropped under a high shoulder. The rifle fire
ceased, and looking back, he saw the sheer rock
lifting black behind him.

It seemed as though he were already safe, and a
great burst of thanksgiving welled up in his soul, but
when he looked down the narrow length of the valley, he could guess that his troubles might be hardly
more than beginning.

So he wound down to the foot of the valley, and
from this point he could look back at the house of
Parmenter on the rock above. It looked an incredible
height. Lights flashed like angry eyes, darting past

windows and he could guess that the whole hive was astir, now.

Other lights appeared on the very roof of the house, twinkling in groups, which changed, and he guessed that a message of some sort was being sent off. So he stared down the valley. Yes, there was answering flashes from either end. He was in a box, with both ends of it sealed!

Gritting his teeth, he determined that he would slip up as close as possible and then strive to bolt through, using the great speed of the stallion, but as anger ceased to blur his eyes, he realized that this was impossible. What other way, then?

He looked across the valley to the mountainside beyond, and there, too, he saw lights moving. It was as though this trap had been specially prepared beforehand by the all-wise foresight of Parmenter.

At that, he reined in the stallion.

Something must be done, and at once, but what could he do?

A horse laboring up a slope, slowly of necessity, made a target that no child could miss—and the least of these people was a hunter.

Then he looked back to the big house, and the village lights that spilled out from it, lower down and to either side. There were little winding paths that led up into the town on either hand. They were watched, perhaps. But then, again, might not the fighting men take it for granted that no one would be fool enough to double straight back into the heart of his enemies?

The Sleeper, though his heart turned cold, decided to start at once. He did not pick up the nearer path, but deliberately rode on past the house and took the way on the farther side, up which he had seen the laborers toiling from the fields at the end of the day.

How infinitely long ago he had seen and enjoyed that picture!

He dismounted and walked. It steadied his nerves. It gave him a chance to rub the nose of Ironwood and speak gently to the stallion who was continually raising and shaking his head, not as in fear, but as in disapproval of those wild cries which rang from the height and passed wailing down the wind.

A chill wind it was that blew upon the Sleeper. He sighed as it bit deep and made his body tremble. That did not augur straight shooting, when the time for shooting should come.

The higher he mounted on the path, the more he could see of the valley, and the more certain he was, by studying the moving lights, that escape would have been impracticable in any direction other than this, though perhaps this was the most impossible of all.

Yet he went on steadily, in a calm desperation.

Once he thought he saw heads bob into sight over the edge of the wall and disappear again—at the very place where he had leaped from the stable yard. Well, whatever lay in wait, that he must meet. He reloaded the two empty chambers of the revolver as he went. It was no magic gun, to be sure, but twice it had driven bullets to the mark; it was far better than empty hands.

He finished the winding part of the ascent. Before him extended a straight, moderately sloping way, up which he led the gray through moonshine and shadow. The small shrubs that grew out of the rock above him, he could envy them their life of heat, and cold, and quiet. They had nothing to fear from guns in expert hands!

He passed the last turn of the path and saw before him the narrow gate of the town—literally bristling with rifles!

Yet, having started in this direction, he dared not turn back. It was ended, and death lay only a few steps or a few seconds away from him, but he went on. A clock will keep ticking while the ship sinks, and the legs of the Sleeper kept steadily along the path.

He came close. Two or three rifles were raised and covered him.

"Who goes?" called a loud Mexican voice.

He went straight on.

"Answer or I shoot! Who goes?"

He made two or three more paces, not rapidly, but neither did he lag. It seemed to him that he was walking on the verge of eternity. The hollow depths of the valley were for him the abyss of all future time.

"Shoot what, you fools?" he demanded crisply.

"You—who are you?"

"Shut up, donkey!" said a woman. "That is Señor Perry. I know him perfectly well!"

"Clear a way, then."

The Sleeper could breathe again!

He saw the little crowd press back on either hand.

"Pardon, señor," said the loudest of the challenging voices. "I thought, in fact, that you might—"

"You thought what? Clear the way! You worthless scum!"

The Sleeper strode in among them.

"It is not Señor Perry," said one hastily. "It must be Señor Chipping."

"No, no, he is down the valley, I think."

"Look, do you see? It is the horse of the great señor!"

"Is it? No, it lacks half a head of his height!"

"It is not, it is much taller."

The Sleeper walked past the last man.

Yes, down the street he went, with the voices merging behind him, walking slowly. He made himself whistle, but before the first note had left his lips, just as he came to a corner of the little, narrow street, he heard a boy's voice screaming:

"Help! Shoot him down! Help, help! It is the new gringo whom they hunt! Ten thousand pesos—you have heard? And there he walks away! I, I have seen his face! I swear—"

The corner came behind the shuddering back of the Sleeper. He looked back, saw the honest wall instead of the threatening gleam of steel, and flung himself into the saddle.

In answer to the boy's scream of alarm—was it not strange that the youngster had not been able to be sure until his back was turned and he was walking away—there broke out a roar from that little crowd like the roar of a surf. Swift were the orders of Parmenter, if he had been able to spread both the alarm and the promise of the reward so quickly after the alarm!

The Sleeper was in the saddle, however, and the gray stallion leaped forward with such a bound that the rider nearly lost his saddle. He had ridden good horses before, but this creature went with the leap of a kangaroo, it seemed.

Behind him, a volley of shouts went up, roaring like echoes down a canyon, and a well-aimed bullet touched his shoulder with a little jerk. Then he was around the next corner.

But the noise of the shod hoofs upon the pavement of the town seemed enough to rouse the whole people and tell them where the fugitive rode. It was like a maddening alarm drum. It was speaking words, and pointing with an accusing hand.

The Sleeper groaned and shook his head. There was nothing else for him to do but to keep ahead!

A man rushed out in white night clothes. He darted from a doorway with a rifle in his hand and presented it. The Sleeper struck him down with the barrel of his revolver and went on.

It seemed to him that he had felt the skull spring and give beneath the weight of the blow. A dead man, perhaps, but what was that to the Sleeper?

He had gained another free hundred yards, and the stallion was now floundering and skidding on the terrific downward pitch of the street. The iron shoes screeched upon the paving stones. Again and again he staggered and almost fell on the irregular steps which had been set in to master the pitch of the ground.

The Sleeper deliberately reduced his gait to a trot and then to a walk!

Yes, with the moon shining full upon him, and with the roar of the crowd speeding behind him like a wave, still he persisted in going slowly on. A horse with an injured foot or a spoiled leg would be of no use to him in such an emergency as this.

Then a door at his side yawned.

It was the door of Pedro's *cantina*, and a woman's voice was screeching:

"It is he! It is he! Ten thousand pesos! Pedro, shoot—Vicente, shoot!"

And the Sleeper saw the steady gleam of two rifles!

CHAPTER 38.

WITH BROKEN REINS

THEY WERE TOO CLOSE to be avoided. He put the stallion into a trot, and poised the revolver, but now he could see nothing except the spitting flame from the lips of two rifles.

He could hear Pedro yelling, "Shoot the gringo dog!" And Vicente, grunting and puffing like a fat pig, and shouting: "For ten thousand pesos! We share, Pedro! Ten thousand pesos! We are rich! We are famous in Guadalupe!"

The Sleeper had time to wonder at this thing. Here where he had first paused in Guadalupe, he would make his last halt of all, in this life! Every instant he expected the thud of a heavy slug striking his body, like the blow of a fist. But the instant did not come.

How could they miss?

Moonlight, to be sure, but men do not miss at five yards, point-blank, shooting from a rest!

Yet miss they did! Deer fever, perhaps—the greatness of the reward had unsteadied their hands!

No, he knew suddenly, as he turned the next

corner and gained a new hope of life, what the thing was that saved him. It was the gratitude and the respect which they felt for him! They had to fire, with the woman there to urge them on. She in an ecstasy of hope, wringing her hands in the bliss of ten thousand pesos—like ten thousand heavens to her poverty-stricken life. He thought of the dingy *cantina*, and its wretched poverty. He could guess what such a reward would mean to poor Pedro, also. But still the little man would not shoot to kill. He and Vicente sent their bullets in clusters, hissing through the air, but always safely wide of the mark.

Heavens bless them, then! There was virtue even in *cantinas* which money could not smutch!

The corner was behind him.

What of the next gate, then?

He kept the stallion at a trot, the blows of the iron-shod hoofs ringing loudly on the pavement still, and the shouting of the crowd growing louder and hoarser behind him, but above all he could hear the dreadful screeching of Pedro's wife, as she saw that paradise of money fading from her hope!

The gate appeared. Behold, there was not a soul in it. It stood open. He passed under the low, narrow arch with a strangely vivid feeling that he was passing out from a tomb. Before him lay his first honest hope of safety.

There was no longer pavement. He had earth which the stallion's feet could grip more securely and silently. Behind him, he heard other horses coming crashing and slithering over the cobbles, then a dull sound which he would have sworn was the fall of horse and man, and a helpless, howling cry of agony.

Aye, they would remember the Sleeper in

Guadalupe long after he was far from it! He had done harm enough among them!

But he was far down the slope of the hill, and the heavenly gloom of the woods stretched just beneath him when the rout of the pursuit burst in single file from the little gate.

They came rushing out on the brow of the hill. He was dipping into the shadows of the woods when he heard behind him the outcry of so many demons—so many red Indians on the warpath.

But now he had good going. The stallion's strength had been saved and husbanded well. He was fresh for a run, and he was eager to be off. It seemed as though he well knew the meaning of those bullets that went crackling through the trees, like the sound of a fire in very dry wood. But still the Sleeper restrained him, and the words of an old song continually rang in his mind:

He who gallops too early will walk very late!

He kept the stallion to a steady trot, and so they wound along up the bottom of the valley, making excellent time, but with the rush of the mounted men first streaming loudly down the hillside, and then settling onto the trail behind him.

Let them rush if they pleased. He knew this way. He knew there was shelter, and too many windings to give long-distance shots. If they winded their horses in the first rush, so much the better for him in the end.

Steadily the good gray mounted that slope. And how the hunters yelled behind! Those loud whoops echoed shrill or deep from the faces of the mountains on either side.

The Sleeper came to the top of the first long grade. There was level going before him. The trees were merely scattering, and therefore, he he let out Ironwood in a strong, steady gallop. He had to sit tight, gripping hard with his knees and keeping a strong, steady pull on the reins, for Ironwood was now fighting for his head, and out of the thicker woods behind came the front of the pursuit, running their horses at full speed.

They screeched all in one breath when they saw the fugitive. They yelled to encourage one another, but when the Sleeper looked back again, he saw that the distance between him and the forefront of the Guadalupe riders steadily was increasing. Ironwood at half speed was dropping them steadily behind him.

What a horse—what a machine!

They opened fire—sure sign they recognized that they were beaten! But the bullets had no chance, except a pure hit of accidental luck. And every moment the noise descended behind the Sleeper.

Again the way grew steep, and again he resolutely pulled the stallion back to a jog trot.

It lost them ground. It brought the howling mob on their heels again, but it saved the priceless breath of the good horse, and when they came to the broken but open country of the upper Tinnio Pass, the men of Guadalupe could not live for a moment with the pace which the stallion set.

With that flawless, long-reaching stride, he made the rocks and trees waltz past him. Up the slight grades, and down the short ones he flew. And the noise of the other riders grew muffled, grew thin behind. It came at last only in meager bursts. Then it was heard no more at all, and there was only the open night, the whispering of the cautious wind in the trees, and the naked, moon-washed face of the sky above them.

The Sleeper pulled back the stallion to a walk.

He was eager to get through the pass. By this time, no doubt, the fire signals from Guadalupe had been passed far down the valley and if there were watchers this far from the stronghold, they probably had read the news.

Yet when he came to a small stream working across the trail, he dismounted, gave the stallion two swallows, and dashed the icy water over his legs, for he was naturally hot from that uphill work.

"I had one chance in ten thousand when I sat in my room," said the Sleeper to the stallion, patting his neck as he mounted again. "I had one chance in five thousand when I reached the courtyard, and one in a thousand when I reached the stable. I had one chance in a hundred when I leaped the wall with you and got into the valley, and not much more when I turned back to Guadalupe. One in fifty when I got through the village gate, and one in ten when I went by the *cantina*. But now I've shaken off the body of 'em. They have two chances to my one, still, but with you in the scales, we'll win through. Old Morice shall have you, and Evelyn will rub your nose and feed you sugar. And Parmenter?"

He thought back to the sky-blue, unnaturally bright eyes of the bandit. All the rest of Guadalupe had grown dim and cloudy and unreal to him. But Parmenter remained a growing fact in his mind, a danger that seemed to slide through the air above him and keep pace like the soundless wings of an owl. And there was the white face of Chipping, too, which was worth remembering!

He kept the stallion now at a good, steady trot. At that gait it was easy to keep watch before, behind, and to either side. He could study the trail, as well, but after these years in the mountains, the stallion seemed to have eyes in his hoofs.

He passed straight up the trail as he first had crossed it. He came by the place of Hazy Pete, and there was a sudden shout from that unlucky man:

"Hello! Hello! Stranger, have you seen any wagons comin' up the— Aw, you're comin' the wrong way! Hey—hello—"

The Sleeper, with a pang, went on.

There was nothing that he could do for that unfortunate. No man in the world had a hand strong enough to help him.

The trail now began to descend, though easily, winding from side to side, and again he made a halt to tighten the cinches a little and then went on at a walk or a jog. He would not risk the shoulders of the great horse by trying a too rapid descent.

And so he came out of the pass, and saw the dark mountains reclosing behind him like soldiers in rank that have opened and come together again at a word of command.

The steepness ended. The pass was well behind. Before him lay the opening, rolling hills which rapidly would smooth out in the level of the desert, and the Sleeper, with the taste of victory in his very soul, threw back his head and drew in a great breath of relief.

It was that very certainty of success which, perhaps, made him suddenly turn his head, and as he did so, he saw half a dozen riders stretching their horses across the open and angling toward him; they threatened his retreat.

The Sleeper, dizzy with this stroke of danger when he had thought that all trouble must be at an end, spurred the stallion. The result was a mighty bound that made him lose both stirrups.

He swung on the side of the racing, maddened animal, one hand luckily gripping the scanty mane, the other holding to the pommel. The reins flew wildly, tossing here and there.

They flopped to the ground, and the gray stepped on them. There was a jerk, a floundering, and Ironwood almost toppled to the ground.

The jerk, also, came within an ace of finishing the dismounting of the Sleeper. Wild with excitement and fear, he hung by a very finger nail, then managed desperately to claw his way up the side of the gray and into the saddle safely again.

He reached for the reins.

They were gone.

Instead, from the bit of the stallion, on either side dangled a few inches of the broken reins, and the Sleeper had lost all chance of guiding his mount, except by pressing a hand on his neck, or swaying his body in the saddle.

Would that serve his end?

He could not tell. But he knew that now the gray was running as straight as a die, and full of confident courage. And at such a rate of speed as the Sleeper had not dreamed possible.

He looked back with a grim smile toward the others, and then gasped with amazement. Three of them, to be sure, had fallen well back, but the other three hung in their places, and all that wild burst of speed from Ironwood had not gained him the advantage of a single stride!

CHAPTER 39.

PARMENTER'S COMING

IT WAS SO INCREDIBLE a thing that the Sleeper shook his head to clear it of the nightmare. But when he stared again behind him, he made the same discovery.

The leading three had not lost ground by an inch. If anything, they were gaining!

Was it possible that here in the wilderness there were three horses which were the peers of the famous thoroughbred?

He could think of another explanation a little later. Perhaps these were relay horses, kept at a last station in the foothills, and the riders might have changed mounts twice between Guadalupe and this point of the Tinnio Pass. They were fresh and full of running; therefore, it was that they held Ironwood level. Moreover, their riders could control and help them with a steadying pull on the reins, whereas the Sleeper was a helpless, useless bulk in the saddle.

For a mile they strained along. Every moment, he looked for Ironwood to turn to one side or to the other, to flounder, to blunder into a hole in the ground, to leave the trail and become bogged fetlock deep in the softer sand on either side of the beaten way; but the gray ran true as a flying bird, never diverging.

For a full mile they struggled, and then the pace of Ironwood told. He was no sprinter, but he had given these other long-legged creatures a taste of his quality during a real race. Perceptibly they fell away. And again it was the clang of a rifle that announced the failure of these latest hunters.

The Sleeper ventured another glance. It was true that they fell back, though not suddenly as the mustangs of the first horde had done. Perhaps the blood of these horses was as pure as that of Ironwood. Certainly they kept well up, and though they lost in the race, they ran with true hearts, and the stallion could only gradually forge ahead. Then the Sleeper harvested the rich reward for care and caution in the first part of his flight. For in spite of the long distance traveled, he had under him a well-warmed, rather than an exhausted horse.

There seemed no limit to the powers of this great-hearted creature. It no longer kept to a racing clip, but unurged by the Sleeper, it struck out a gait that seemed heartbreaking, yet when he leaned and listened to its breathing, the stallion was in no trouble whatever, but the breaths came home without whistle or roar, or without that strange bubbling sound which sometimes tells that a good runner is badly spent.

Still, machinelike, he devoured the miles before him, and still he refused to slacken his gait!

Then the Sleeper knew that he was not riding a

mere creature of flesh and blood, but that he was mounted upon an idea, to the forging of which one old man had contributed his money, his time, his thought, his prayers, the happiness of his child, the whole of his energy, love, and ambition during a long life. The gray was not failing, because, in the first place, old Adamant had had enough bottom to carry a mountain. The gray was not slow, because, with delicate and prayerful care, old Morice had added to that original stock of endurance the fine flight of speed which was in Ironwood like wings. And it seemed to the Sleeper that mere horseflesh did not account for the composition of the mind of Ironwood. That cheerful and undaunted air with which he carried his head, and sometimes turning it a little, looked back at his rider with a bright content with life, reminded the tramp of old Morice again. As though something of the man had passed into the line of his horses!

They ran across the night into the gray of dawn and then the rose of it, while the desert smoked with purple, and behind the Sleeper there was no sight of the pursuers except a thin cloud of dust which was rising far away, like one of the pillars which the wind builds in the thin air.

He knew that the heart of that column contained the six riders. Or, at least, the foremost three were sure to be there, for they had clung to his trail with a grim and purposeful insistence. He wondered if he could account for that bull-dog firmness in the pursuit by the appearance of one of the riders, for it had seemed to him, when the three were nearest, that the broad shoulders and the big head of one of them were reminiscent of the great Parmenter himself!

Far off, now, he could see the faint haze of smoke rising over the town of Alcalde, though that village itself was still not in view. But at this moment, Ironwood fell to a trot, and then to a walk.

He had endured wonderfully well, but after all he was not made of iron entirely. There was flesh which must grow weary, and very weary was the famous stallion now. Even in his walk he dragged. He had run his race and now needed rest.

The Sleeper looked back at the thin dust cloud so far behind.

It seemed to him that from moment to moment he could see it grow in visibility. They had been able to rate their horses along, and still they could raise a good gallop. Or perhaps Parmenter was bringing them along at a good round trot, which saves the strength of a horse more than any other gait.

The Sleeper, reluctantly, spurred the flanks of the gray.

Ironwood merely shook his weary head.

Again the Sleeper spurred, and the tired horse broke into a dragging, lazy trot, like some old plow horse coming home in the evening after a long day of lugging into its collar. Yet the Sleeper dared not linger on the way. He knew, now, that he never could make the complete safety of Alcalde and its throng of honest fighting men. He would have to pause at the first way station, which was manned by only a one-legged old man, and a helpless girl!

The thought drove him frantic.

It banished his own weariness. He dropped from the saddle to the ground, and seizing a broken end of a rein, he tugged Ironwood along after him.

Again and again he looked behind him, as he got

into the straight Alcalde road, that diminished to a shimmering point in the distance; and every time he looked back, he saw the dust cloud mounting higher and whiter in the morning air.

Parmenter was to win, then, after all!

To the Sleeper, considering everything, this appeared the only logical outcome, for such a man as the bandit could not be expected to lose to a mere tyro, a worthless tramp—

Jogging panting down the road, the Sleeper saw the trees, saw them grow in size until he could distinguish the individual shapes, the trunks, the leaves turning and winking silver in the rosy morning light.

A delicious morning to waken into from sound sleep, and if he must die, a proper morning for that, also.

He went in under the trees, pulling the exhausted horse after him, and as he went he called, his voice thick and harsh, while in the distance he could hear the cheerful piping of the girl as she called the chickens:

"Chick, chick, chick! Here, chick, chick!"

"Hello! Morice! Morice!" shouted the Sleeper.

He heard a screen door slam.

"Well, well, well, he's come back!" said the familiar voice of Morice.

Clear, clipped, matter of fact, that voice banished half the fears of the Sleeper at one stroke. And again he remembered, as he had so often of late, what Parmenter himself had said of the little old man in the plains—the one man in the world, the one power that he feared. Behold, that one-legged old tyrant had found means to draw back Ironwood to him in spite of all the legions of Guadalupe!

So the Sleeper came out from under the trees.

He saw old Morice standing at the back door, filling his pipe; from the barnyard came the tingling cry of joy and astonishment from Evelyn Morice. She was running to meet them. She wore the same faded calico dress, almost white with many washings. There was only the inharmonious dark blue of a big patch in the skirt of the dress.

What would old Morice say? Somehow, the Sleeper could afford time to wonder about that.

Behold! The old man went on with the lighting of his pipe, tamping the tobacco down, and applying the match again and again to get a good fire on top of the tobacco, and emitting great puffs of white, and in between puffs a few casual words:

"Well, Sleeper, how—did—the old hoss—carry you?"

"Ironwood! Oh, you darling!" said the girl.

She came up and threw her arms around the wet and dusty neck of the stallion.

"Walk him up and down, Ev," said the father. "Give him a walk up and down, will you? Them that get out of danger most usually has their temperature raised a mile, and even Ironwood looks kind of warm. Walk him and cool him, Ev, will you?"

He added to the Sleeper: "Step in and have a cup of coffee, you might be a little fagged yourself."

"Do you hear me, man?" cried the Sleeper, as the girl began to lead the horse up and down.

"Yeah. I hear you tolerable clear," said Morice.

"He gave you the horse?" asked the girl eagerly. "I knew he would! I knew that he would!"

"Listen at her," chuckled old Morice. "That lover of hers up in the mountains, he couldn't do a wrong thing. He couldn't make a wrong turn. Just for play, and out of high spirits, as you might say, he's done a mite of stealin', rustlin', bank-robbin', and a few murders here and there. That's all. Just a few. What would you have a young man do, anyway? They's gotta be some spice in life, don't there?''

"He's coming now!" exclaimed the Sleeper. "Have you another horse that I can ride into Alcalde? Quick, quick, Morice! Parmenter himself is coming. You talk of danger. He'll be full of it, now!"

"You see about Parmenter," said old Morice. "You gotta chance now, Ev, to see the great heart you been talkin' about—a soul different from other folks, eh? Well, he's different. And you're gunna see the difference. You'll see whether he prizes you higher'n a hoss or not."

"But have you got another?" cried the Sleeper. "Or shall I go ahead on foot? Speak to me, Morice, before I go mad! Did you hear me say that Parmenter and his men are coming?"

Old Morice tamped his pipe and drew at it methodically before he spoke.

"How many men might there be?" he asked.

"Six!" shouted the Sleeper, growing frantic with impatience.

He looked askance.

There was Evelyn Morice, brown-faced, clear-eyed, more like an exquisite child, but more like a woman, too, than ever. A shadow had fallen over her since the Sleeper had last seen her. That unconscious look was gone, and something of sorrow looked gravely out at him.

Still, obediently, she was walking the horse up and down, and Ironwood, recovering his spirits a little, was nuzzling at her shoulder with his dripping muzzle. He had not forgotten.

By the coming of Parmenter, would not she, too, be swept away into the wilderness, into the wild and inaccessible fairy-land of the Tinnio Pass and Guadalupe? The Sleeper had gone there once and borne away a prize from them all, but neither he nor any other man ever could do so again.

Yet, with all these obvious prizes at stake, old Morice still tugged at his pipe, and drawled at ease!

CHAPTER 40.

ON AN UNKNOWN SEA

"SIX!" SAID THE OLD MAN. "It's a lot—of the kind that ride with Parmenter. A mighty pile, I'd call six of them free-swingin' fire eaters that—"

"There may be only three. What difference does the number make? I'm asking you again, man, if there's a horse that I can bolt into Alcalde on?"

"Well, suppose I give you a hoss," said old Morice, "what good would it do?"

"Is the saving of your horse—and the saving of your daughter—is that anything?" shouted the Sleeper, more maddened than before.

"Something? Yes, that's something," admitted Morice thoughtfully. "But now I wanta ask you something. Did you ever mention Parmenter in Alcalde?"

"What about it? Are you trying to drive me insane with this time wasting?"

"If you ever mentioned Parmenter in Alcalde," said the old man, "you'd've been pretty sure to notice that the boys are likely to look around over their shoulders, as though all at once they was a draft blowin' up their spines. They get mighty uneasy, and begin to feel like home. They just sort of drift away. Mind you, I ain't sayin' that they ain't fine, up-standin', brave men in Alcalde, but just the same, they got limits. And one of them limits is Par-menter."

"Do you mean that they won't come? But I'll swear they will! And whatever we try to do, we must try to do it as quickly as possible! Don't you see, man, that—"

"Oh, I see that the tail of your coat is smokin'," said old Morice calmly. "But it ain't gunna do any good to get excited about it. Lemme tell you the truth. Those boys there in Alcalde, sure they'll come out and fight agin' Parmenter, but they'll need time to go and organize their party. They wouldn't be such fools as just to get half a dozen or even a dozen of 'em together and go rushin' out to catch Parmenter. They wouldn't do that, because they've tried it before, and they've mostly got pretty well spanked before they got home ag'in. Is that clear to you, son? They'd have to do everything regular, which takes time. They'd have to call for opinions. They'd have to elect a leader. They'd have to pick out the hosses that they'd least mind losin' by gun fire. They'd have to get hold of a deputy sheriff or something like that for advice. They'd have to clean their guns and load them. Then still they'd hang around for a few minutes.

"Can't you hear 'em talkin'? 'Wait a minute, boys. Jeff Peters, he's gunna be with us directly. You wouldn't want to start off without old Jeff, would

you?' And then another one says: 'We'd oughta fetch
that riot gun. There ain't nothin' so useful as a riot
gun, when you get to close quarters with a bunch of
shots like them Parmenters! Where's Tim Phealy and
his riot gun? Does anybody around here know where
Timmy is?'

"That's the way that they'd be talkin'. And it
wouldn't take 'em more'n an hour to clear out of
Alcalde and take the trail; but by that time, if I can
reckon anything nigh true, Parmenter will be here
and gone again, and the wind blowin' his sign off of
the sand!"

The Sleeper listened in amazement.

He could see that this probably was a true diag-
nosis of what might happen, and he was enormously
troubled. If that were the case, then Parmenter indeed would be here and gone, and with him Ironwood, and the girl.

"What can we do, then, Morice?"

"What can we do? Why, you, Sleeper, can take a
walk and get yourself out of danger, because I reckon
that there won't be any life taken around here except
yours. Just jog along. I ain't got another hoss to
mount you, nor nothin' but that cow, yonder, and
judgin' by the way that I've seen you sit the saddle,
you wouldn't last long on the back of a buckin' cow,
which the Old Nick himself comes and tells the ornery critters how to pitch. Clean out, Sleeper.
You've done your job about as well, I reckon, as any
man under the sky could've done. But it won't do.
And Parmenter wins once more!"

The Sleeper listened. It seemed to him that he
could hear the throbbing of hoofs far away across the

desert, but he could not be sure.

Then Evelyn Morice left the head of the stallion and stood before him:

"Can you tell me in half a dozen words what happened?" she asked.

"I can. I didn't give Parmenter your letter. Not after one look at him. I tore it up and threw it away. Then they tried to murder me, but I didn't walk into the trap. They offered me a membership in the band. I refused that. Then they voted me a dead man. I ran for it, got Ironwood, and here I am. That's the store. Parmenter had found the torn bits of the letter and pieced them together. According to his way of thinking, I was a traitor because I hadn't given that letter to him. That makes short of a pretty long story."

"Yeah," drawled old Morice, "pretty short, I reckon. But he give you a chance of joining up, and you should've done it. They would've treated you pretty good, I think! You should've joined up with 'em, because that would've meant the easy life for you!"

The girl caught her breath, and looked at her father in horror.

"On one thing," she said with a flushed face. "Are you sure that Charles didn't—purposely—let you get away?"

"He raised the house and all Guadalupe," said the Sleeper calmly, seeing again that night picture. "He sent fire signals up and down the valley. There were lights on all sides. I'd gone down to the bottom of the valley. I saw I was in a box, so I went back up the slope and bluffed out the Mexicans who were guarding the gate. They recognized me after I was through it. They started shooting, and there were bullets, more or less, all the way through the town, but Ironwood carried me through. Ironwood is the cause of my being here. But Ironwood won't be here long! Parmenter will take him. And, by Heaven," went on the Sleeper with a growing excitement, "He'll take you, also!"

"He never will!" cried the girl.

"Listen," said the Sleeper solemnly, "I've sat with him and watched him smiling and polite at the very time when he was planning the murder of me. He sent a girl to draw me into the trap!"

He had saved that blow to the last, and it turned her white. Her head fell, as though something had died in her that moment. And Sleeper felt little enthusiasm for his victory. Parmenter might be snatched from her life, but what would fill the void?

"Come inside, son," said old Morice, "if you ain't gunna get out of the way."

The Sleeper looked up at the bright morning sky, and far away, carried by the wind, this time he unmistakably heard the pulse of hoofs in galloping cadence. It would be simple, as old Morice had said, for him to escape. In their necessary hurry, the Parmenters would not search far for him, no matter how rabidly they might desire his life. Moreover, if he ran on toward the town, cutting across the fields, and then following down the river bank, he might be able to organize a pursuit mounted on horses swift and fresh enough to overtake the outlaws.

This was the promise which hope held out to him, but yet he knew that hope was a liar.

Somehow, it was impossible for him to imagine Parmenter failing twice. The thing simply could not be.

Parmenter would come, snatch up the stallion—

already the breathing of Ironwood was easier and he began to show signs of interest in the watering trough not far away—and with the stallion he would surely take off Evelyn Morice.

He, the Sleeper, in the meantime would be free. He had done enough, as Morice had said. And he had the reasonable excuse of hurrying for help against overmastering odds.

Suddenly he said, "Morice!"

"I?" said the old man.

"If you were in my boots—"

"Which I ain't!"

"If you were in my boots, I say, what would you do?"

"Me?" said Morice. "That's a thing that I can't answer very good, it's such a spell since I was young!"

And again, into the interim, rolled the beating of galloping hoofs, nearer and nearer.

The heart of the Sleeper shrank small and cold.

His lips grew dry, and his knees weakened so that they were as much as in a nightmare, when one strives to flee and cannot.

"You must go," said the girl suddenly. "There's nothing that you can do here. Please, please go! You've risked your life for Ironwood, and for father. And you were a stranger to us—"

Her breath caught in a sob.

"Now, listen at her and watch her," said the wonderful old man, his voice as calm and unhurried as ever, though well he knew the meaning of those galloping horses that swept down the highway toward the little house. "Listen at her how she's getting a change of heart! There ain't nothin' like a young girl. She'd carved that Parmenter out of a cloud and poured the statue full of sunshine. But now she sees that even handmade clouds can rain and turn black. Well, she's gettin' a change of heart and beginnin' all at once to look up to Mr. Sleeper, that brave young man! Look at her, Sleeper—"

"Be quiet!" said the Sleeper, moved.

"No, young feller, I can't be quiet. My tongue is hung on unbalanced hinges, and it's gotta rattle and clatter in every breeze that blows, good and bad. But I wancha to see how girls are—like sailors on an unknown sea, and every loom of land they think might be India! The same with girls and men. Somewhere is the fairy prince. If he's got freckles across his nose, it's nothin'. It's only a mask, d'you see? Fairyland is what they're hunting for, and now it looks like she's findin' it in you, Sleeper!"

The Sleeper raised a hand to stop the tirade.

But he knew that the eyes of the girl had risen and that she was looking steadily at him.

Suddenly, his heart grew stronger. There was a rush of courage all through his body.

"I'll go inside with you, Morice," said he.

Old Morice stood aside from the doorway.

"Come in, lad," said he, "and welcome."

The Sleeper entered that narrow, low doorway as though passing into a tomb.

"I've had big men out here to look at Ironwood," said old Morice. "But I never seen one before that made that doorway look no smaller than what you do. Come in, son!"

It might well have been taken as a mere tribute to

the width of the tramp's shoulders, but the Sleeper himself guessed that something more was intended.

He entered the house, and knew that there he must wait until the battle rushed suddenly up and closed upon them.

CHAPTER 41.

IN THE DUST

"WHERE ARE YOUR RIFLES, Morice?" he asked eagerly.

"The rifles? Never keep any, my son. The day used to be when I could eat rabbit and squirrel with any man and do my own shooting. But a peg leg don't help a hunter, and you can't hunt ground squirrels from a buckboard. So I give up rifles."

"Revolvers, then?"

"Nope. Not a one."

The Sleeper, amazed, took out his revolver. That one weapon stood between them and the Parmenters! And a small, useless thing it appeared.

"Morice," he said, "what under heaven can we do?"

Morice looked calmly at him. "You brought the hoss away, but Parmenter has certainly beat you!" he said in the end.

"Why do you say that?"

"When you went up there," said the horse breeder, "you could've faced any man, any two men—and three wouldn't've made you lose much temperature; but now even the idea of Parmenter, let alone the rest of 'em is enough to upset you, ain't it?"

"Yes," said the boy frankly. "You're right."

"Your hand would be pretty likely to shake, son, I reckon?"

"Yes, I would probably find it shaking."

"Then what happened to you up there?"

"To take my nerve?"

"Yes. That's what I mean to say."

"I'll tell you," said the Sleeper. "A thing happened to me up there that nobody would believe. Not even you, Morice. I can't talk about it. It's between me—"

"And Heaven?" said Morice.

"Yes. Now, what is there that we can do, and what's the best way to defend the house—with one gun?"

"It can't be done," said the other calmly, as always.

"Are we to lie down and let them walk over us?"

"Heaven, that you're talkin' about, has charge of us and of all our days, son," said Morice.

That was the key to his being, then. Under his hardness, his patience, his grim enduring of suffering of mind and body, there was a bed rock of fervent religion.

"Call in Evelyn!" said the Sleeper, growing colder and colder of face and of heart.

"What for?"

"She won't run. And Parmenter—he'll have her in the end, but not till he's finished me!"

Morice shook his head.

"That's good big talk," he said. "When I last seen

you here—then you wouldn't've said anything. You wouldn't've had to, but you would've done the thing without the talkin'. You've gone downhill, son. Parmenter's broke your spirit, I reckon.''

The Sleeper quivered like a child under the lash. He said nothing. He could not say anything.

"And when you know that he's close to you," went on Morice, "you'll begin to weaken. The thought of that eye of his will finish you off. It ain't an easy eye to meet, I reckon!"

The Sleeper shuddered again.

"No," he said faintly. "It's not an easy eye to meet. Will you call Evelyn inside?"

"Call her yourself," said the old man, with a grim scorn in his eye. "But I wouldn't want her around, if I were you, to have her see you take water and—"

The Sleeper was startled with rage at this constant annoyance.

"Are you trying to help him break me down before he comes?" shouted the Sleeper. He ran to the door.

"Evelyn!" he called.

He had no answer.

"Evelyn! Evelyn!" he called again.

He ran outside. The noise of the hoofs rang in his ears. It was like passing into the presence of leveled guns, to hear them. And turning the corner of the house, he saw the form of the girl hurrying before him through the trees and out toward the road. And far beyond her came the riders. Not six. Not three, even, had been able to endure the length and pace of that grim ride, but two men were coming, and one, beyond any doubt, was the great Parmenter.

He could see the plan in the girl's mind.

She would hurry ahead to meet the brigand and

offer herself to him, as she had offered herself before.
She had been willing enough, that first time, carried
away by the strength and by the romantic interest of
this strange man. But the Sleeper remembered how
her head had fallen as he tallied up the repeated
villainies of Parmenter in Guadalupe. She was going
now to meet him, and offer herself in exchange for
the horse and for the Sleeper himself, no doubt. A
sacrifice that shook him to the soul!

"She's gone!" he gasped.

And from behind him, at the door, came the harsh,
rasping voice of Morice:

"Well, let her go. What's a girl, more or less, to the
world, or to us? Come inside and make yourself
snug. If they swaller her first, likely they'll forget
about Ironwood, and you!"

The Sleeper turned on him with a groan.

"Dang you and your insults!" he said. "If I'm not
man enough to stop them, I'm certainly man enough
to die trying!"

And with this, he ran straight forward through the
trees.

He called as he went, and she, hearing, turned and
waved him desperately back, and pointed down the
road toward the two riders.

But he went on.

She had reached the road. It was there that he
overtook her. She ran on, crying out at him over her
shoulder to turn back. But he caught her in his arms
and stopped her.

Straight at him came the two riders, still at the
gallop. He on the left was Parmenter; and the other,
on a smaller horse, showed the pale face of the gunman extraordinary, Chipping. Once that man had

been shamed by the matchless effrontery of the Sleeper; he would not be ashamed again on this day! A naked gun was already in his hand, poised, the muzzle tilting toward the sky, ready for a snap shot at long range.

"Go back!" panted the Sleeper. "If you give yourself to him, you give yourself to misery. I'm nothing. I'm a tramp. A waster. I'm no good. But let me stop them if I can! Evelyn, I love you enough to die without pain!"

She twisted a white, stricken face toward him, then with a wrench she was free, and running on with arms outspread, as though to shield him, and the Sleeper in pursuit. A strange chase down that dusty road!

She tripped. She was down.

And the Sleeper ran straight past her, gun in hand, to meet his fate.

He thought he could see a smile on the face of Parmenter. The gun tilted down in the hand of Chipping. The streak of sunlight on the barrel narrowed and shortened to a blinding point, and the gun spoke.

It was as though a fist had struck the Sleeper inside the left shoulder, with a force that half turned him, and dropped him to one knee.

It was Parmenter who fired the second shot, as he pulled his horse to a stop in order to steady his aim. That bullet sang past the Sleeper's temple.

Then he fired and turned.

He could not understand why he made Chipping his target, except that somehow the lesser man must go first. Then Parmenter for the finish.

But as he kneeled there in the dust of the road, looking through that other dust cloud which had been knocked up by the sudden stoppage of the horses, the very soul of the Sleeper sang with joy. For he was calm. There was no tremor in brain or in body. The pain that ripped and tore at his shoulder as though new bullets continually were driving through the flesh, now was like something read in a book, and unrelated to his own body. All that mattered was that he had a good right hand uninjured and in his revolver, six shots.

So through the dust cloud he fired at the dark silhouette of Chipping.

He knew that he had not missed. It was as though a divine assurance had been whispered at his ear, sending that bullet home to the mark; but only slowly Chipping swayed in the saddle. The gun dropped from his hand. He leaned toward the ground as though he were stooping to pick it up again from the dust, but the Sleeper knew that from that fall the gunman never would rise again.

He had given half a second to that shot.

Then he swung his weapon toward Parmenter.

Behind him, down the road, the high-pitched voice of the girl was screaming terribly. He saw the face of Parmenter convulsed with black hate and rage. There was reason for it. He had been sure of the girl's love, before—or must have thought himself sure of it. What could he be sure of except loathing when she saw him do a murder in cold blood, with odds of two to one in his favor?

In the tenth part of a second, as he drew his bead on this face, the Sleeper could think of this. Then the gun of Parmenter spoke again, and the leg of the Sleeper was knocked from under him.

He had been shot through the thigh. He fell forward face down in the choking dust, while another bullet, still, struck the road before him and sent more blinding dust in his face.

Yet still he had the revolver in his hand.

He rolled on his side, twisting his body back like a bow, so that he could shoot again, and the fourth bullet from Parmenter's gun hissed again by his face.

"He is dead!" said the Sleeper to himself.

And without doubt, with a perfectly calm assurance, he pulled the trigger.

The horse on which the bandit was mounted reared as though the slug had smitten into his own flesh. He whirled on his hind legs, while Parmenter, like a loose image stuffed with rags, slid out of the saddle and fell in a shapeless heap on the road.

All this in how long? In two heart-beats, perhaps?

For the voice of the girl still was coming toward them, shrilling.

The scream stopped.

Would she go to Parmenter?

No, it was by the Sleeper's side that she dropped to her knees. It was his head that she took in her arms. It was his lips, blackened by the dust, that she kissed. It was of him that she asked how desperately he was hurt.

All pain left him, washed away by the sound of her voice and by her touch.

"Hurt?" said the Sleeper. "I'm only marked a little, so that I won't forget the day!"

CHAPTER 42.

THOROUGHBREDS

TURF MEMORIES are short.

Race horses themselves are brittle stuff. The two-year-old hero of one season becomes the broken-down cripple of the next. The three-year-old champion retires with a bowed tendon. And the handicapper, as he studies form, realizes that the horse which did a mile in one thirty-six Monday, may work hard to do one forty on the Sunday following. Only now and then some great Eclipse, Lexington, Colon, St. Simon, or Man-o'-War, proves to be made of iron and defies defeat. The public comes to love such horses, for they are "honest" in an almost spiritual sense. Flesh and bone in them will not fail, and their hearts will not fail, either. No matter what weight is heaped above their withers, or how grueling the drive down the stretch, though they are passed, they come again; though they are challenged, they never stagger, but stretch out straight and true; they work unfaltering to the end, nostrils flaring red, eyes glaring with pride and disdain of defeat. They are world champions, and they know it.

Such a horse was King Cole; and for all of these reasons, he was loved by the racing public. Men and women who never had seen a race before traveled long distances to view the "King", as he was called by every one. Like a king he was in stable, in paddock, or ready at the start—noble in beauty, noble in soul, he disdained flightiness, tricks, or trouble of any kind. His heart was as great as his speed, and the world knew it. Therefore, it loved him, rejoiced in his victories, shook its head in disbelief or two or three unimportant failures when weight had anchored him on muddy tracks, and now swarmed to the track to see his last triumph at the end of his four-year-old form.

It was the Goodwin Stakes, and fifty thousand dollars would go to the winner of that race. Of that sum, if Jockey Hillgore won on the King, he was to get a flat bonus of ten thousand. He had had other bonuses when he took his toes out of the golden stirrups with which he always rode the King. But never had he been so perfectly sure of his reward as now.

For the King was fit, and the race was his. The distance was long, but he had done a mile and seven furlongs before, and done it well. His defeats, in fact, had always been in sprints. The track was perfect for speed, neither too hard nor too soft. And the handicapper, as though shamed by memory of the long series of crushing impositions which he had placed upon the back of the great thoroughbred, now loaded him with only a moderate weight.

There was Amethyst, the good Irish mare, in under a feather and picked by some to win on that account. There was that notorious in-and-outer, Bib-and-

Tucker, whose legs were pronounced sound for this meet, and the old gelding, when he was right, was considered as good as the best. He, too, was greatly favored by the weights. In addition to this pair, the great stake horse, Black Knight, had been entered. Thrice before defeated by the King, still his owner persisted in declaring that the Knight never had been at his best in the other contests. He took ten pounds from the King and was trained as fit as a fiddle. Money was certain to go down on Black Knight, even though he had been beaten thrice before. These three were the only contenders, with the exception of one stallion whose name was now being considered in a newspaper held by a pair of slender brown hands in the grand stand.

Ironwood, gray horse, by Forester, out of True Iron—

He was aged. He was almost unknown.

It is an imposition to enter such a horse in such a race. Ironwood, after two full seasons of campaigning, had the honor of winning one race! It is true that the race was a long one, and that in the same contest was entered one of the best racers of the season. But the season was poor, and Ironwood was apparently having the one great day which, according to the superstition, comes to every race horse. Even so, on that occasion, he got up barely in time to win.

On that day, his victory caused a sensation because he was considered such a hopeless outsider, and because of his true, hard running in the stretch, and particularly through the last six-teenth. However, that day was several years ago. Ironwood is now aged. If he is not left at the post, it is to be hoped that his addition to the number of starters will not cause any bad racing luck to more legitimate performers. It is not too much to say that the day never was seen when he was worthy of mention with such clever runners as Amethyst and Bib-and-Tucker—when the last-named gelding is fit to be seen at all. This is not to mention that sterling thoroughbred, Black Knight. Of course, King Cole stands by himself as a superhorse, and it is perhaps foolish to give any attention to the other entries when the grand stallion's name is listed.

He is perfectly fit, trained to a hair for the greatest day of his life. Unless rain falls in the middle of the day, the track is entirely to his liking, the distance is his own, and it is expected that he will hang up a record which will break hearts for a long time to come.

There was more talk, but no more about Iron-wood, and failing to find that name farther along in the columns devoted to the Goodwin, the small brown hands lowered the paper and folded it care-fully, with the slowness of an absent mind. Then the girl turned her face to her companion.

He was a big-shouldered, handsome fellow, with black eyes, and a rather swarthy skin. A pair of crutches leaned against the seat beside him. But he sat as erect as a knight in the saddle.

"They say that Ironwood hasn't a chance," said the girl. "They say it now, at the last minute. What do you honestly think?"

"Honestly?"

"Yes. Without trying to comfort me. I don't care if the place has been sold to bet on him. I want to know the truth."

"Well," said the big youth, "the odds are good. Forty, and fifty, and even seventy to one. One can't ask for much more than that!"

"That's not an opinion," said she. "It isn't the money that I really care about. We've always been poor. We can be poor again."

"You want what I think?"

"Yes. Exactly that."

"Well, then, I think that Ironwood's a great old horse. A great *old* horse, mind you. He's been off the track for years. He's been out of training. Hacking up and down the mountains of the Tinnio can't have improved his shoulders a great deal. Out there in the West—well, he was a wonder. He is a wonder, across country, I'm convinced. And if this were a ten-mile race over hill and dale, why, I'd swear that he couldn't lose. But what they call a distance race—less than two miles—is really a sprint, for Ironwood. I don't think he'll get warmed up. He's sluggish. You've seen these other thoroughbreds dancing on their toes; they're like violin strings in tune!"

"You don't think that he has a chance?"

"Not one! These experts are not fools. They know that he has run one good race already, but they're betting fifty to one, to-day!"

"Then why did you put up every penny that you

could borrow, or scrape together in any way?"

"Why? Well, I couldn't go back on a horse that had saved my—"

"Mr. Sleeper?" said a voice.

They looked up. A policeman was leaning above them—one of the private police of the track, in a natty gray uniform. He had lowered his voice—just sufficiently to enable everybody within ten feet to hear what he had to say.

"Yes," said the Sleeper.

"Everything all right, sir? Not seen any suspicious faces?"

"Not one," murmured the Sleeper. "Everything's all right."

"Just wanted to ask. I'm here to protect you, sir. Special orders. Let me know if anything goes wrong—"

He withdrew, but whispers continued around them.

"That's William Sleeper."

"Who's he?"

"Don't you read the papers?"

"Well, what about it?"

"Why, you've heard of Parmenter, I suppose."

"You mean the bandit, in the West? I thought he was dead?"

"Sleeper's the man who killed him!"

"You don't mean it!"

"Of course I do. Talk lower, or he'll hear us. Shot twice. Brought down Parmenter and Parmenter's best man. Broke up the worst bunch that ever raised the dickens in the Southwest—and they've had their share before now. The whole outfit went crash, with Parmenter gone, and it's said that all the remnants of the band have sworn vengeance on Sleeper—that they'll kill him, sooner or later—''

The Sleeper, hearing, covertly laid his hand over that of the girl. She looked up at him with a pale, strained, anxious face.

"Rot!" said the Sleeper. "There's nothing in that. Newspaper talk never has anything in it, Evelyn."

She tried to smile, but the smile faltered.

"Now, I'll tell you," said the Sleeper, "we're here to watch the race, and not to watch anything else. Forget the chatter, dear!"

"Oh, yes, I'll forget it—"

A trumpet blew.

And out on the track came a man in a red hunting outfit leading a procession of five thoroughbreds. And, at the head of the list, came King Cole.

Nothing else was seen.

His head proudly bent, his chestnut coat as red as fire, he paced along with infinite dignity, and the stands went wild. The hardest bookies shouted. They expected to lose much money. They hardly cared. For one dollar on anything else, there were eight on the King. Eight to one—and yet in a real race. That was the racing public's estimation of that marvel. Eight dollars on him, to win one.

Then came Amethyst, dainty as a débutante, graceful, with her wicked eyes glittering from side to side. Some said that they wanted to change their bets when they saw her. Behind her walked with a gangling stride that long-legged gelding, Bib-and-Tucker. He had no middle piece. But then he was made fore and aft to please the finest eye, and that was all he needed, when Fate sent him his day. After him came Black Knight, black as his name, gloriously shining, far the most beautiful of that array. He went dancing, eager, leaving too much of his race in the parade, perhaps, but a thing to fill the eye this moment, and the mind forever, with an exquisite memory. Blood certainly would tell.

Last of all came a long-drawn-out gray, low, heavy, close to the ground, a little pigeon-toed. He moved his head in and out on his ewe neck at every stride. One ear would cock forward, the other swing back, alternately. The jockey, blushing, had to keep jabbing him with his heels to bring him up with the parade.

When people forgot their enthusiasm about King Cole, they sat back and laughed—at Ironwood!

CHAPTER 43.

THE STUFF THAT LASTS

THEY LINED UP at the start quietly, except for Black Knight, whose owner was twisting and groaning as he kept the glasses glued to his eyes.

"Leaving his race at the post!" he muttered, as the stallion, backing and filling, threw the line into disorder.

And then an old man with a wooden leg, leaning on the rail, heard a man beside him say:

"And that gray goat, out there. Not a chance in a thousand. Disgrace to have such an entry—"

"I got a hundred dollars and a watch that says he's got a chance—at a hundred to one," said the man with the wooden leg.

"You're a fool," said the other, a little disconcerted. Yet he moved off a bit.

"A race ain't over until the numbers are posted," said the man with the wooden leg, elbowing away one who tried to crowd him from his place on the rail.

Then a great, short, hoarse roar went up from the crowd, like the groan of wounded animals:

"They're off!"

No bets could be changed; none could be withdrawn or increased now; let the better judge win!

"He's left. The gray plow horse's left!"

It was true. Three good lengths separated the other four from the long-drawn gray stallion before the latter's head was jerked around and he was sent away by an indignant, groaning jockey. Even an apprentice could feel the bite of shame; even a burly, overgrown apprentice, whose only instructions had been:

"Don't carry a whip. Steady him hard, that's all. Ask him, and he'll do what Fate will let him do!"

He remembered those instructions now and sat still, helpless, hopeless. Before him the flickering line of beauties fled away.

It was a great race from the start, because it carried from the beginning a staggering surprise. King Cole, whose early burst of speed usually strapped all contenders—King Cole was a poor second, and in front, across the round field of the eager field glasses, floated and bobbed the shining body of the little filly, Amethyst.

Oh, why had they not had sense? A grand racer, and in under a feather!

"She's going to run away from them all!"

There were some who had put up only a dollar or two. These could sit back calmly.

"The King will come at the end," they said.

Then they sat back and laughed at the long, awkward bounds of the last in the field, the clumsy-bodied gray stallion, Ironwood.

Then panic seized upon that crowd.

A mile went by, and the filly was still there in front. She had eight open lengths between her and the nose of Black Knight, who then began to rush up on the outside, though under a hand ride from his jockey.

Beautiful Amethyst! She had set a dazzling pace.
And where was the King? The great King was running third, and not under any great restraint.

"He's been overtrained! A thrown race! Danged
outrage!" groaned the loyal and indignant crowd.
"Such a record to be spoiled by a ham of a trainer!
The yellow pup!"

They turned the mile and a quarter. Black Knight,
beautiful, shining like a dark star, had his nose at the
saddle girth of the filly.

"She'll go to pieces, now. She always does under a
challenge."

She did not go to pieces. She ran like a demon, and
the Black Knight could not gain on her. Locked
together they ran. The field was nowhere behind
them.

What was the matter with King Cole?

His jockey sat like a statue. Was the race crooked?
So blatantly crooked?

Long-legged Bib-and-Tucker came up and lapped
himself on the King. They ran side by side, stride for
stride. And still the pair in front hurled on at dizzy
speed.

And less than half a mile to go!

The Sleeper touched the girl's hand.

"Look!" said he.

She brushed away the big tears which were rolling
down her face.

"With a fair start—with half a chance—" said the
Sleeper.

The gray horse which tagged the field no longer
lost distance. His enormous bounding stride kept
him even. Or, was it not an illusion that he actually

gained ground on the King?

"They've drugged the King!" shouted nervous bettors. "They've drugged him, the dogs!"

Around the last turn flashed the filly, and the Knight beside her. They straightened away. King Cole was coming, now, and Bib-and-Tucker came beside him, but what a late, late move! Then, as people watched with agonized faces, the filly threw up her head and stopped to a stagger. The Black Knight went on alone!

The race was his. He had shown the early foot, he was showing the uncracked stamina now—

No, a quarter from home he swerved. The hip of the jockey rose and fell. He lurched. And suddenly he seemed to be laboring up and down, jumping like a jack-in-the-box on one spot. And the King and Bib-and-Tucker swept past him, left him in their dust.

Ah, how great he seemed, then, the King—the good old King, the dauntless one! And what a jockey sat in those golden stirrups, his withered monkey face drawn by an expectant grin of triumph.

Yet Bib-and-Tucker held on, gallantly. Let him hold on! Let him be gallant! The crowd laughed, and tears came to their eyes. It was the King again, of course. All the experts had said so. Only once in a hundred years such an upset. Perfectly rated off the pace, now he was taking the race to himself— A length away from struggling Bib-and-Tucker!

All that the Sleeper saw was the gallant chestnut straining in front. And then a startling voice from an old man in front of him broke on his ears:

"By thunder! Look at the old gray come home!"

The Sleeper looked, and that was how it seemed. Ironwood, perhaps, had not increased his pace. He seemed to be going along with the same gigantic, sweeping strides. But the field came back to him. Stretched out straight and true, he caught the poor filly, Amethyst, bobbing along at a mere canter. And then that weary Black Knight went to his rear.

Far in front toiled the King himself, and with him the good gelding, whose fame was greater for this day's work than for a lifetime of honest racing.

Gallantly, gallantly they fought, but far on the outside, doubling himself up with effort, rushed Ironwood.

They had reached the mile and a half, and they had passed it. That was his distance. From now on, he came to himself. Thanks to the bottom of Adamant!

Furiously they whirled down the stretch. A quarter from home, and he came on like wildfire.

The crowd saw him, now. A wild screech went up from fifty thousand throats. Then they were silent.

For the drama was too appalling. The King to go down before this old "aged" horse!

They could not believe it. They were frozen in their seats. But literally Ironwood was walking over the field.

A scant furlong from the finish he came up with the good gelding, Bib-and-Tucker. Tucker went behind.

He caught the King.

Oh, mighty King! One glance from his proud eyes, and then he was coming again, as though the race had hardly begun. The frightened apprentice on Ironwood, with fame lying in his lap, with bulging eyes, incredulously saw the great chestnut brushed to the rear.

A whole sixteenth with nothing in front of Ironwood except the wire, and wildly he went for it. A length, two lengths, three lengths in front of the king of the world of horses!

"Won going away, after a poor ride, and practically left at the post, with an unknown apprentice on his back!" So said a newspaper reporter as the race finished.

And up from the crowd came a great, deep-throated wail of dismay and of wonder.

To be beaten, yes—but beaten in this fashion! All the laurels of three seasons of glorious racing were stripped from the head of King Cole and heaped upon the gaunt neck of Ironwood.

Then madness came over the assembly. They yelled and they shouted:

"A wonder horse!"

Well, afterward there were streams of reporters, of racing enthusiasts, of men who wanted to offer a bid for the great gray, and they surrounded a one-legged old man who still leaned on the fence.

"I reckon," said he, "that Ironwood ain't gunna race no more. Me and Ironwood, and my boy and girl, we're gunna go home."

In the crowd, Evelyn and the Sleeper found him.

Each took an arm, the Sleeper hobbling along on one crutch.

And the old man looked with a faint smile into the horizon sky, drenched with mists that promised another rain.

"Adamant," said he. "She had to win. She was the stuff that lasts! Like you, Sleeper!"

And he turned and looked the tramp full in the face, and the boy knew, quietly, proudly, humbly, that the old man was right again. He would last, to the end.

Raw, fast-action adventure from one of the world's favorite western authors

MAX BRAND
writing as Evan Evans

0-515-08571-5	**MONTANA RIDES**	$2.50
0-515-08527-8	**OUTLAW'S CODE**	$2.50
0-515-08528-6	**THE REVENGE OF BROKEN ARROW**	$2.75
0-515-08529-4	**SAWDUST AND SIXGUNS**	$2.50
0-515-08582-0	**STRANGE COURAGE**	$2.50
0-515-08611-8	**MONTANA RIDES AGAIN**	$2.50
0-515-08692-4	**THE BORDER BANDIT**	$2.50
0-515-08711-4	**SIXGUN LEGACY**	$2.50
0-515-08776-9	**SMUGGLER'S TRAIL**	$2.50
0-515-08759-9	**OUTLAW VALLEY**	$2.50